THE
GRAVE
KEEPERS

ELIZABETH
BYRNE

HarperTeen is an imprint of HarperCollins Publishers.
The Grave Keepers

www.epicreads.com

ISBN 978-0-06-248475-8

Typography by Heather Daugherty
This book is set in 11-point Adobe Caslon Pro
17 18 19 20 21 PC/LSCH 10 9 8 7 6 5 4 3 2 1
❖
First Edition

To my parents
and my sister, Amy

THE TENETS OF GRAVE KEEPING

1. A grave is to think.
2. It matters not what is in another's grave.
3. A grave is for the keeper alone.
4. Your grave is your true and only everlasting home.
5. Your everlasting home must be ready to receive you, just as you must be prepared to go.
6. Your grave key is your key to life.
7. A key is unique to the individual; as there is no second you, there can be no second key.
8. Everlasting rest requires patience and practice.
9. Parents shall keep their children's graves until the children reach their thirteenth year.
10. The seal of a grave is an everlasting seal.

A GRAVE IS TO THINK

You should know that I died a long time ago, and that I was young when I died. But that doesn't matter much to me anymore. I've been in the Catskills far longer than Rip Van Winkle. I've seen a town flooded for a reservoir. I've watched beetles chew leaves all summer until the mountain's scalp showed. I've seen people step out of second-story windows in snowshoes and walk down the middle of Main Street; I've found a lost child hours before the authorities and waited with him until the first ranger arrived. I watched the great Hudson Hotel rise on the cliff and then, decades later, I watched its skeleton emerge as fire consumed silk wallpaper, potted palms, several thousand dollars' worth of Cuban cigars. Trails became turnpikes, and rivers, creeks. I've learned all the contemporary vocabulary: hybrid, cell phone, hydrofracking, brunch, terrorism, Ross and Rachel, transgender, Miranda rights, Polaroid, friending. I learned even more once I started following Laurel and Athena around.

Chapter 1

"ONE CHICK, TWO CHICK." LAUREL WINDHAM COUNTED by feel. Her brother's old baseball T-shirt hung almost to her knees, where scabs—from trying to bike down to the creek and failing—were coming off in flecks. Soft pink shadows, fresh skin, showed through underneath. She pawed through a cheeping mass of chicks, warm and soft, fragile as eggs. Twiggy wing bones poked from under the down. If she didn't set them aside as she counted, they re-mingled with a ruckus. Seven chicks present and accounted for—where was number eight? Laurel ducked out of the hut and stooped to look under the gangplank. Number eight had fallen before she got there, must have been keeping a lookout for her. Its yellow fluff was still warm but its head dangled at an odd angle. Laurel folded number eight into her basket beside the eggs.

Her animal graveyard on the far side of the barn was a perfect replica of the human one her family tended in the old orchard behind their house. At the hatching of each and every chick, she'd dig a hole and top it with a curl of birch bark, a door lying over a ready grave just as people did for newborn babies. River-rock headstones marked the resting place of a litter of rabbits, buried together because Laurel couldn't bear the thought of separating them. They rested beside the carcass of the first turkey she'd bagged, returned to her after her mother had finished boiling it for stock. Rows of graves stretched for yards. The head and spine of every trout she'd ever caught, every sparrow Emily Dickinson (the cat) left on the doormat. This was why she was up so early—to tend her own cemetery in her pajamas.

Laurel pulled a pretend key from her pocket and pretend unlocked the pretend doorknob on number eight's pretend grave door. "Little chicken, your grave is your true and only home," she said as she lowered it into the ground. "Welcome to your everlasting rest." She scraped dirt, two-handed, onto the yellow fluff, and when it was nearly filled, she pressed the birch bark into the hollow. Her scalp twitched under a shiver as she thought about what came next, the mysterious finality she wielded. With a sprinkling of grass, she said, "Be at peace. The seal of a grave is an everlasting seal."

✧ ✧ ✧

Laurel shuffled into the kitchen from the back porch, yawning, knuckling her eyes. Her mother, Claudia, licked her fingertip, turned a page of the morning daily. The sun fell through the back-door window, catching the black satin of her eye patch. "Morning," she said without taking her good eye from the page. Her silver-white hair was still in its nighttime braid, snaking down her back like a getaway rope.

"Morning." Laurel rinsed and dried the eggs, poured a dollop of coffee into a mug of milk. "Did Athena leave yet?"

Her mother ignored the question, copying details from the obituaries into her ledger. Laurel knew better than to interrupt. It was one of the unspoken rules of the house, along with no TV after nine (her father was a light sleeper) and no stepping on the second step down to the cellar (the wood was spongy with rot, and no one had gotten around to replacing it yet).

A fresh blueberry muffin, waiting for her sister Athena, sat beside a basket of tomatoes and summer squash on the counter to be washed. Laurel's mouth slimed over at the sight of more squash. She'd had her fill, many times over. Laurel plucked the fish food off the windowsill, held it over the bowl. As she tapped flakes for the goldfish with her right hand, she dipped her left hand into the water and pinched a few stones from the fake ocean floor. Gently, one by one, she pressed the slimy pebbles into her sister's muffin, then dried her hand on her shirt.

Overhead the bathroom door slammed open and Athena shouted, "Sorry!" just as her mother yelled, "Take it easy!" Laurel slid into her seat with a bowl of cornflakes.

Athena pounded down the stairs. "I'm late, I'm late, I'm so-o-o-o late," she chanted as she threw an empty water bottle into her canvas bag. "Hey, Sissy." She wrapped a cloth napkin around the muffin, dropped it in with the water bottle.

Laurel smiled. "There's my beautiful sister."

Athena glared. "What did you do?"

"It's gonna be a hot one today. Got your sunblock?" Claudia's pen never stopped moving across the ledger.

"Yup."

"Hat?"

"Yup."

"Pool pass?"

"The Houlahans keep all the pool passes together. They're pinned on their pool bag. You know this." Athena's eyes were still squinty from sleep. Laurel noticed dried toothpaste in the crease of her mouth.

"Well then. Have a good day. Stick to the shade."

"I will, I will, bye," she said, shooting a final laser look at Laurel.

"Bye." Laurel waved to the closing back door. Through the lace curtains she watched Athena toss her bag into her bike basket, kick off and throw her leg over the seat all in one fluid movement. She would have liked to see her take a bite. Just one bite.

"Hello?" someone called from the front hall.

"Back here, Suze."

"Oh no!" Laurel skittered off the bench and ducked around the corner.

"What's the matter with you?"

"I'm still in my nightshirt, Mom!"

"You were just out in the yard like that, cuckoo bird."

"Nothing I haven't seen before, sweetie pie," Suze said, entering the kitchen and helping herself to a mug from the cabinet. Her funeral director's uniform was half-complete—flip-flops with her dark skirt suit. Heels and pantyhose poked out the top of her gigantic purse. She was there to finalize the details of that morning's funeral with Claudia. The Windhams owned the cemetery, but their work was limited to grave openings and groundskeeping. Coordinating the hearses and wakes and sealing ceremonies was Suze's jurisdiction.

As she ran upstairs, Laurel heard her mother say, "She's at that age, you know. When suddenly you realize other people can see you."

"Puberty," Suze said. "Poor thing."

Laurel left through the front door. Shoelaces untied, hair and teeth unbrushed, she untwisted her bag strap along her shoulder and stuck a pencil through her ponytail. A steady *clink-clink-clink* came from the open barn door—her brother, Simon, was already well into his day of stone carving.

This is what she heard: a carpenter bee helicoptering under the eaves, a bullfrog in the gully refusing rest, her brother carving headstones by hand, Clover Honey (the dog) trotting over. This is what she didn't hear: tongue-shaped leaves sucking in lungfuls of sunlight, ants chewing new tunnels through the dirt below her knees, the dogwood's roots tapping water veins underground.

"There you are, nosy." Laurel scratched her dog down the length of her back. "We're on grave duty in the northeast quad today, far away from that funeral. This way, c'mon." Laurel went the long way around the house for a taste of damp shade, past the garbage cans and a giant mushroom shaped like an ear. On the back wall of the house, a salvaged window frame held a mirror taller than Laurel. She couldn't help watching herself as she passed.

The work truck idled somewhere in the orchard cemetery, impossible to see for all the trees. Probably her father, hauling dirt and grass seed up to today's gravesite for the sealing. Her parents and siblings always attended the sealing ceremonies, good representatives of the cemetery, and sometimes they were the only mourners. They stood in the back, hands stuffed into pockets, as the grieving family dropped the grave keeper's key through the door's mail slot onto the dead person's coffin, ensuring that the grave door was locked for eternity. That was her father's cue to wheel up a barrow full of dirt for mourners to scatter on the door, symbolically sealing it with soil and seed. It all made Laurel's throat close, the top of her head feel ready to cave in. She made herself scarce during sealings. No one ever missed her.

"Good morning, Mrs. Tisch." Laurel waved to a woman with an impressive stoop and steel-wool hair. One of the devout, Mrs. Tisch had visited her grave each morning for as long as Laurel's memory existed. No longer able to climb down the ladder into her grave to think, Mrs. Tisch sat on a folding lawn chair and tapped her feet on the door.

"Laurel, sugar, will you check on Mr. Colvin? He's going to have a stroke trying to open his door one of these days."

"You bet." Laurel changed course, setting off at a jog toward Mr. Colvin's grave.

Laurel found Mr. Colvin's door propped open, stray cobweb strands on the beveled panels twitching in the breeze. A few feet from the grave, she cupped her mouth and yelled, "Mr. Colvin? Are you there?" In the stretching silence, dark possibilities multiplied in her mind. He could be dead at the bottom of his grave, or knocked unconscious, bleeding from the head. She would have to check, look down into the deep well of his most private existence, toeing the edge of the grave. And if he was fine? If he simply wasn't wearing his hearing aids that day? She would have to throw herself back from the doorway and pray that he hadn't seen her peeking. He would tell her father. She would have to make it up to Mr. Colvin, whose picture was in the dictionary next to the definition of *crotchety*.

"What?" he finally shouted. "Who's bothering me?" A buckle clicked in place, followed by mechanical whirring. "What do you want? Can't a man"—his voice grew louder as his motorized chairlift carried him to the surface—"in his own grave be left alone to think?" He paused the chair as soon as his head topped the grass. His skin was liver-splotched and creased with discomfort, he had no eyebrows or eyelashes, and what little hair was left hung in wisps from his temples. His skin was so thin, it seemed stretched over nothing but bone. In the full force of the sun, Laurel could practically see his skull underneath.

"Sorry to bother you. Mrs. Tisch just asked me to check—to make sure you didn't need anything."

"Actually, yes. I do. I need some privacy! I need some peace and quiet!" His egg-like noggin descended, still spouting directions at Laurel. "You go back to Mrs. Tisch and tell her to mind her own business." The chairlift shuddered to a stop. "Just because she isn't thinking inside her grave anymore, doesn't mean she can go poking in other people's. God almighty."

Laurel backed away. The thing about her family was that they of all people—the ones tasked with upholding the Tenets by virtue of owning and running the cemetery—had rights to see into others' graves, and did on a regular basis. No one acknowledged it, or even seemed aware, but her dad, Walt, and her brother, Simon, helped the undertaker lower the caskets. They engineered holding walls to keep the grave shafts from collapsing and making victims of their owners. They pulled out chairlifts and ladders and lighting. They didn't merely peek in; they set foot in other people's graves.

The devout were a dying breed. Daily visitors had dwindled to a handful of the elderly and one or two younger people who came weekly, usually with either an aging parent or a child for whom a good example must be set. One girl, a little older than Athena maybe, came more often than most. Her schedule was erratic. Laurel would catch her grave door open at six in the morning on a Sunday, or lunchtime on a school day.

If the devout's days were numbered, she hoped that Mr. Colvin would go first, and when they ripped the elevator chair out of his grave before the sealing, she'd ask them to save it for Mrs. Tisch.

Chapter 2

ATHENA'S BRAKES SCREECHED AS SHE COASTED DOWN Orchard Hill toward town. This was her favorite part of the day: full-bodied wind, sun still low and cool, long hair streaming behind her like a banner. The only time Athena ever felt graceful—felt what it might be like to be Roxanna Dover, who swept down the halls of school as effortlessly as she sprinted across the soccer field—was when she rode her bike. On two feet, Athena felt body-bagged. Arms tight to her sides, legs stiff, pigeon-toed. A layer of pudge coated her body evenly, smudging away any trace of a collarbone, blurring the line between hips and waist, camouflaging her jaw. Her body was as unsure of herself as her mind was—could this be a shoulder blade right here? I dunno, maybe. Other girls grew in the arms and legs, stretched out like Elastigirl. Athena grew like a miniature dinosaur that you submerged in water overnight: she was simply bigger in all directions, but overall no different than she'd looked or felt in eighth grade, or fourth grade, or third. On two wheels, coasting toward the library, not late at all but actually an hour early for babysitting—which her mother didn't need to know—she didn't think at all. She was one long strand of exposed nerve endings.

At the bottom of the hill, Athena stopped in the right-turn lane at Greene Falls' single stoplight. Two blocks long, Main Street was a sorry excuse for a downtown: three storefronts stood vacant, with old newspaper pages taped to their windows; the rest of the stores included Sally's Antiques & Gifts, the library (which had been Our Lady of the Mountains Church before being recycled by the town), Vandeveer's Funeral Home (also Suze's house), a tattoo parlor, a Chinese takeout place, and Black Diamond Saloon, which also advertised GIRLS GIRLS GIRLS. Her brother, Simon, rented a room at Suze's, and he had left his windows open wide that morning. One curtain billowed out over the street.

A block to the left, the high school stood at the top of the best sledding hill. A fleet of sinister school buses waited in the front circle. *Two more days. Don't think about it.* The library had a decorative flag flying: an apple and a piece of chalk dancing before a blackboard that said *Back to school!* Everywhere she turned, the town was giving up on summer. Sally's had electric jack-o'-lanterns in the window.

She studied the silhouettes of mounted deer heads and moose antlers on display inside Sally's. A sunbleached poster advertised *Grave Goods & Gifts—Just in Time for Grave-Opening Season!* The poster curled at the edges, fried to a crisp. Grave-opening season was practically over. For the millionth time she wondered what kinds of grave goods Sally's offered to the town. Her parents' disgust for what they called "the commercialization of grave keeping" still hadn't completely lost its hold on Athena. She was curious, but wary. "If anyone sees us in Sally's," her mother had explained, "they'll lose all respect for our business. What we do goes deeper than that grave goods nonsense, those cheap blankets with a map of New York State embroidered on them." Under no circumstances, save life-or-death, was Athena ever to go in.

It was strange to think about giving someone else something for their grave. Hers had been decorated entirely by her mom, and then slowly redecorated by her as she grew out of her sunflowers phase. She couldn't imagine choosing something even as boring as a flashlight to give a grave opener. What if the person was super orthodox and wanted an electricity-free grave?

I guess their parents would probably mention that on the grave-opening invitation somehow: "Candles only, please." But still, the grave opener unwraps every gift in front of the entire party; everyone oohs and ahhs at each little fountain pen or digital voice recorder.

How do you avoid giving the same gift as other people? How do you choose something worthy of being held up like a trophy?

As Athena waited for the light to turn green, the standing-still sun laid into her. Beads of sweat budded along her upper lip. *Mom was right; it's gonna be hot, hot, hot.* She was still staring at the antiques store when its door jingled open and out walked Roxanna Dover, swinging a gift bag and sliding her aviators up her ski-jump nose. *She must be buying something for her sister—for her grave opening tomorrow. Tomorrow! Tomorrow she will be at my house.*

Roxanna Dover wasn't the most popular girl in school, but she was the coolest. It had taken Athena a while to understand this because so often popularity was mistaken for coolness. In reality, popularity and coolness ran along two different axes. There was a point of intersection, but you could be one without being much of the other. Coolness was gained, in part, through aloofness; a certain degree of unpopularity was required. Athena had the unpopularity part of the equation nailed. The coolness bit was harder to come by. When everyone knew—or thought they knew—everything about your family, no amount of aloofness could compensate for that. As the third Windham kid to make her way through the Greene Falls school system, teachers asked about her brother and complimented her mother's baking. Her sisters shadowed her like rumors—Lucy, the tragic cautionary tale every kid grew up hearing—and Laurel, hidden away from the world and therefore infamous. They were weights tied to her ankles, dragging her down, down, down into the depths of social outcasts.

Roxanna's coolness stemmed from her lack of regard for

virtually everyone and everything in the entire town, including her social status. She wasn't cowed by the popular girls, whose coolness was limited by their dedication to uniformity. She was moderately popular without trying. She wore Swedish clog boots and bracelets made out of Starburst wrappers. She had a black-and-white Sleater-Kinney sticker on her violin case. She carried a tiny mermaid-green Diana camera with her at all times; it dangled from an old-ladyish eyeglasses necklace. She had over five hundred followers on Instagram, but she never reposted the same photos on her blog.

Roxanna disappeared around the corner of the building. Her 1995 Saab convertible was probably waiting, top down, in the parking lot behind the Chinese restaurant. Maybe it was the sun, or leftover adrenaline from the bike ride, but a thousand thoughts fired through Athena's brain and funneled into one: *I could follow her.* Her sweaty hands suctioned to the handlebars. *Just for a little while, I could.*

A car horn blew and Athena jumped. She waved in apology to the impatient car as she pedaled into the intersection with new determination, past the Peter Pan bus stop, whose weekly schedule she might or might not have memorized. The Houlahans and the community pool and the rest of her day waited for her in the opposite direction; she wasn't ready yet. She pedaled toward the library, toward the point where Main Street dissolved into the county road, with the ski slopes in the distance like green scars crossing the face of the mountain.

Chapter 3

GRASSHOPPERS BURST FROM THEIR HIDING SPOTS, small and green as Mike and Ikes, fleeing the giant's path through the orchard. Laurel knew Mr. Colvin read the paper in his grave, the grouchy hypocrite. So much for time spent with his thoughts. She ripped a leaf from the nearest apple tree and sliced flesh from the veins with her thumbnail.

She did well with the devout, mostly. They were the old people of the town—prehistoric birds—who grew up unquestioning. Back then families still visited their graves together each Sunday, the boys' hair wet-combed, the girls in buffed Mary Janes. Now, those visits were reserved for holidays like Christmas or New Year's—days when swarms of people would take the time to sweep up the doors in their family row, leave a potted poinsettia at the head of a sealed grave. On those obligatory days Laurel either stayed inside completely or went out very early in the morning. She'd learned the hard way that people knew who she was, knew her name even if they'd never met her. She was part of the reason they came to the cemetery in the first place, to catch a glimpse of the tragic fairy-tale girl. She hated their roving eyes. Pitying looks from adults, fascination from kids. She was the only homeschooled kid in the mountains, and therefore a weirdo, a Boo Radley. The youngest sister of the girl who died, whose parents snapped the family shut tight after the accident. Her older brother, who grew up in the Before, had been a Boy Scout and basketball player and member of the jazz band. Laurel and Athena grew up in the After, small lives whittled even smaller. Forget the fact that it wasn't her choice, that when Lucy was killed, Laurel hadn't even been born yet. Forget the fact that she was just as curious as they were. Their stares made her squeamish, and the only way to avoid the stares was to avoid being seen.

She turned up the Champs-Elysées, which ran north-south down the center of the orchard, the main trunk off which all the rows branched. Her grandfather had named the rows to better direct workers and grave-opening guests alike. Neat hand-painted street signs stood at intersections. At Fifth Avenue Laurel turned left and slowed her pace. Grass tickled at the hole in her sneaker toe. Her eyes roved from ground to apple trees to headstones, in search of anything out of place: a mudwasp nest, a chipped grave door, a sealed grave whose grass top was beginning to sink. Her dad always said she was vital to the health and well-being of their customers, not to mention the business. Laurel was his eyes and ears; she reported back from the field with a list of graves that needed tending.

Clover doubled back, ran ahead, paused every now and then to stalk an invisible critter. Twigs and burrs clung to her belly and tail. Laurel kept to the rows, noting every door hinge, every decorative shrub. She knew never to take pebbles off the tops of headstones, but she stopped to deadhead a few marigolds or collect a handful of leaves that had settled around an unused grave door, packing them into her brother's old paper-route bag.

The sun was getting strong. A few graves ahead, Clover was sprawled in a patch of shade, tongue flapping out the side of her mouth. Laurel patted her heaving side. "There's a good girl. You stay here and nap." For a long time Athena and Laurel had tag-teamed grave duty, walking rows side by side like horses in a harness. That went out the window when Athena finally won her campaign to go to school, and then when her grave opening came around. After that, she only cared about her own grave, and their parents were only too happy to indulge her newfound devoutness. "She's taken to that grave like a fish to water," their father said one night as Athena ducked out the back door after supper.

"Like a fish to water," Laurel mocked now, wiping sweat from her forehead. She was half certain that the main reason Athena loved her grave so much was that Laurel couldn't follow her there. "'A grave is for the keeper alone.' So stupid." Her skin was sticky under the strap of her bag. She glanced over the last few rows, then back toward the house. "Good enough for me." Her father would be occupied with the funeral for another couple of hours at least. She jogged to the edge of the woods, where her mandatory orange hat and vest hung over a branch, rain-specked with dirt. Without giving them a second thought, she ducked into the trees and headed downhill to the creek.

Laurel walked down the center of the creek with one dirty Ked in each hand. When she neared the swimming hole, she picked her way over to the side. Her legs were numbed to the point of senselessness; she stopped, closed her eyes, and listened, trying to separate and identify the different melodies of the water. Bubbling, from the shallower, stony part; a bass line *glug-glug-glug* from up above in the deeper hollows; a steady shushing, like long skirts; a more rhythmic surging sound, the water's heartbeat. She waited, listening. It was a feeling she had often at home: she wasn't alone. But that was always true in the woods.

She opened her eyes, and a flash of movement in the trees across the water caught her eye. Sometimes she saw pheasants munching in the berry bushes, but this was far too big and bright to be a pheasant.

It was a boy. His round face dimpled as he waded into the stream fast, determinedly. "Oooh! Ahh! Cold!" he chanted, until he was knee-deep in the pool above with two hands on the first stone of the retaining wall.

What in the world is he doing? Swimming with his clothes on? Laurel stood perfectly still, aware of every contact point between her body and the ground, rooted, breathing slowly. *He hasn't seen me. He doesn't know I'm here.* He reached a leg out, trying to get footing on the ledge.

"Don't!" she yelled before she realized what she was doing. "It's too slick, you'll fall!"

The boy staggered backward into the pool, arms flailing to find balance. He took one step too many and the silt brought him down with a splash.

"Oh my God." Laurel scrambled up the bank and waded into the swimming hole. "Are you okay?"

Shivering and blushing, he stood up on his own, his sopping shirt clinging to his skinny frame. "You scared the crap out of me." He stalked back to his side of the creek. "Where did you come from?"

"I was here all along; you just didn't notice me."

The boy glowered at her from the tree line, wringing out the hem of his T-shirt. "Who are you? You don't live around here, do you?"

"In the woods?" Laurel laughed. "No way, I live—" Damn it. She couldn't tell him, there was no way. If he lived in town, then he would know she didn't go to school, and he would know exactly who she was, and he'd disappear with a story.

"Did you forget?"

"No, I live a ways away. You probably wouldn't know it. I'm just here visiting family, thought I'd take a walk."

"Okay," the boy said, unconvinced. "I thought you might be—never mind."

"Do you live in town?"

"No, I um—" He made a show of bouncing on one leg to shake water out of his ear. "I, uh, live up near Albany, but my family rents a house here every summer."

Phew, he's just a tourist.

"I'm Charlie. What's your name?"

"Laurel."

"Laura?"

"Laur-el. Like the tree."

"Huh. That's weird."

Laurel thought, *Is it?* And at the same time, *This is the first boy I've ever spoken to.*

"Are you going to stand in the creek all day or what?"

Laurel had barely noticed the water rushing around her shins. She skirted the deepest parts and still her shorts got wet. Standing on Charlie's side of the creek, the hems of her cutoffs dripping water down her legs, she said, "Sorry about, you know, scaring you."

"It's okay. I probably would've fallen anyway. I could hardly feel my feet."

"Yeah." Laurel looked back at it as if to remind herself. "I mean, yeah it's cold. Not yeah you're a klutz." She slapped a mosquito from her knee. "One time I found a six-pack some teenagers tied to a rock. They hid it in the water to keep cold."

"I thought you said you weren't from here."

"Oh, this was near my house. Creek water everywhere is cold."

"Uh-huh." Charlie shook his head, spattering Laurel with droplets. "Well, I've gotta get back. My mom will kill me if she catches me soaking wet like this."

"Me too, actually. I totally lost track of time." Her head said, *Move it!* But she didn't budge an inch. "Maybe, uh, I'll see you around?"

"Sure. See you around, Laurel."

"Bye, Charlie."

As soon as he turned and headed back into the woods, she was off like a shot, dodging trees, leaping roots, barely letting her feet touch the ground.

She found the orchard exactly as she left it. All in all it hadn't been a bad morning—with her laundry list of fixes, her father would never suspect her extra-long detour to the creek. Laurel whistled for Clover and headed down to the meadow where the barn was. Her dad was there in the yard—alone—sleeves rolled, wrestling a chicken onto the block. When his ax fell, it took a beat for the dull *thunk* to make its way to Laurel.

"Hey there," he said. "What's the good word?"

"Nothing much. Found a broken doorknob." She squinted up at him. His hair was slick with sweat, and a few curls clung to his forehead. Thick glasses magnified his eyes.

"Well, you know what to do. Go pick out a new one." Walt

motioned into the barn with his ax. "I'll save the chicken head for you to bury later."

The barn felt hollow without the noise of her brother, probably gone for lunch at the diner. She plucked the tiniest chisel off the wall, felt its sharp curve, thin as a fingernail, and weighted her list to the table with it. Her father's worktable was routinely covered in a collection of chewed yellow pencils, rusted screws, various spray cans for apple scab outbreaks, open tubs of brass polish, and thin strands of newsprint clipped from the obituary section.

In the corner under the sawhorses, Clover scratched her back in a pile of wood shavings. Laurel said, "Knock it off, weirdo," but Clover ignored her.

The barn's stalls, emptied of animals long ago, held slabs of marble and granite and fieldstone. A tired angel stood outside a stall of doors whose hinges shone gold. Dozens of ladders were strung between the rafters overhead, and one solid wall was covered floor-to-ceiling-beams with drawers. The fluorescent light over the desk droned, flickering from time to time.

Laurel dragged an old milking stool over to the wall of drawers. The rafters creaked, watching her. The first drawer took three tugs before it scraped out. Thumbtacks and grass seed sifted around on the bottom; a few glass knobs, too delicate for the heavy door on 504, winked back in the light. The next drawer held a collection of sandpaper rubbed soft and bald, and doorknobs too small, with plates no bigger than Laurel's hand. Finally she found a solid candidate with a white enamel knob that would stand out nicely against the polished walnut of grave 504. Its key hung off its neck by a green ribbon.

As she dragged the stool back to its home, a ladder broke free from its hook and sliced the air between Laurel and Clover. The clanging crash sent Clover bolting out into the yard. "You chicken!" Laurel yelled after her, but she had screamed, too.

Walt rushed in. "Are you hurt? Did it hit you?" He held Laurel by both shoulders, checking before pulling her to him for a hug.

"I'm fine. It fell next to me." They looked up at the rafters and saw the hook still intact, thinking the same thing and saying nothing.

Chapter 4

A SINGLE PUBLIC COMPUTER SAT IN THE FRONT LEFT corner of Our Lady of the Mountains Public Library, next to a soft cardboard box of old hymnals. Athena logged in to her email: coupons to ShopBop and Walgreens, yesterday's weekly update from Ticketmaster. Over her shoulder the librarian sisters, Norma and Noreen Blackistone, shared a slice of pound cake and sipped tea from Styrofoam cups at the front desk. "Vitamins," one said to the other.

"I'm not taking those things. Makes my hair hurt."

"For the love. I give up."

Their dentures nuzzled in an ashtray.

Athena slid the stinger of her headphones into the computer

console and called up Spotify before returning to her ritual. First email. Then Facebook. Her profile, cloaked in privacy settings, allowed her to browse the pages of her classmates—those who were stupid or vain enough to have them set on "public," anyway. For people like Kristy Mellon, a day without an update was a day that did not exist. Pictures of dinner plates and nail polish designs and yet another day at the pool with Hannah and Jessie; Athena saw them in real life, stomach-down on beach towels in the back corner behind the lifeguard chair, bored and half-asleep behind their sunglasses. But the pictures on Kristy's profile—posing in straw fedoras, Airheads sticking out of their mouths like blue tongues—sent a completely different day at the pool glowing back at her from the screen. "Loving life!" said one caption. "Me 'n' mah girlzzz," said another.

Friendship. To Athena, it was a library of sweet-smelling books with their pages glued together. She figured it was something you learned in preschool: how to build a history with another person. How to call that history Friendship. Athena couldn't find her way to it. She hadn't started attending school until seventh grade—the perennial new kid, no history with anyone.

Kim Deal was singing in her headphones, "And this I know, his teeth as white as snow," in her sweet Muppet voice, calling Athena back. After a Facebook check came the lifestyle blogs written by women in Brooklyn and San Francisco and Portland, posts about baking miniature doughnuts and refurbishing found furniture, a dozen photos of a bar stool. How did you make a life look like that? She imagined the graves of these women, outfitted with crocheted throws and striped paper straws to drink out of glass Coca-Cola bottles. Grave keeping through an Instagram filter. They would have a field day at her house—it was the epitome of vintage, but accidentally. Her parents still used the percolator given to them at their wedding because it still worked. The girls grew up in retro boys' clothes because their mother believed in darning and mending and hand-me-downs, because anything with any potential use was saved, squirreled away. Athena wore barrettes that had belonged to her grandmother. Laurel played with porcelain dolls wearing fingerless lace gloves aged to the color of tea. Each night they ate off plates that had *1896* stamped on their undersides. Vintage was a generous way to say old.

The double doors of the library parted in the middle. It was Athena's classmate Maude Gelwick, scuffing to the front desk in her duct-taped sandals, her long hair tied back with a bandanna. "Good morning, ladies," she said to the Blackistones. "How did you sleep?"

"Like hell."

"Sleep? What's that?" Noreen smiled and rolled her eyes at herself. "Old bones don't settle well."

Athena took one earbud out but kept her eyes on the screen. This was more library action than she'd seen in the last six weeks.

"I'll bring you more of that tea after lunch. I wish you would let me buy you a heating pad. Just one! You can fight over it," Maude said.

Norma reached across the desk and shook Maude's hand by the fingers. "You're a sweet girl. The shelving cart is back by the biographies."

Maude works here? I've never seen her here this early.

"You're Athena, right?" Athena spun around in her chair so fast she accidentally pulled her second earbud out. "I think we had chorus together, maybe?"

Half the school is in chorus. Good guess. "Yep. Hi." Athena waved pathetically. "How's it going?"

"Pretty good. This is early for me, but I'm trying to get back on a school schedule, you know?"

Athena nodded. "Me too."

"Today feels like a two-cups-of-tea morning." Maude rubbed an eye. "Well, I better get to it. Good to see you, Athena."

"Yep, see ya soon." When had she adopted her father's mountain-man monosyllables? She had no reason to be intimidated by Maude, or feel any need to impress her. Her heart rate begged to differ, though.

With both earbuds securely back in place, Athena made her way to Roxanna's blog, her last stop. Dove-gray background, cherry-red font, *Rox Talks* unspooled across the header, which was a thumbnail picture of one of Roxanna's eyes, lined in black. The one upside to being back in school? Potentially having math with Roxanna again. Reading her own experience recast in an entirely different perspective, searching the screen for mention of her name, or the back of her head on the edge of a photo—it was like a *Where's Waldo?* of her own life. High on Athena's list of personal goals was being mentioned on Rox Talks.

The closest she'd come was Roxanna's documentation of a Pi Day party that their math class had held the year before. On March fourteenth, kids from the honors class had crammed into their classroom to watch the first thirty minutes of *A Beautiful Mind*. Someone had brought a tray of cupcakes decorated to look like Mr. Glahn. Each frosted top sported glasses and a walrus mustache. Roxanna had written:

Pi Day shenanigans were ridic, as expected. We ate cupcakes instead of pie—I mean, come ON. A Beautiful Mind *was all Princetonian and Jennifer Connelly's eyebrows. He rode his bike in a looping infinity sign, which was kind of cool. Got to split a second cupcake with someone, which was cooler.* [Black-and-white photo of cupcake wrappers piled in the trash.]

That someone had been Athena. She had split the cupcake.

No new post from Roxanna this morning. She was not in the habit of updating for the sake of updating. Her readers could wait.

IT MATTERS NOT WHAT IS IN ANOTHER'S GRAVE

The tail end of August in Upstate New York was an unreliable segment of summer—days were still hot and baked-feeling, but nights were cold, and the crickets chirped louder in panic. In my day, autumn was the height of production, a race against time to harvest and dry and store. You could feel your life shrinking with the season, your world reduced to the perimeter of the fire's warmth. Laurel felt this as well, but to her it wasn't life shrinking; it was a reduction, like a potion—all components boiled down to something more potent. She looked west to where Hunter and Plateau mountains met in a notch, cloud shadows patching them dark green. They feel it too, she thought.

By the time I was Laurel's age, I was busy wishing years would stretch, wanting to heap birthdays into a rowboat and push them out toward the horizon, unreachable. I loved being thirteen. I refused to quiet. I refused to surrender my time in the trees for the good of the work. How could anyone expect me to spend all day carrying water or plucking chickens when there were eagle feathers to be found on the cliffs by the falls?

I was the first grave keeper born in the New World. I lived my life under the influence of England, a place as foreign to me as the moon. The New World was supposed to be Eden for the grave keepers. Their journey, it turned out, was a self-fulfilling prophecy. Harsh seas became a grave for many before they even arrived, which is not to say they weren't prepared for that possibility. If your grave was your true and only home, as they believed, and your temporary home was a boundless unknown, wouldn't you take comfort in your grave? Wouldn't you devote yourself to the one certainty in life? Death comes for everyone; it's nice to have an idea where you'll end up. The belief knit itself into the fabric of a newly forming nation.

As the centuries wore on, and living became more likely than dying, graves were reclaimed for the individual. With the newfound time, people felt they had to prepare more. Graves became rooms; rooms became shrines. Leaving flowers on the grave of a loved one is no different from decorating the inside of your own grave; both are thought in action. The First Tenet of grave keeping, after all, is "A grave is to think."

I have dipped in and out of more graves than I care to admit, accompanying Laurel on some spying missions, but mostly satisfying my own curiosity. The sealed graves are far more interesting, as you can imagine. I sought answers, and then clues, then any tiny fragment of a reason why a grave might keep one person and not another. Graves, there were plenty; but ghosts? I was the only one.

Chapter 5

FROM LUNCH UNTIL ABOUT THREE O'CLOCK, LAUREL had Self-Guided Study Time. She and her mother sat in the dining room with the lights off. Condensation beads slid down their glasses of ice water. Laurel lifted one sticky leg at a time from the chair, eyeing the computer at the end of the table. Claudia used the old desktop to run finances for the cemetery, but lately she had Laurel practicing typing with her fingertips on specific keys, like the world's most torturous, tuneless piano lesson. She was supposed to practice by typing out letters to her pen pal in Korea, Darlene. For months Laurel had been sending and receiving ruffle-edged notebook pages full of questions: *Have you heard of Michael Jackson? Do you wear glasses or braces?*

What is your favorite beverage of choice, if you had to pick just one drink to drink for the rest of your life? But now, when Laurel looked at the printed page with answers to Darlene's many questions, it felt like a lie. Anyone could've written that letter and signed her name to it. Her mother insisted typing was the way forward, end of discussion. The day before, she'd had Laurel type "A grave is for the keeper alone" twenty-five times. It was murder.

Claudia pushed her crochet hook through an unidentifiable tangle of yarn. "Before I forget, we need some meat for supper tonight."

"What about the chicken?"

"I put it in the freezer for Suze, as a thank-you for the funeral today."

"You're giving her a whole chicken? For doing her job?"

"It was an important one."

"A whole chicken? We haven't had chicken in ages. She can just buy it at the Price Chopper." *Like normal people,* she didn't say.

"Without Suze, we'd be in dire straits." Claudia adjusted the elastic of her eye patch, pulling long strands free from her bun in the process. "What's next on the reading list then?"

Laurel could barely stand to look at the wool yarn in her mother's hands. Winter seemed so far away in such heat. "Grimms."

"More fairy tales? Don't you want to sink your teeth into some science writing for a change? Botany? Outer space?"

"No thanks."

"What about some legends that hit closer to home? You've never read 'Rip Van Winkle,' have you?"

Laurel shook her head and made a face.

"It takes place right here! Rip Van Winkle Trail is the road up the mountain. It could be a fun way to fit some history in, too."

"Maybe after the Grimms."

Her mother sighed. Laurel loved making her mother sigh. She headed upstairs to her father's study, taking the stairs two at a time, testing the new length in her legs. With each step she chanted in her head, *Rich man, poor man, beggar man, thief. Doctor, lawyer, merchant, chief.* It was the rhyme her mom had said when buttoning her coat when she was little. There were only four buttons; Laurel always got the thief.

The back bedroom had once belonged to Laurel's brother, but years ago her parents had reclaimed the room. Claudia's grandmother's enormous gilt-framed mirror hung over her quilting table. Walt had built bookcases around three walls and a threadbare wing chair sat under a brass floor lamp, looking out across the open floor. As sloppy as he was in the barn, when it came to his books, Walt was meticulous. A rectangle of sun stretched across the floor. Laurel planted her bare feet in the middle of the warmed hardwood and looked for the spine she had memorized from all those bedtimes, all those nights of begging for one more page, one more story.

Her gaze landed on the curly, knotted font of *Irish Myths and Legends*, roved over the Vikings and the Aztecs to a green hardback without a title. The binding crackled, opening reluctantly. Plain print on the title page read *The Complete Fairy Tales of the Brothers Grimm*. Laurel looked at the tea-colored paper, the hardback wings suspended between her hands. Even though it had been around since Baby Simon, the book was a relic of her own childhood, too. After Lucy, routines and traditions started anew with Athena and Laurel. Very few things, whether books or toys or extracurriculars, had had the staying power to last from Simon to Laurel.

She was constantly surprised by things that turned up under her own roof, even more so because she was forever on the lookout for them. Laurel had never known the house when it was full, when there was another kid between Simon and Athena. Her brother had grown up and moved out before her memory began. She went looking for remnants of her family, feeling for loose floorboards as she walked, closing herself into closets to rummage through shoeboxes of keepsakes that meant nothing to her. Her siblings' rooms still held memories of them in the walls. On the back of the door Simon had carved *YANKEES* with a pocketknife, and in the closet there were dozens of water-wrinkled *National Geographic* magazines, tubes of acrylic with hard marbles of paint rattling around inside, and a ball glove hanging from a nail, filling the closet with the scent of oil. She had always felt like a historian, like the age of her family had come and gone without her.

Laurel carried the book to the end of the hall and the door that was always open. She liked Lucy's room because it didn't really belong to anyone, and no one would yell at her to get a life or mind her own beeswax. Plus, the bed sat next to the window—exactly where Lucy had kept it—and Laurel liked reading with pillows under her head while a breeze carried blue jay squawks through the screen. With one elbow resting on the windowsill, she opened carefully, two-handedly, to the dedication page and read the inscription underneath out loud. "For Lucy, with love from your big brother, Simon." It was in her mother's handwriting.

"'Once upon a time,'" she began, and the pile of picture books on Lucy's dresser flew one by one across the room. "Lucy, knock it off." Pages gusted open and crash-landed in crumpled heaps. "I'll stop reading out loud, okay? Will that make you happy?" The books stilled.

Laurel turned back to her book, tracing each line with her index finger.

Over the years I watched the farmhouse accumulate people and empty, crescendo and fall quiet. I found my place in the house after Lucy died. Fewer and fewer windows held light in them after dark. A constellation formed between the blue of the TV room, the candle flicker of Lucy's room, and the faint glow of the girls' attic bedroom. To round out the figure, I would turn lights on in the bathroom or the basement. Occasionally, when I felt loneliness press in around me, I went through the house turning every single light on, no matter the time of day. When it got especially bad, I turned on every electrical appliance, too. The hum of a current comforted me.

I spent a good chunk of time in Lucy's bedroom, which was probably the one way I could be a comfort to anyone. They all thought that I was Lucy, banging cupboards and turning faucets on and off during dinner, begging to be included. Lucy's room, in a sense, was where I was supposed to be, if not in my grave. Claudia kept an electric candle in the window year-round, well after the Christmas decorations went back into the crawl space behind Laurel's bed. Lucy's hairbrush lay belly up on her dresser, still woven with white-blond strands. A blue field day participant ribbon hung from the lampshade on her bedside table. Her sheets had never been changed, her hamper never emptied. It was as if Lucy had touched a cosmic pause button by mistake—at any minute, she could return and pick up right where she left off, moving her Venus flytrap with the shifting sun and taping Pokémon cards to the back of her door.

It comforted me, too, that a family would preserve a memory that way. To Laurel, the only family member who hadn't met Lucy, the room was a museum to explore. When she was little, fascination triumphed over fear of punishment for disrupting things in there. Now that she had the room completely mapped out, its draw was privacy, quiet. A place to think. Claudia spent the most time in Lucy's room. She sat on the bed most evenings, sometimes to tell Lucy stories, sometimes to remember. I would open the music box to show her I was listening.

Chapter 6

By three thirty Laurel was out the door and back into the woods, taking the long way down the road to their mailbox. She was free to roam the woods as far and wide as she pleased, so long as she didn't go into town. A few years back she could be found in the sliver of woods behind the playground almost every afternoon, watching recess after recess come and go, and in the summer she took up a post at the fence of the community pool, peering between the wooden slats at boys cannonballing off the diving board and girls in red swimsuits whipping silver whistles around their fingers. (And of course at Athena, bobbing the littlest Houlahan in the baby pool.) She still went back occasionally, but nowadays it depressed her more than entertained her.

She checked the mailbox every day, toting the stack of bills and junk mail back to the dining room table and stashing her own haul under her bed for night reading. Athena smuggled *Seventeen* and *Teen Vogue* and, bizarrely, *O, The Oprah Magazine* down to her grave to memorize horoscopes, turn pages slowly, rub perfume samples against her wrist. But Laurel had Delia's and Scholastic Books and Hammacher Schlemmer, and they were full of things she could make her own, things she could wrap for birthdays or display on her dresser. Not everything fit her life—for example, an electric tie rack would be of very little use to her—but she could imagine the lives made easier by those things, the different people who would look at an electric tie rack and think, *I know just who to buy that for!*

That day happened to be a rotten mail day, nothing but plain white envelopes addressed to Mr. Walter Windham, so Laurel took the creek down to the broken dam to check her traps for dinner.

She pulled four frogs and half a dozen crayfish from the darker water at the end of the broken cement wall, the deepest, coldest corner. She was lucky: critters never raided her traps the way they did her father's. Laurel found her traps either empty or full, and more often than not, full. Her mother didn't know she fished Dibble's Dam. It wouldn't sit right with her, to think of Laurel tightrope walking out to the fattest part of the creek, leaning way over to haul up her traps. Luckily, her mother never asked for specifics.

Laurel found her in the kitchen, stirring a big pot of milk. "Here." She handed Laurel a glass of orangeade and the wooden spoon. "I'll trade you." Claudia heaved the bucket into the kitchen sink and ran cold water into it. "Only babies today, huh?"

Laurel nodded, gulping her drink so fast the undissolved powder scratched her throat. "I'll fish tomorrow if you want. Or maybe Dad'll let me take the rifle. I keep seeing pheasants. I could—"

"Stir the pot. Freddie picked a good week to forget and deliver us milk twice. Let's just hope he forgets the extra bill, too, huh?"

Laurel ran the wooden spoon through the milk. "If I have the rifle with me, I can get a rabbit, maybe. Or like I said, a pheasant. Maybe a turkey?"

"Sweets, do me a favor? Tell your sister it's time to come in, and then set the table: forks and knives."

The family graves lay all in a row, her parents in the middle, Simon to their right—unmarried, yet to be relocated to a marriage plot—the three girls to their left. Grass bisected the family's row of doors, planted over Lucy's door, sealing it for eternity. Laurel's grave was at the end because she was the youngest, the headstone smooth except for her name, carved in deep by her brother's chisel.

Athena's canopy, intended for a twin bed, stood out from the headstones like a skyscraper; its floral curtains twitched in the breeze. Athena clocked so many hours in her grave that the usual deterrents didn't faze her. She would simply close her door most of the way and sit in her stuffy grave as the sun or snow or rain beat down, bundled in old quilts with a thermos of tea. The canopy was her mother's idea, waterproofed and erected by her father, so she could think in her grave any time of day or night, any type of weather.

Athena sat inches away from the lamp with a magnifying mirror and a pair of tweezers, studying the half inch of skin between her eyebrows. Her hair being as blond as it was, eyebrow hairs were nearly impossible for her to spot, but that didn't stop the scrutiny. Finally she caught a stubborn strand—*yoink*—and sneezed. Tweezing always made her sneeze.

"Athena!"

"Yeah?"

"Mom says it's time for supper and you have to set the table." *Did you bite down on the stones in the muffin?* Laurel almost asked. *Did you break a tooth?*

"I'll be there in a minute." Athena squinted at the palm-size mirror. She could tell Laurel waited, listening.

Laurel parted the rosebud-printed canopy curtains with one finger, inched her forehead into the shade. From within, the curtains felt like a tent in a field. For a moment Laurel lost her bearings. Sunlight set the rosebuds in stark relief from their cream-colored background. Athena's door was propped against the opposite legs of the canopy, the underside the same bright green as the top. Laurel hadn't been down in Athena's grave since the spring, when Athena was securely at school for the day.

Since then her sister's grave must have morphed; with all the thinking time of those long summer days, an entire geological era could have gone by. To see into Athena's grave, she'd have to step under the canopy, right to the edge, but slowly, slowly. If Athena—or worse, her mother—caught her peeping, she'd be dead meat. A person's grave was the most personal, private part of her life. It was her own preparation for death, values and loves and passions manifest in decorations and collections. Secret desires, hopes, and goals—a person's grave was a window to her innermost thoughts. To go into another's grave was like eavesdropping on someone praying—it was beyond improper; it was flat-out wrong. But you could only be wrong if you got caught.

Is she—? Athena craned her neck, half expecting a sun-dried snake to fall through the air. The quiet was too quiet—a forced silence that hid more people than comfortably fit. When she realized what Laurel was doing, Athena snapped off the light. Given the choice between a peeping Tom little sister seeing inside her grave and a dead snake landing on her head, she'd take a rain of reptiles.

Laurel had one boot through the curtains when Athena's ladder started to twitch. Sheer instinct: Laurel ran. Boots *ka-thumping* against her shins, she tore down the hill to the back porch, took the stairs in two strides, and was through the back door before Athena's curtains even flickered.

Her mother raised her eyebrows. "What, you see a ghost?"

✧ ✧ ✧

Laurel buttered her biscuit once, twice, three times, four, collecting and redistributing the spread like a plasterer working putty into a cracked wall. She got the Gumby silverware that night, the fork and spoon she could bend into a U. Great-grandma's silver—what was left of it—was reserved for her parents at supper. Used to be there were silver pieces enough to go around, but over time butter knives and salad forks had gone missing like socks in the dryer.

"Walter, that's enough salt." The pink shade on the lamp at the center of the table quivered when Claudia set down the stew pot.

"Sissy, pass the biscuits," Athena said.

"Don't talk with your mouth full. Walter, I'm serious! Give me that." She swiped at the saltshaker. The lamp clicked off, dropping dinner into darkness. Claudia felt for the switch and turned it back on. "Lucy," she said to the air in the room, "don't be fresh."

Athena took the basket from Laurel, untucked the dishcloth, and felt down to the bottom for the warmest one.

"Claudia, I'm a grown man. I can salt my food however I choose." Walt slid the saltshaker into his shirt pocket.

"Suit yourself." Claudia chased a hunk of potato around her bowl with her spoon.

No one said a thing, but Laurel knew what they were all thinking. She stole a peek at her mother's numerous chins, her chubby, ringless fingers. "Can I go back-to-school shopping with you?" Laurel asked.

"I don't think that's such a good idea, sweet bay."

"No, I think it's a great idea. She can go instead of me. No one will know the difference." Athena loathed back-to-school shopping; it all took place at the Goodwill down in Catskill, which smelled like mothballs and basements and garage sales. And as for school supplies, they came one at a time: one notebook, one pen, one pencil. When she filled one or drained the other, only then did she get more.

"Athena, don't start."

"Please?" Laurel begged. "I promise I'll be so quiet no one will notice me. No one will even see me."

"And if that works, maybe she can start going to school for me, too."

"Athena," Walt said with a warning in his voice.

"Sorry, honey. Not this time. Maybe next year."

"I'll go to school for her! Send me to school instead."

"School is so inconvenient."

"Athena, knock it off. Laurel? Both of you. That's enough."

Walt drew a wedge of biscuit around his bowl, chasing the leftover stew, picking out shell shards and tiny frog bones with his fingers. "School is overrated, sweet bay. At school they only give you one desk. One desk that you have to sit in all day long."

"Yup," Athena said.

"At school there are people my age, and class pets, and I can have a lunch box."

"Class pets are for the little kids. Get real."

"Shut up, Athena. I'm not talking to you."

"Here, you've got so much space, so many options," Walt said. "And just think: you can't take a dog with you everywhere you go at school, can you?"

"Nope," Athena answered.

"But I could have a locker, and I could sing in chorus, and I could ride the bus."

"You've got the run of the land! You've got the life every kid dreams of!" Walt punctuated his argument with jabs of his fork.

Laurel felt a patch of cold on the back of her head, seeping through her hair. It felt like someone had pressed an ice pack onto a bump that didn't exist; it soothed her. "Fine," Laurel said, and went back for one more pass at her buttered biscuit.

For a few minutes everyone chewed in silence. Athena pinched bites from her biscuit and tossed them into the air, catching them in her mouth until one hit Walt and he told her to cut it out.

"Well," he said, "not to change the subject, but how are things going with the grave-opening prep? Only two left in the season."

"Technically one in-season"—Athena held up a finger—"and then one in September."

"Let's not split hairs."

"She's right, Walt," Claudia said.

"It's a matter of four days." He held up four fingers. "Four days."

"It's a grave opening in September, Dad. It's out of season."

"It's opening a can of worms, is what it is," Claudia started in. "What if the IRS started telling people, 'Sure! Send in your taxes a day or two—or four—late.' What if kids decided to take the SAT four days late? If you let one person do it—"

"Those are completely different scenarios. This is a legitimate grave opening."

Athena spoke through a mouthful. "So what's the big deal? Why is this kid getting special treatment if he missed his summer?"

"It's not special treatment; it's—complicated. Let me worry about the logistics, and you guys just think about your jobs," Walt said.

There was a moment of tense chewing before Claudia replied, "I should have enough for both grave cakes without needing groceries."

"Excellent. Girls?"

Athena perked up. "I've got both my outfits picked out already. And if Mom can write me an absence note, then I'll be all set."

"Great. I look forward to your carefully curated outfits. Sweet bay, what about you?"

"I'll be around. I'll just help Simon with whatever."

"Yeah, you know the drill." Walt gave her a gentle noogie and the ice pack feeling went away.

"I have some news." Athena looked across the table at Laurel. "I had a visitor at my grave today."

"Oh?"

Athena turned to her mom, hoping for the best, most horrified response. "When I came up for dinner I caught Laurel under the canopy peeking into my grave."

"I did not! Mom, I swear. I've never seen inside her grave, never."

"You did so. I saw you!"

"Girls, all right now, come on." Claudia slid a finger under her eye patch strap and massaged small circles into her temple. "Athena, I asked her to call you for supper. And Laurel, you know you're not supposed to peek."

"I didn't!"

Claudia put up a hand. "It's okay. You're not in trouble, but don't go giving me a reason to change my mind, hear me?"

Laurel nodded, face on fire, furious at her sister, but too stunned with her mother's bored reaction to protest the injustice any further.

"You owe your sister an apology."

"Sorry, Athena," Laurel spat.

"Okay, now everybody drop it."

"That's it? She's not even grounded? Mom—" Where was the yelling, the shaming, the lessons to be learned?

"Athena, drop it." Claudia locked eyes with Walt across the table, flashing their secret Morse code.

"She also put rocks in my breakfast!"

"What? Don't blame ghost mischief on me." Laurel's face wrinkled into a laugh. Athena threw her napkin at it. The cabinets under the sink opened and closed in applause.

Up to her elbows in hot, sudsy water, Laurel scraped the stew pot with a stretched-out, shapeless Brillo pad. Athena leaned against the counter, impatiently folding and refolding the towel. A fat bead of sweat rolled over Laurel's eyebrow, and she swiped at it with her shoulder. "Can you get me a spatula or something? This gunk won't come off." Her fingernails softened and bent in the greasy water.

"Here." Athena offered her a wooden spoon.

"Come on, I said a spatula. Something to scrape with?" she said slowly, making sure Athena could understand. It was moments like these where Laurel was sure they had been born out of order. Athena was three years older, but she was made to be the baby. Prone to whining and pouting, grabbing the clicker, skipping out on shared chores. She'd put up such a fight to go to school that her parents gave in two years before high school, the original start date. And of course, true to fashion, the instant Athena got what she wanted, she didn't want it anymore.

"All right, all right, keep your shirt on." She sighed and went to rummage in the utensil drawer again. Under the table Clover yawned and put her head down. Through the lace curtains above the sink, the sun-stained clouds tumbled over themselves slowly. Walt and Claudia were already in the bench swing under the birch in the front yard, their cups of tea cooling in the grass, talking—or not talking. *A grave opening in September.* They all were thinking about it.

Athena finally brought over an ancient metal spatula with a bent handle and rust blooming along the edges. "Here," she said. "Now try to take a little longer cleaning that pan." She threw the spatula into the sink with a splash, then returned to her post at the counter, twisting the towel around both hands.

Slimy water drenched Laurel's shirt and dripped down the cabinets onto her bare feet. *That brat.* She felt around for the drain stopper, clogged with potato skins and bloated biscuit crumbs. Scooping a handful, she paused as the sink gurgled, gulping the water down. "Thanks a lot!" She heaved the goop, and a pretty hefty amount of water, at her sister.

Athena screamed and semi-ducked, her back and hair taking the direct hit. Her hands curled into fists, her shoulders tensed to her ears. "Oh." She heaved a deep breath. "My. God."

Laurel's feeling of triumph evaporated. Her parents were too far away to intervene. She could be face-first in the toilet in a matter of seconds—she knew it from experience.

Athena seethed, breathing through clenched teeth. Very slowly, she approached Laurel and wiped her long wet ponytail across her little sister's face. Laurel knew not to move. She coached herself, *Running will only provoke her*. "You are dead and buried, Laurel. Dead. Sleep with one eye open." She threw the towel across the room as she strode to the door. "Finish the rest of the dishes on your own, buttface."

Her flip-flops *smack-smack-smack*ed across the yard as she ran up the hill and disappeared into her grave.

Chapter 7

ATHENA FELT THE BACK-TO-SCHOOL PANIC CINCHING itself around her shoulders. All those things she'd daydreamed about in June as she folded loose-leaf into an accordion fan and pulled her hair up off her neck—*this summer I'm going to get a job at the Ice Shack and bike to the bonfire every Friday and learn Mom's recipe for grave cakes.* She hadn't done any of them. All ten weeks had been identical: riding to the Houlahans' house, the lawn chair weave imprinting on her thighs while the kids thrashed and kicked at each other in the kiddie pool, hair drying on her ride home, dinner and dishes and her grave.

Athena stripped off her drenched shirt and slid her bare feet down the yoga mat on the floor of her grave. *I'll take my time getting her back. Let her squirm for a while.* The sunburn peeled along the part in her hair, and she chipped the polish from her thumbnail to keep from scratching. She hadn't even done her summer reading yet! *Damn, damn, damn*. She probably couldn't read three books in two days, even if she didn't have another grave opening to deal with.

She chose a thick red paint pen from her rubberbanded stash and began to doodle over a newspaper article about shale drilling. Summer reading was gross. Anyone who did their summer reading obviously didn't have much else to do for the past two months. Where did they go, people like Roxanna Dover and Lindsay Nathan? They seemed to evaporate into the muggy summer air the day after school ended, teleporting to places like Block Island or Lake George and returning with ankle bracelets and stark white bikini straps ghosted to their shoulders. (And in Roxanna's case, rolls of film to be developed in her private bathroom-turned-darkroom.) It was still so weird to Athena: these people she would see nearly every single day for forty weeks would go away and return in September with different voices and heights, completely new interests and outlooks on life. She'd come to expect the unexpected.

Goose bumps prickled along her forearms and across her shoulders. She pulled her sweater on—it was always cold in her grave. *I should have followed Roxanna. I should've found out where she was going, what back-to-school errands she had to run.* Her teeth found her lip and began to chew. *Tomorrow she will be here, in this very orchard. She has to come to her own sister's grave opening.*

Athena imagined walking through the party guests in her green dress, her long blond hair in a sheet down her back, Roxanna noticing her bracelets (all handmade by Athena) and asking about them, then taking a picture of the party over Athena's shoulder, posting it on her blog. *Crap, what if she invited her friends to the party?* All they wanted to talk about was clothes, or boys, or who was dating certain boys, or why said boys would find anything attractive about those girls. Plus, they looked at her like she was some freak, practically Amish compared to them. And they would never leave Roxanna's side. Lindsay and Jordan would be game changers; they pretty much hated her.

Laurel thought she had the short end of the stick, staying home and helping their dad all the time. She had no idea how good she had it. Laurel never had to wear her hair in a bun for two months straight just to cover up another uneven haircut from their mom, or turn her back to whispers while she changed for gym. Laurel didn't have to lock her bike at the far end of the parking lot where the bushes hid her from view of the kids who had their licenses and were allowed to drive to school (or kids who were allowed to ride in other kids' cars, period).

Athena drew a filigreed border around the newspaper photo of what looked like a rickety knockoff of the Eiffel Tower. *Eleventh grade. This year, then one more.* Two more years and she could make her final retreat, go home to her grave-digger daddy and eat grave cake at every meal, like those girls said. Go home to your grave and cry about it.

And the thing was—the thing that really got her—was that

she had been there for all those girls at their grave openings, arranging the gift table, refilling punch glasses, receiving hugs from them at the end of the day before they piled into a parent's car and went to the mall or a sleepover or whatever. All summer long the Windhams hosted grave openings for kids in their thirteenth summers. June through August the orchard swelled with people. Some families brought folding card tables and lawn chairs; others hired party planners to swoop in with upholstered dining sets and strands of electric lanterns that plugged into a portable generator. No matter the person, Walt put on his twill vest and good shoes for the key service, and Claudia baked the honorary grave cake, decorated to match the person's grave door.

After the official key service and grave-opening ceremony, the grave honoree sliced into the cake, symbolically opening their grave to the rest of their family and friends. Of course it was all a bunch of hooey. None of those cake-eaters would ever be permitted in that kid's grave. To enter someone else's grave, to breathe the air and leave your thoughts there, corrupted the grave as well as its keeper.

While everyone ate cake and the little kids fought for the candy-coated doorknob, the grave opener would start in on the presents. Traditionally, the gifts were to ornament the grave or somehow make it more comfortable. Candles were common, as were lanterns and headlamps and fire extinguishers. Some people gave diaries, others gave blankets and pillows. Athena could walk the rows, pointing at grave doors like a fortune teller. "Cassidy got three strands of twinkle lights. Joe got a beanbag chair." She remembered so much—grave openings seared into her memory—because for one day at a time, she was in. She was involved. And it wasn't that long ago either! Three years, give or take, since they told her, *I like your headband! Very Blair Waldorf*, which she didn't actually see as a compliment, considering Blair was evil. But she had said, *Thanks! I'll see you around the graves!* and continued to wear the headband every waking moment of the following three months. A couple of girls came back to their graves maybe once or twice, pressured by their parents into using the new gifts they'd received. But they never bothered to cross the orchard cemetery and find Athena's grave. They never knocked on her grave door or slid a note through the mail slot, written on a page of their new "From the Grave of" stationery. And at school there was a collective memory loss whenever she waved hi to them in the hallway, wearing their grave keys on necklaces as if they actually ever used them.

It didn't matter. Athena circled random words in the newsprint: *booming*, *stream*, *zoned*, *coffers*. In two years she would never have to see them again, and in the meantime, she would do her grave-keeper duty. She could feel her mother's warm hand holding her own as she recited the Tenets of Grave Keeping, and when she was done, not a single mistake along the way, her mom had spun her around and fastened the thin gold chain of her key necklace.

"Congratulations, sweet pea," Claudia had said, tears shining up her eye. "You're a grave keeper now. Happy birthday—thirteen, hard to believe."

Athena had smiled and run the key back and forth along its chain. She thought her grave opening would make her feel older, wiser. Thinking back now, as she colored in the newspaper photo, that was the feeling of her twelfth birthday, a year too early. All that excitement for nothing. Twelve had been a hard year, starting school, blossoming with acne, her eyeteeth at odd angles while it seemed everyone else's mouth was ringed with metal.

But turning twelve, Athena remembered how freeing it felt—she would be going to school! Finally, she didn't have to stay home; she was getting her end of the bargain. The deal had always been there, but just out of reach, bounding ahead of her like a white rabbit. First it was understood that Claudia would keep her home and teach her for kindergarten and first grade. Then it was thought best that she help Walt with the orchard cemetery and look after Laurel, so fourth grade would be the year she started school. But the deals never stuck; every few years her parents renegotiated, worry overtaking reality.

Laurel had caught some of that worry—the excessive wariness of strangers, the caginess. She wanted to go to school, she wanted friends, but she wouldn't even leave the car at the grocery store. She'd asked to go back-to-school shopping knowing the answer would be unequivocally no. It was as though she wanted nothing more than to live her life behind a two-way mirror. Their parents worried that without homeschooling, the girls would veer off into an unforseeable future. Accidents happened in that future; cars ran red lights. It was so easy to send your daughter to school and never see her alive again. Laurel's worries were simpler: that the kids wouldn't like her. That the reality would never rise to meet the expectations. Athena saw the nervousness well up in her little sister on the morning of every grave opening, when the thought of kids traipsing through her own backyard terrified her to the point of throwing up. Their parents had carved the fear in so deep.

The year before Athena's grave opening, they couldn't delay it any longer: they had to promote Athena. She was finally needed in the business, and not just to walk the rows with Laurel, picking up twigs and raking leaves for days every fall. *God, that was awful. No ten-year-old should suffer from back pain.* Grave-opening ceremonies were growing bigger and more elaborate every year—what they needed was an assistant, someone to straighten up throughout the parties and direct guests to the bathroom. What they had was a chubby blond twelve-year-old with jagged fingernails and a cowlick that made her hair shoot up from her considerable forehead. Athena was never asked. She was told. In exchange for school, she would help run the grave openings—a reward of work for work.

"Forget it!" She threw down her paint pen and went at her sunburned scalp with both hands. "Ahhhh." Flakes floated down onto the newspaper, but Athena didn't care. Who did she have to impress? Who was going to see her in her grave?

Chapter 8

After suppertime in the summer was Laurel's favorite time of day. Athena retreated to her grave for the last few hours before bed, and Laurel, barefoot, took her Fla-Vor-Ice and climbed out the window of her brother's old room onto the roof of the back porch. It was high enough to be out of the mosquitoes, and no one but Clover knew where she was.

She could see the whole orchard spread out before her like an orderly forest. She looked over toward row ninety-two in the southwest quadrant, where the next day's grave-opening ceremony would take place. It felt like the whole sleepy orchard was wallowing in the calm before the storm. Tomorrow dozens of people would drive in and turn the yellow-green meadow into a parking lot.

The screen door slapped the house. She heard the faucet turn on with a rush, teacups clinking in the sink.

"I don't know, I'm worried about her," she heard her mom say.

"It's normal for a kid her age to be curious."

"I agree, but curious about her own grave, maybe. Not other people's."

Wait, what? They're going to punish me after all? Laurel's toes gripped the shingles, waiting for the response.

Claudia pressed on. "What harm could it do? It won't cost anything. At least think about it, will you?"

"I will if you'll think about the last opening."

"Walt, I'm not comfortable with it. It isn't done, and people will find out, and I'm not comfortable."

"It's not just the money, they have good reason—"

"It's enough that it's partially about the money."

Garbled TV voices floated up to Laurel from the living room windows. The hectic theme song of *Wheel of Fortune* drowned out the rest of her parents' conversation.

Laurel shimmied to the edge of the roof and followed the orange extension cord from where it bit into the wall outlet all the way to where it disappeared between Athena's grave curtains. Her sister would be down there even if she couldn't have a lamp. She'd bring lanterns and flashlights, or she'd just sit there in the dark. *What does she do down there all this time? What is so interesting about her grave?* Laurel had been down there. It wasn't that great.

✧ ✧ ✧

Summer reading guilt brought Athena out of her grave and to her father's library. She found *Siddhartha*, *Antigone*, and *Romeo and Juliet* in the study and flicked the reading lamp on. Handwriting filled the endpapers of each book, notes from English classes when someone else had had the same summer reading books. Athena read, "Themes: search for enlightenment, love, inner compass." And below it, in cursive: "Important symbols: water, the ferry."

Simon's handwriting isn't here. Typical. It wasn't that he didn't like to work hard—it was that it was more important that he appear not to work at all. He had been captain of the basketball team, got asked to the prom all four years, made friends with kids whose parents had ski houses in Stowe and beach houses in the Hamptons. A social schedule like that was a full-time job. Their father called Simon "the mayor" because every time Simon went into town, he knew everyone by name, and they knew him.

Feet pounded up the stairs. Laurel yelled, "No!" Then more slowly, Claudia made her way upstairs. Athena looked up as Laurel ran past into the bathroom and slammed the door.

Like clockwork. Athena checked the other two books to make sure there were notes on the inside covers. Inside *Romeo*, in bubbled, girly handwriting, someone had written, "Wherefore art thou Simon?" The question mark was dotted with a heart. *There we have it—the only evidence of Simon.*

Claudia knocked on the bathroom door, catching her breath.

"Laurel," she said, "so help me," she said, "I'll lock you in there all night if I have to."

"No."

"You are far too big to pitch a fit like this every time."

"I'm old enough to make my own decisions, then."

"You have to take a shower."

"No."

"Do you want me to call your brother and have him come over here and throw you in naked? 'Cause he will."

"I don't need to shower today. I'm not that dirty."

Athena yelled from the study, "You stink, Laurel! Take a friggin' shower!"

"You haven't been using the deodorant I gave you. You've got to wash, and you've got to do it more often now. You could get away with this when you were little, but you're not little anymore." Her mother slapped the door—"Do it, Laurel"—and walked downstairs.

Athena thumbed Juliet's upturned face, angelic, creased where the cover was bent. Who would write that in Simon's book? *God, that's so desperate. She might as well have written her phone number.* The shower taps squeaked; hot water pipes clanged.

In the bathroom, Laurel tore her clothes off, throwing each piece at the hamper with all her fury. When steam curled across the ceiling, she stepped into the tub and stood under the water with her arms crossed. Little gray rivulets dribbled down her legs. She

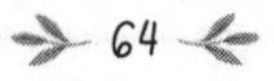

wasn't going to cry. Her hair melted into a thick curtain over her face. Finally she offered her pits, one at a time, to the shower, took her father's hunter's soap, and rubbed.

She wasn't going to cry.

That night a thin strand of tension stretched across the girls' attic bedroom, from the front-facing eave and Laurel's bed, over the clothes-strewn floor to the orchard-facing eave, where Athena had fortified her things. Laurel removed the dolls from their places against her pillows, carefully laying them out on a blanket on the floor, smoothing their hair and closing eyes as she went. Across the wide room Athena sat on the edge of her bed, massaging lotion into her elbows. In between was a no-man's-land speckled with coverless paperbacks, bent hair clips, dirty underpants, blue jay feathers, chlorine-scented beach towels, and Clover's stuffed mallard. Below them, their parents' voices grew louder and they stopped taking turns speaking. Laurel hummed to cover up the shouting.

Athena tried not to think, *Tomorrow is my last day of summer. There are only twenty-four hours until I have to go to bed with my alarm set and my lunch premade in the fridge.* Her stomach seized. *Don't think about it, not yet.* She watched Laurel put her dolls to bed, envious. On Laurel's nightshirt, a damp patch spread where her hair ended.

"Can you believe it—a grave opening in September?"

Laurel shrugged. "The weather's still good for it. No big whoop." She tapped at the mason jar lying sideways on her night table, and her toad froze. "Good night, Norman."

"No big whoop? Are you kidding?" Athena snapped the lotion bottle shut. "It goes against tradition—grave openings are a summer rite, period. How could Dad let them get away with this? The family must be really rich, maybe even famous. I wonder who it is."

"You'll find out soon enough." Laurel found the bookmark in her green book and pushed Clover down toward the foot of the bed. "You'll actually be there for the first-ever September grave opening." She stared up at the poster of constellations pinned to the ceiling above her bed. Fragile white lines connected the beads, filling the deep blue with gods and crabs and ladles.

Athena climbed under her covers and turned out her light. "Soon it'll be your turn, Laurel. Then you'll have to work the grave openings, too. It's not as much fun when you have no choice."

An oscillating fan clicked back and forth on the dresser top.

"I guess."

"That reminds me—Mom was asking about you the other day."

"What do you mean?"

"She's worried that you're not interested in your grave. She said she asked you if you had been thinking in it lately and you said no."

"What, should I lie?"

Athena considered it. "In this case, yes."

"So what if I haven't been thinking? It's not like I'm going anywhere. I have all day every day to pop in and out of my grave. I have literally nothing better to do."

"That's what I said."

Laurel's heart beat so hard she felt her T-shirt twitch.

"Laurel, don't stress about it. Maybe mention to Mom how you'd like a chain for your key, or extra batteries for your flashlight. If you bring it up before she does you'll deflect her, she'll forget all about it. One of the many paradoxes of dealing with parents."

"Okay."

Athena heard a page turn. "What is that you're reading?"

"Fairy tales. For Momschool."

"Oh, that figures—Mom asked me to get you a book at the library, some sketchbook thing. I miss being able to choose my own homework. Geometry nearly killed me."

"Mm-hmm." Laurel had a chunk of hair in her mouth, sucking the water out.

Clover squeaked a yawn and Athena turned toward the wall. *No more days at the pool. No more squeezing Ellie's feet into those awful water shoes. By next summer she won't fit into them anymore, and she'll be in the minnow classes with Jeffrey, and I'll be seventeen, and a senior.* It was like peering through a keyhole into an alternate universe—how did she get there from here? The sheer number of days between then and now made Athena sigh and bury her face in her pillow.

How many years had she felt exactly the way Laurel felt now? She ached for school, for friends, for protractors and report cards. She watched her brother bring home track medals and A+ Scantron sheets and homecoming pictures, and she thought, *I will never have that. I could never be that lucky.* Of course at the time what she meant was *I will never have the chance to go to school and play sports for real, not just in the yard, and I could never be lucky enough to wear a long strapless dress and get a bracelet made of flowers from a boy.*

But now, as the lotion cooled on her skin and the crickets fought the racket of the cicadas, Athena thought, *I will never have that. I could never be that lucky*, and it meant something completely different.

Downstairs, Lucy's music box tinkled softly while Claudia sat in Lucy's room, thinking. "Mom's in her room again."

Laurel pulled her hair from her mouth. "I don't get what difference the room makes." She gestured toward the ceiling, the walls, the floor. "She's still here. Everywhere."

Athena screwed an earbud into her free ear and set her Discman to repeat. Across the attic, wide awake, Laurel lay thinking about her grave, tensed and ready for Athena's revenge.

YOUR GRAVE IS YOUR TRUE AND ONLY EVERLASTING HOME

Around the time Walt and Claudia took over the orchard cemetery from his folks, the pendulum of tradition was swinging toward change. The once-sacred marriage plot—two graves side by side for the newlyweds, new space for everlasting rest to go with till-death-do-us-part—splintered with the divorce rate. People remarried, or moved across the country, changing graves three or four or many more times. Cemetery developers, running out of options in New Jersey and Connecticut, kept up a ceaseless assault on the Windhams and other cemeteries in the mountains. People no longer settled for the town cemetery—they liked to shop around. Plus, it was no secret that New Yorkers had to travel to keep a grave. A grave rush was under way—too many people in the cities, too few cemeteries. Many avid skiers had bought plots in the Catskills decades earlier, and more continued to, year after year. I helped where I could, directing the strangers in their Zipcars down wild roads that veered away from the slopes. They arrived at the Windhams' confused, not knowing how, exactly, they got there.

Laurel heard her parents talking about the city slickers trickling into the orchard each winter—vacation grave keepers. During the week between Christmas and New Year's, Laurel sat in her room and watched families trudge through the snow in their bulky ski pants, lift tickets fluttering from zippers. To her mind, they came from an elegant place, as foreign to her as Morocco, as glamorous and coveted as Manhattan: the suburbs.

People were the problem, and the solution. Laurel had swallowed the fear without the reasoning. Her family held the truth about Lucy like a closely guarded secret, the only way to bring privacy to such a public loss. Everyone in town knew the story, had read the driver's plea in the paper and seen the courtroom sketches on the nightly news, so why did the Windhams ever have to talk about it? Lucy Windham, age nine, hit by a car walking home from school the year before Laurel was born. She'd stayed after for clarinet lessons, or band tryouts. No one mentioned the end; facts were hard to verify. The hard-shell case had burst open in the road. Sheet music, muddy and torn, was gathered and returned with the missing piece of clarinet. The crossing guard had already gone home for the day, that much Laurel knew. Her mother hadn't allowed Lucy's grave to be seeded for over a year. She knew that much, too.

What she didn't know: who hit and killed Lucy. Did it really matter? To her family, having the name changed nothing. Was there comfort in the fact of a drunk driver, as opposed to a distracted driver, or an elderly driver? How did the loss change when the person at the wheel—a stranger—became the murderer, or when the driver-murderer was a friend? The ending was always the same, and Laurel knew better than to ask. She also knew that because Lucy had died, she couldn't go to school. Town was off limits—the library, the playground—forbidden.

I preferred it that way myself. Though in no way bound by

property lines or counties or even walls, I found myself needing the orchard cemetery the way animals need a territory. I couldn't stray far for long. Having Laurel nearby was the only solace, but even that was wearing thin. I had one year left before she started high school, slashing her hours in the orchard, the woods—her hours with me. School would crack Laurel's world wide open the same way it had Athena's. After centuries on my own, I had finally found a companion for one sliver of a decade. A plan was forming and gathering urgency. I needed to secure her place at the orchard, the way mine had been secured centuries before: far more permanently than preventing her from going to school. Laurel was connected to the mountain the same way I was. My connection outlasted my life. The question was: would hers?

Chapter 9

CLAUDIA SHOOK LAUREL IN THE DARK. "HONEY BEE, time to get up. Dad needs you in the barn." She disappeared back down the stairs without waiting for an answer, the old wood groaning under her feet.

Clover found Laurel's hand with her wet nose. "Five more minutes," she whispered. She hadn't slept well. She was in no way dumb enough to fall asleep before Athena did, not after that soapy threat her sister had made. Laurel must've woken up fifty times thinking Athena was standing over her, ready to pounce.

Across the room Athena slept on, dead to the world for at least another hour. The space between their beds felt cold, as though a fog had moved in during the night. Pulling on her jeans, Laurel slipped on a catalog and crashed to the floor with a thud. She held her breath, knowing how furious Athena would be if she woke up extra early on her last day of summer. *She'll beat the ever-loving guts out of me, for real this time.* The fan clicked softly on the dresser. Athena's breathing held steady, and the blankets didn't budge, so Laurel grabbed her nubby sweater off its hook and finished dressing in the hall.

Her mom had breakfast set up on the kitchen table, where she sat with the obituaries and a plate strewn with burnt bits of crust. Through the doorway into the dining room, Laurel could see cake-decorating tools standing around the grave cake, which waited for its finishing touches. Claudia would spend most of the morning carving slabs of fondant and beating drops of red food dye into buttercream icing.

Laurel carried the rest of her coffee-milk out to the barn, pausing at the woodpile to pick up a couple logs for the stove. Clover trotted ahead, her clinking tags interrupting the quiet. *It's never quiet like it is first thing in the morning*, Laurel thought. There was a sharper chill in the air that morning, as if the last week of August were trying to warn them about winter. She followed the smell of coffee and wood smoke across the yard and into the barn. Her dad and Simon were sitting around on an overturned milk crate and sack of grass seed. Everything looked yellow in the glow of the overhead lamps. "Morning." She slumped onto her three-legged stool, dropped the wood to the floor.

"Hey, squirt." Simon's hair stuck out from under his baseball hat like a scarecrow's straw.

"Hiya, sweet bay."

Clover wiggled from one to the next for a scratch, saying her own good mornings.

"Okay, kiddos." Walt wiped his mustache with the back of his hand. "Let's get started." His magnified eyes moved behind his glasses as he read from the to-do list. "The ceremony's at four, so we have a solid chunk of time to get this all done. First thing, I need to make a lumber run. The ground is too soft up by the grave, so I want to make a little platform and walkway. Simon, how's the stone coming?"

"Those feathers—Jesus." Simon massaged his claw of a right hand.

"Well, at least we're charging them for it. You and Laurel should take your stroll while it's still cool, in case you have to spray any nests or whatnot. Come back soon as you're done. We need time to set the stone. The fireworks crew are arriving around three to set up on the road."

Simon whistled. "I didn't think they were serious about the fireworks."

"Oh, they were serious. I don't think even the Prince of Wales had fireworks at his grave opening." Walt's eyes darted between his children. "Don't repeat that."

"*Moi?*" Simon feigned shock. "I wouldn't dream of it."

They left mugs in a cluster on the plywood desk and shuffled out into the barnyard. Clover darted into the orchard, as if she knew exactly which was the ceremony row.

✧ ✧ ✧

Laurel caught a groundhog chewing away at its breakfast, nose twitching anxiously, as she and Simon walked through the cemetery. They each had a pail of tools, his filled with poisons for yellow jacket nests and codling moths, hers crammed with pruning shears and gardening trowels to fill in holes and clean out old squirrel nests. Simon also carried a bucket of water and ammonia to scrub the headstones in the ceremony row. (No one wanted to see dried bird poop on the family graves.) The tin pail squeaked in his grip as they made their way through the orchard.

"Last show of the season," he said.

Laurel snuck a sideways glance at him. *Doesn't he know about the September ceremony?* She heard Athena's voice: *Play dumb. If you're not sure what you're supposed to know, play dumb.* "I know, last one, thank God. I'm getting too old for these early mornings."

Simon snorted. "Is Athena excited to start school tomorrow?" His face broke into a wicked grin.

"Oh, you know it. She's thrilled to death." Athena talked about school as if she were serving out a prison term. Given the choice, she'd drop out and spend all day every day in the bottom of her grave. If she knew Laurel was jealous, she never let it stop her from complaining.

Simon seemed to read her mind. "You know what? I'll swing by the library and get you a fresh stack of books if you want. First thing tomorrow, I'll be there when Miss Blackistone unlocks the front door." He gave her shoulder a nudge. "Sound good?"

"That's okay. Athena's going." They walked along in silence for a few minutes. Laurel knew the first graders went on a spring field trip to get their first library cards. Lucy's library card was in the sleeve of a photo album in the study. Clover came bounding down the Champs-Elysées, a pale streak in the dark, and took off in the opposite direction. Laurel counted steps, counted three stars still winking on the dim horizon.

The sun broke over the treetops just as they made it to row ninety-two. "Jeez, what a sty," Laurel said, and Simon snorted. This family clearly knew how to tend their graves and were sticklers about it. Each headstone had a neat border of pansies, dozens of little purple-white-and-yellow faces turned east, waiting for sun. The ground was perfectly even, no puckers of dirt around their doors or gentle sinkholes over the tops of sealed graves. They even fed the grass! It was so thick and bright, it looked like a green carpet had been unrolled down the length of their row.

The problem with people who were excellent grave keepers was that the Windhams' work had to be extra meticulous. The parents of this particular grave honoree would probably examine the row with white gloves before the ceremony. Today's honoree was Katarina Dover. *If I went to school (which I don't), Katarina would be in my grade.* Laurel had quizzed Athena on her earlier in the week as they set the table for supper.

"Do you know what she looks like?"

Athena gave her a look of pity, like she'd just realized Laurel's brain was the size of a walnut. "No, I don't know what she looks like. She's in eighth grade. At the lower school. I'm in eleventh grade, remember?" She went back to folding napkins.

"But you know everyone at the upper school. Does she have any older brothers or sisters? Maybe she looks like one of them."

"Actually, she does have an older sister, Roxanna, but I have no idea if they look alike."

"What does Roxanna look like?"

Athena sighed. "She has short dark hair, like a bob, average height. She's in my grade. She hangs out with, like, Lindsay Nathan and that group. Why do you care? You don't know these people anyway."

"Just wondering." *So maybe Katarina has dark hair, too. Maybe it's curly like mine.* Laurel was the sole inheritor of her father's hair. Her brother and Athena had some shade of their mother's blond corn-silk hair. Lucy, too.

"Mm-hmm," Athena said, obviously bored. That's when Laurel gave up.

Now, Simon and Laurel walked down the row past all the sealed graves to the doors of Katarina's parents and grandparents. They always worked top to bottom, starting with the trees. Laurel climbed each tree in the row, careful not to scrape off too much bark with her boots. "Nurse," she called down to Simon. "My scalpel, please." He passed up a pair of shears and she trimmed the scorched brown leaves. She went like this from tree to tree, Simon following behind with the rake. At some point Clover showed up and stretched out for a nap in the shade.

Once the trees were neatened and hung with purple glass lanterns, they moved on to the graves themselves. Simon trimmed the grass alongside the doors with scissors to make sure it was even. Laurel snapped on a pair of yellow rubber gloves and dipped a rag in the ammonia water to clean every single letter and carving in the Dovers' headstones. Cleaning the older generations' headstones went faster, just names and birthdates in simple capital letters. She went over the letters with a scrub brush and then washed down the face of the stone with a rag. When she got to Roxanna's grave, though, she had her work cut out for her.

Roxanna's headstone had a border of pine branches carved in such detail Laurel had to use her pointer finger to clean each individual needle. Her last name spread in an arc across the top—*DOVER*—and underneath, in a more delicate font, it said, *Roxanna Grace, Beloved Daughter and Sister, February 17, 2001*. She stepped out of her boots and sat cross-legged on the evergreen door to get closer to the stone. Next to her was Katarina's grave. A long shallow trench waited for her headstone to come back from the workshop. The hot pink door looked headless lying there on its own.

Halfway around the pine branch border, Laurel's fingers cramped into a tight claw. "Why do you have to be so good at the fancy carving?" She cracked her knuckles and slowly flexed her hand. "It kills to clean." Simon could do almost any design a customer dreamed up—angel wings and roses and cursive lettering. There was even one carved to look like Hogwarts Castle. People were getting more and more particular about their headstones; everyone wanted a one of a kind.

"What's Katarina's look like?"

"Flowers and ponies."

Laurel raised her eyebrows like, *Oh really?* and Simon said quickly, "I'm joking, but check out that door! That is seriously pink."

"Okay, say it back to me."

"Garbage bags, paper towels, fancy napkins, fancy plastic cups," Athena read off the list her mother had just dictated to her.

"Yes, and anything you need for school lunches." Claudia scraped chopped chocolate from the cutting board into a double boiler. "Take Laurel. Tell her she can get a snack if she wants. Make her go in with you this time." Simon pinched a fleck of frosting from the bowl, and Claudia swatted his hand away. "Go on! People will be arriving in a few hours, and I'm sure Dad will need you back well before that."

Simon, Laurel, and Athena climbed into the cab of Walt's truck and bounced down the gravel road, Clover Honey chasing behind. "Be careful! Don't hit her! Slow down!" Laurel craned to watch out the back window.

"Clover's too smart to get hit," Simon told her.

At the end of their road, where it met Orchard Hill, Clover skidded to a halt and watched the truck shrink out of sight.

The parking lot of the Price Chopper was nearly empty, just a few cars with out-of-state plates, down from the campgrounds to stock up on ice and hot dogs. Athena slid out of her seat belt. "You coming in this time or what?"

"I think I'll just wait here."

"Mom said you could get a snack. What do you want?"

"Fruit Roll-Ups. No, wait! Strawberry Pop-Tarts. With the frosting."

"Suit yourself." Athena cranked the window down a few inches before hopping out. Halfway across the parking lot, she looked back at the truck. Laurel had two hands in her hair, ripping knots apart; she seemed to be studying a minivan parked in the next row.

They made their way up and down each aisle, Simon draped over the handle of the cart like a ninety-year-old man.

"Why doesn't she ever come in? It doesn't make any sense." Athena smoothed the list against her leg.

"She doesn't want to, I guess."

"Of course she wants to."

"Here, we need these, too." He dropped a box of animal crackers into the cart.

"Mom's gonna make you pay for that."

In the paper goods aisle, Athena squatted to get the store-brand garbage bags from the bottom shelf. "What is she afraid of? It's a grocery store. It's not like we're asking her to escape Nazi Germany with us."

"Oh, and you're so brave, Miss I-Hate-High-School-Don't-Bother-Me-I'll-Be-in-My-Grave? That makes you really unique, you know, the fact that you hate high school. No one in the history of the world has ever had a hard time in high school before you came along."

"Why are you mad at me?" They moved down the aisle, scanning for fancy napkins. "I didn't say anything about you."

Simon was quiet for a long moment, thinking about the truth and whether to say it out loud. Finally he said, "Never mind."

"No." Athena blocked the cart. "I really want to know what I did to piss you off. Is it that I missed the Yankees game last week?"

"It's not the game, Athena."

"I told you I had to babysit, so—"

"It frustrates the shit out of me to see you moping around all the time. Do you know how easy your life is? You spend almost every day in a herd of people your age, friends and boyfriends—or girlfriends—for the picking. You don't have to pay rent or cook your own suppers or do your own laundry."

"Um, have you met Mom? Of course I have to do my own laundry."

"You know what's expected of you and where you're meant to be," Simon continued. "The toughest thing you have to worry about is a trig test, which—hate to break it to you—is not going to have that big an impact on your life, so it doesn't really matter anyway."

"In case you haven't noticed, I'm sixteen. That's the average lifestyle of a sixteen-year-old you just described, so lay off."

"I'm just saying that you could appreciate the little things more, instead of being such a Holden Caulfield all the time."

"Who?"

"From *The Catcher in the Rye*."

"I haven't read that yet."

"Well, he's a legendary emo baby."

"I'm not an emo baby!" She threw one packet, two packets of fancy napkins into the cart. "This isn't about me, anyway. You just miss your glory days. And you think *I'm* too self-centered? Next time you want to relive your wonderful high school experience, why don't you go hang out at the Black Diamond instead of taking it out on me?"

Simon wheeled the cart around and backed her into the shelf of ziplock bags. She tried to dodge her way out, but he had her cornered next to a display of plastic wrap. He spoke through clenched teeth. "Listen. I know you're unhappy. I know you're not making it up. But you need to be honest, too. How many days a week did you eat lunch in the cafeteria last year?"

Athena had both hands on the cart. "Simon," she said. "Come on."

"I'm not letting you go until you answer me."

"I don't know. What does that have to do with anything? I ate in the cafeteria most days." Simon pushed the cart closer and Athena knocked several boxes off the shelf. "Okay, maybe a few days. Here and there. Mostly I went to the art room to work on projects. I had stuff to do."

"And when you had to do that group project about religions of the world in Carter's class, how many times did you meet with your group?"

"A few."

"How many times did you—?"

"Twice—in class. I picked a part to work on by myself and we put it all together on the day of the presentation."

"See my point? Those kids aren't entirely to blame; you're making the choice to be alone. Stop acting like such a charity case and grow a pair. Talk to people. Get out of the house. Do you think, if given the chance, that Lucy wouldn't trade spots with you in a heartbeat? That she wouldn't take full advantage of this God-awful hand you've been dealt?"

Athena pushed back on the cart with both hands, throwing Simon off balance. Ziplock boxes tumbled down the aisle. "Don't you dare make this about Lucy."

"I'm just saying. You might actually have fun, between the agony and mortification."

Athena gathered the boxes and shoved them haphazardly into empty spaces on the shelf. "Great bullying—I mean, pep talk."

"Don't forget the fancy cups." Simon strolled down the aisle, hunched lazily over the handlebar once more.

Athena didn't speak for the rest of the shopping trip, or the car ride home. All she could think was *Talk to people. Get out of the house.*

Roxanna Dover will be in my orchard in three hours.

Chapter 10

CLOVER BARKED AT EVERY RIFLE SHOT OF THE NAIL gun as Walt and Simon cobbled together the platform for the Dovers' row. Custom cutouts allowed it to fit over the graves in the next row, which only meant one thing: it was going to be a huge party.

Digging through the clutter of her dresser drawer, Athena felt for her silver barrette, the one with little green jewels like emeralds. It would match her green grave-opening dress perfectly, and Roxanna Dover would notice a detail like that. This grave opening was the only chance Athena had to make an impression—at least, more of an impression than *awkward girl in hand-me-downs* or *dork at the chalkboard fumbling through a geometry proof.* This time they were on her turf, and she was hoping for a rave review on Rox Talks.

She had shaved her legs and washed her hair to get rid of any sunburn remnants. After blow-drying with a round brush (to coax the ends under), she'd set up the ironing board in the sewing room and carefully pressed every pleat on her favorite sundress. Glancing in her great-grandmother's mirror, she noticed that the steam from the iron had set the flyaways in tight ringlets around her face, so leave-in conditioner had to be applied. She'd flossed after lunch to make sure there were no offending particles snagged in her teeth, and she even rinsed with her dad's mouthwash, gagging and gasping.

The clanging bell, her mom calling Laurel for the second time, sent needles of anxiety shooting through her. Less than an hour. *Why won't this stay?* The barrette slid down over her ear, leaving her thin hair drooping like a stage curtain. *Not cute. Forget it.* She threw the barrette on top of her dresser, among the regimental rows of lip gloss and ChapStick, the only makeup she was allowed. It had been two years since Athena had realized that it was no longer good enough to look the way she looked. Eyelashes needed varnish. Skin needed camouflage. If hair was straight, it needed loose curls at the ends; if hair was curly, it needed straightening. By eighth grade she was one of the last girls with fine golden hair on her legs that caught the light like spider strands. No one had told her she needed to shave. She'd found out by being left behind.

Now, a Jenga tower of magazines stood in the corner of her

grave, manuals on how to be a teenage girl. There was so much to learn! So many ways she could have gone wrong. *Seventeen* recommended showering in the morning, because going to bed with wet hair increased the growth of dandruff-causing fungus. *Teen Vogue* advised the hot nail polish colors for fall, and how to apply powder without looking like you'd done a face-plant in a barrel of flour. Athena saved her babysitting money in envelopes labeled by month, each with exact change for that month's issues. She knew it was cheaper to subscribe, but her mother would have thrown them in the garbage, unread. "Trash for the trash," she'd said, when she found an old issue of *Nylon*.

Athena couldn't be mad at her; it was like getting mad at Clover for chewing the handle of her hairbrush. *She doesn't understand. It's not that these things don't matter, it's that they don't matter to her.* Athena had learned fast: only go to the bathroom during class, and only if absolutely necessary. In between classes, bathrooms turned into dressing rooms. Girls lined the mirrors, retouching their eyebrows with tiny pencils and blotting oil from their foreheads with squares of toilet paper. Even though she knew none of them noticed her, even though it would have taken a small explosion to force them to look past the zits that needed concealing, Athena would wash her hands with her head down, feeling like the "before" to their "after" pictures.

For Katarina Dover's grave-opening ceremony, since she couldn't line her eyelids or dust her cheeks rosy with her parents around, Athena needed her lips to be at their shiniest, and for that she relied on a heavy coat of cotton candy–scented sheen.

She pursed her lips and kissed at the mirror, then smiled shyly. *There. Now if I just keep my lips closed when I smile, no one will see my gnarly stalactite teeth.*

Her breath smelled like medicine. Her legs smelled like vanilla. Her hair smelled like Screamin' Tangerine conditioner layered on top of Peachy Clean shampoo. Adjusting the pleats in her skirt, she paused and raised an arm. Powder fresh, just like the ads. Standing in front of her mirror, she tried her hands folded in front of her, one hand resting on her hip, both hands clasped behind her back. *No way—I look like Nancy Drew.* She twirled once and her skirt opened like a parasol before swishing around her knees.

Laurel led Clover up the Champs toward the far end of the orchard where she wouldn't get into trouble with the platform builders. They almost never went there on their walks; hardly anyone set foot up there at all. Graves were sparse—it was more orchard than graveyard, and Clover was the only frequent visitor.

A permanent shade settled over the orchard. *It's not going to rain, is it? Dad didn't mention anything.* Laurel trotted along after Clover, not really trying to keep up. Every few minutes the dog circled back with a stick for her to launch, and Laurel thought, *I have my own furry boomerang.* When they reached the fork in the path, Laurel turned right where the open lawn was, but Clover happily galloped to the left. Laurel whistled. "This way!" Clover stopped, looked at Laurel, looked back down the path, and took off running. "Where are you going? Wait!"

Laurel about-faced and followed her row after row into the far corner, the oldest part of the cemetery. Thick roots laced the row, pushing headstones out of joint. Overhead, silver-green leaves met in great connecting canopies, and the bark, nearly black, cracked and peeled in slashes. Ivy carpeted the ground, winding its way over headstones and up tree trunks. Unlike the rest of the cemetery, the headstones in this corner were Laurel-height, all different shapes and sizes, some pillars with writing on all four sides, some just tiny wafers of stone that read *BABY*. Laurel passed a statue of a saint—something had clobbered it, a tree branch, or maybe a hard freeze. The whole bottom half of its face—nose, mouth, and chin—were completely gone. Two eyes stared out at nothing. Names and dates on most of the stones had been washed away by centuries of wind and rain. One or two still had the ghosts of engravings, and at the top, winged skulls watched over the grave keeper.

What's the point of having wings but no feet? Laurel could just make out the skeleton teeth, grinning as they flew away. *Is that what happens to you after you die? Your head flies away?* She snickered at the thought of Athena's head popping off like a Barbie doll's.

Where is that dog? She stood still and listened.

Nothing. Dead silent.

She whistled high and loud, *woop-woop-woop*. Waited for Clover to come crashing through the bushes. Nothing. *Please*, she thought, *please don't let her be in a skunk den.*

Brambles and saplings and poison ivy forests filled the gaps between headstones, so she picked her way up and down the rows carefully, calling Clover's name. Raindrops hit her shoulder, her cheek. She turned the corner and there was Clover, munching on a sandwich, an entire slice of white bread flapping out the side of her mouth. "Clo-ver! You come when you're called, you hear me?" Clover continued chewing, unconcerned. "Whose lunch did you steal, you thief?" A few yards away, a brown bag lay on the ground, its guts spilling out: an apple, a can of soda, a plastic baggie of chips. "How did you sneak that all the way from the house?" She scooped the rest of the lunch into the paper bag, and as she stood up, her eye caught on something a few feet away. In the oldest part of the cemetery: an unsealed door.

The door was weatherworn and grayed with age, lying under a few bent weeds. The small places where rain had landed were darker and soft-looking, as if the wood were melting. The headstone above it read:

HERE LYES Ye BODY
OF TAMSEN QUINN

But she knew it wasn't true. No body could lie in an unsealed grave. Could it?

Looking around for answers, she noticed a knapsack tucked behind the headstone and a jacket hanging from a tree the next row up. "Hello?" she called, continuing down the row. "Anyone there? I think my dog ate your lunch." The jacket swayed creepily in the breeze. Rain was moving in. She turned to glance back over her shoulder. The unsealed door was still there; it was a car on the highway with no driver, footsteps in the hall without feet to put them there. The impossibility of what it meant—that either Tamsen Quinn hadn't been buried properly, or that she had had to bury herself, climb down alone and close her door one last time—made Laurel's skin crawl. It wasn't right. And there were no dates on her headstone, not even a birthdate. Laurel knew that there was a time, not all that long ago, when birth records were a luxury and people gave their age by how they felt, how many winters they could recall. But these other headstones—the ones she could read—had birthdates with years like 1682 and 1703. Clearly someone was keeping track. What went wrong with Tamsen's?

Unsealed graves were even rarer than September grave openings. A sealed grave was proof that a body was taken care of and resting in its everlasting home. The unsealed grave was just about the cruelest and saddest thing Laurel had ever seen. She couldn't stand looking at it any more than she could stand those heart-wrenching commercials for animal shelters. Tossing the rest of the bag lunch into the brush, Laurel took off for the woods, crossing the width of the orchard and cutting into the trees where the path was wide and smooth. Orange-vestless, she plunged into the piney shade. She didn't stop until she reached the pool where Charlie had fallen in. Laurel stilled her breath, listened for footsteps, the creaky snap of twigs. Picking through the trees, she scanned for movement, a profile, anything resembling a boy, but there was nothing. She was alone.

✧ ✧ ✧

About an hour before people were due to arrive, Claudia rang the bell on the back porch, signaling Laurel to help her with the last of the cake. She was the fact checker: was the icing true to the wood stain on the door? Did the lettering match? Was there anything left out, like a knocker or plaque?

Claudia was reaching for the bell for the third time when Laurel came sprinting down the Champs. "Where have you been? I was beginning to worry."

"Sorry," Laurel heaved. "Forgot. The. Time."

"I'll say. Scared me half to death." She ambled back inside.

Thankfully, Laurel had the gravesite memorized: Katarina's looked exactly the same as Roxanna's, except her headstone border was made of four hawk feathers, long and delicate. Simon's chisel had articulated every filament and barb. The font was even more elaborate: *Katarina Victoria, At Home in Our Hearts, August 28, 2004.*

Laurel sketched the design with ballpoint pen on an old envelope. Claudia drew the pastry bag across the tabletop, practicing the headstone lettering on a piece of parchment paper. Face creased in concentration, her eye patch crept up her forehead.

Laurel slouched behind the computer at the end of the dining room table, allowing as much space as possible between her and the cake station. "I'm so sick of grave openings."

"Oh?" Claudia moved back and forth between the table and the stove, pausing to drift into the kitchen and stir the bowl of chocolate melting over a pot of boiling water, then returning to stir dark droplets of food coloring into a mixing bowl of icing. Streaks of hot pink shot through the white icing like tie-dye. "This one should be pretty good. The Dovers are—fancy. Fancy people."

"Fancy?"

"There will be fireworks! Didn't Dad tell you?"

"Yeah," Laurel admitted. "He did." On grave-opening days, Laurel did her row prep in the morning and then didn't leave the house again until after-party cleanup began. She sat at her bedroom window in the orchard-facing eave of the attic and watched the parties through her yellow binoculars. "Maybe this one will be worth making popcorn for," she said, trying to ignore the pangs of jealousy that surfaced on every ceremony day. It was pointless to feel jealous. She couldn't even identify who exactly she was jealous of: the honoree? The guests? Athena?

Everyone. Every single one of them.

"Oh good, it's clearing up," her mom called from the kitchen. "Your father was fit to be tied, thinking he was going to have to tent everything in a downpour. And now it's sunny! What a strange day."

Laurel wanted to hate her mother and father. She wanted to throw everything she'd missed in their faces, evidence of the punishment she'd already had to endure at the hands of their self-preservation instincts. She'd seen Athena do it for years, pushing back on every decision, begging to go to school and then begging to stay home once she got her way. It was pointless. She recognized defeat when she saw it: saw it in Athena's attempts to stay home sick; saw it in Simon's talk about traveling; felt it in her arms and legs, her aching shoulders, every morning when she left for the orchard instead of the bus stop.

She sighed. The anger never stuck. Her thoughts wandered back to Charlie. Would Athena know him from the pool? *He looks like he's maybe my age, maybe younger. I can't tell.* She folded a corner of the tablecloth into itself. Sometimes she still daydreamed about having a teacher and a classroom, having a playground for recess and jumping rope under a long clothesline instead of the ratty old dog leash. She imagined drinking milk from a miniature carton and carrying her own library card and learning to decipher the rambling black tally marks on sheet music. It wasn't her place, though: her dad needed her in the orchard, and her mom needed company at home.

Charlie could've told me about school, what having a desk felt like, if he'd ever seen a baseball game in person. He was gone, and she felt certain she'd never see him again. She knew he didn't live anywhere nearby. Between the orchard cemetery and the state forest, the Windhams were surrounded by hundreds of acres, most left wild, all uninhabited except for their house and one old recluse living in a cabin. Charlie would've had to walk miles to make it to the creek. *How did he know where to find it?* She replayed the splash, the noisy getaway. *He was real, wasn't he?*

Her mother was back at the table, spreading a pink crumb layer across the cake. Athena passed through toward the back door, trailing a scent like fruit salad.

Claudia ran a toothpick along the edge of her cake, straightening the line between door and chocolate earth. "Athena, it's roasting out there. You must wear sunblock."

"No, I'll be fine. I'll stay in the shade."

"If you stay in the shade you'll be no help to us, and once you start moving around with the trays you're going to be in the sun. Sunblock, now."

"No."

"Laurel will get your back."

"No, I'm fine."

"This isn't up for discussion, Athena."

"Mom, I'm telling you—"

"Athena!" Claudia turned on her, slicing the frosted door with the point of her toothpick. "Jesus, Mary, and Joseph, look what you made me do." She dipped a palette knife in the bowl of icing and blotted the cake's wound. "If I see you walk out that door without sunblock on, you will be grounded from your grave for a month. Do you hear me?"

Great, now I'll smell like Water Babies and look all sweaty and greasy, Athena thought.

"I'm serious, one month minimum. And don't forget the part in your hair."

"Okay."

"Laurel, go help your sister."

Laurel slunk out of the dining room and followed Athena upstairs to the bathroom cabinet. Athena smeared two streaks down her arms and handed the bottle to Laurel. "If you get any on my dress, I'll kill you."

"You mean like—" Laurel squeezed hard and the bottle farted out a palmful. "Oh, whoops! Sorry, Athena."

"Stop goofing around! The family will be here any minute, and I have to be outside to meet them with Dad." Her stomach galloped. *Roxanna Dover will have to talk to me. This could be my in. This time tomorrow, my life could be totally different.* In spite of her sticky lip gloss, she grinned hugely.

Seeing her sister's reflection, Laurel thought, *What a lunatic. Everyone's losing it today.*

Athena stood next to her father at the entrance to the Dovers' row, watching him polish his glasses with his handkerchief, hold them up to the sky for inspection. She knew how he felt, eager and yet unprepared, excited but expecting the worst. Glancing down, she checked her shoes for grass, plucked a dog hair off her dress, swiveled her necklace so that the clasp rested precisely on her spine. *Where are they? Let's get this show on the road.*

As if on command, the Dovers' black car turned into the drive and parked in the meadow. She watched them all climb out: Mr. and Mrs., young and fit-looking even from that far away; Katarina, in a flouncy purple dress and towering heels that forced her to high-step her way across the grass like a stork; and then Roxanna, the last to slam her door, striding forward in a short cocktail dress and Chuck Taylors, an enormous leather bag over one shoulder. As they walked up the Champs-Elysées, Mr. Dover helping Katarina to walk, Athena deflated. *Oh God, look at me. I look like a ten-year-old compared to her. I look like Skipper and she looks like Barbie.* She looked down at her cotton sundress, its narrow brass belt buckle gleaming at her waist. *I look like a nun! Is my hair frizzing out?* She quickly tossed it behind her shoulders.

"Welcome! Congratulations, Katarina. Peter, Natalie, you must be very proud." Walt shook their hands.

"We've been looking forward to this day for quite some time, right, Kat?" Mrs. Dover put one of her heavily braceleted arms around her daughter's shoulders. Katarina smiled and nodded at her mother, squinting against the sun. *I remember girls like you*, Athena thought. *So cutesy and polite when adults are around.*

"Thank goodness it turned out to be a nice day," Mr. Dover said. "I kept picturing the entire party rained out."

"Oh, we would've tented the party before anything had a chance to be ruined."

"Is that right?" Mr. Dover seemed genuinely surprised, as if Walt had just told him that he could make the tents appear out of thin air with a twist of his mustache. "I didn't know you had the capability."

"Yup." Walt shifted his weight. "We have a standing order at the Home Depot, just in case."

Mr. Dover laughed like a sitcom dad. "Well then, I shouldn't have worried."

"Shall we?" Walt led the way, as if the Dover family had never been to their own graves before. Athena fell in behind her father, wanting desperately to smooth the back of her dress and at the same time not wanting to touch her butt in front of those people. *He didn't even introduce me. How am I supposed to get to know Roxanna if we're never introduced? This is a disaster.*

In the grave row, Katarina squealed at the sight of her newly carved headstone. Athena stared very hard straight ahead, not blinking, watching Roxanna through her peripheral vision. Roxanna, for her part, pulled a crossword out of her bag and began filling in cubes with a golf pencil.

The ceremony went ahead without a hitch. Gasps from the crowd as Athena and her mother carried out the grave cake; Katarina only stumbling once over the Eighth Tenet, remembering, "Everlasting rest requires patience and . . . ," and then standing there giggling with one hand over her mouth going, "and . . . and . . . and . . ."

Athena wanted to shout, "Practice! It requires patience and practice." *No surprise she can't remember "practice"—I'd bet my life that she visits her grave once in the next year.*

After she finished her recitation (finally), Walt presented Katarina with her key and a variation on his traditional speech: "There will be many things you care for in your life, Katarina—pets, friends, children, parents—but the most valuable one of all is your grave. Treat this key with the love and reverence it deserves." Athena could practically mouth along with him.

The key was the last part of the official ceremony. Once the honoree had the key in her hot little hands, the party began. The guests couldn't care less what Walt said—they wanted cake. Giggling the entire time, Katarina cut an enormous slice for herself as everyone raised their glasses and toasted her coming-of-age. Mrs. Dover teared up and made a big show of fanning her face with both hands, bracelets jangling up a racket. It was during this part of the event that Athena and her parents vanished into the background. Sometimes, if the party was small, or it was for a family they knew a bit, they would be invited to have cake and sit at the table with the guests. Mostly, though, and that day was no exception, the honoree's family completely forgot they were there.

Athena stood beside her usual apple tree, centering the belt of her dress. What had begun as the culmination of an entire summer's daydreams turned into another humdrum grave opening. *How did I ever think that Roxanna Dover would want to talk to me, or even notice me? She doesn't need any more friends. In her world, I'm the equivalent of, like, a fourth grader. Simon doesn't know what he's talking about.* She glanced up at the attic window, but Laurel's yellow binoculars weren't there. *Even Laurel's bored with this one.*

"Hey, it's Athena, right?"

Athena jumped (*Did Roxanna notice?*), but recovered quickly. "Yeah, Athena" was all she could say because out of nowhere, there was Roxanna, alone and shoeless.

"I'm Roxanna."

What could she say? *I know who you are*? "Nice to meet you. Congratulations on . . ." She waved toward Katarina, who was unwrapping the first box from a large pile of gifts.

She shrugged. "Thanks. Actually, I was really glad to be

coming here today. I was so happy on the car ride over." Athena could smell her gum.

"You were?" *Really?*

"Totally, I can't wait for this thing to be over. I'm so sick of hearing about it, all the planning. Know what I mean?"

Surveying the scene—lanterns hanging from the trees, real candles glowing in the early dusk on the tables, Katarina reaching for the next box from a dwindling mountain of gifts adorned with feather-patterned wrapping paper or real hawk feathers—Athena said, "Totally."

No way is this happening right now. No way! She tried to think of all the things she could bring up that she and Roxanna might have in common, like a *Nylon* subscription (though technically Athena's was less a subscription and more a disciplined purchasing habit), or an interest in photography (Athena was starting Photo 1 with Mrs. Adelaide this year, inspired by Roxanna, but she didn't have to know that), or perhaps even the shared drudgery of having a job ("I can't imagine the kinds of people you have to deal with at the Gourmet Bean—ugh."), but she was terrified of seeming too eager. Cool was the opposite of interested. And if she was honest with herself—which she was, on occasion, usually around hour two in her grave—she was downright scared of Roxanna Dover. In the halls of Greene Falls High School, Roxanna had the power of the Queen of Hearts, but the laws of the land were far crueler. If she didn't like something about you, your death was not a swift beheading; you faced torture every morning at 7:05 when the bus doors screeched open like the jaws of some ghastly animal.

Roxanna held her little camera to her face, twisted the lens, and snapped a photo of the empty end of the table: abandoned chairs and dirty plates. *I should clean that*, Athena thought, but she didn't move. She bit her lip and sticky gloss came off on her teeth. She ran her tongue over them as casually as she could, letting her hair swing down in front of her face and then flinging it back behind her shoulder. *I know so much more about her than she knows about me. That's weird, right? That I know her dogs' names and what her desk looks like and what grade Mrs. Bair gave her on the* Julius Caesar *paper?* Roxanna found a spot of dried icing on her arm and began picking at it. Athena was in agony, her posture ramrod straight, thinking, *There's no one here to see us hanging out together.*

Katarina kept unwrapping present after present: framed pictures of her and her friends, a bedazzled flashlight, a giant pillow shaped like an owl, a Do Not Disturb sign, and a pair of speakers that she immediately tore from their packaging and plugged into her waiting iPod. All the eighth-grade girls sprang to life, dancing and wiggling and leaping across the specially designed platform into the next row. Athena and Roxanna stood there watching the show. Athena's shoes were starting to feel tight, but she didn't care. She would stand there all night. Maybe the photographer would catch the two of them in the background and there would be evidence of the night that Roxanna Dover pretended to be friends with Athena Windham (or was it the other way around?). *Say something. Say something!*

All the easy banter from her daydreams dissolved into what felt like heartburn.

Out of the corner of her eye, an animal moved behind the trees. And then the animal cinched its ponytail and ran in a crouch to the next row. *Laurel. What the hell is she doing?* Athena quickly turned back to the party, watching everyone and keeping an eye on Laurel at the same time. The party continued merrily on its way, the adults sitting around in a cluster at one end of the table, swatting mosquitoes from ankles and bare arms while the kids capered around the iPod. Good, no one else had noticed Laurel. *What's she trying to do, crash the party? Steal some cake?* Her parents were nowhere to be seen, probably in the kitchen beginning the long cleanup.

"So how many of these things have you been to?" Roxanna turned to her, facing the direction of Laurel's escape.

"Oh, gosh." Athena moved a few steps toward the party. *Pay no attention to the girl in the orchard.* "Dozens. Hundreds. Too many to count."

"Must get boring after a while."

"Eh." She continued shifting until she had her back to the party and Roxanna had her back to Laurel. "Some are better than others."

"Well, I don't know about you, but I'm so bored right now I could die."

Oh.

"I tried to swipe a glass of wine earlier, but my mom caught me, and now she won't take her eyes off the drinks table." She crossed her arms and looked around. "So I guess we have to get creative. You want to take a walk or something?" She turned and headed straight up Laurel's path. "C'mon."

"Oh! You know what?" Athena was almost screaming. "Let's go this way, the orchard is kind of creepy at night."

"Exactly. Let's check it out. I bet I can get some great pictures." She waved her camera necklace. "C'mon."

"Um, but . . ." Athena couldn't think of a reason why not, not without ruining the one and only chance she might ever get to hang out with Roxanna, to see what she was really like, to earn a mention on her blog. School started the next day, and then Athena would be just another blur in the hallway. *Get out of the house. Talk to people.*

"Why not?" she said. "Lead the way."

Chapter 11

LAUREL HADN'T PLANNED TO SNEAK OUT. SHE HAD planned to rent an R-rated movie from On Demand and eat ice cream straight from the carton and blame the mess on the ghost. As the guests arrived, she sulked upstairs to her room with the empty bowl of icing, to lick it clean while watching from her window, as usual. When the coast was clear downstairs: TV. Ice cream. Mess.

People wandered into the party in family clumps, or elderly couples, with only the occasional solo friend. There were equal numbers of boys and girls—Katarina must've been popular, or at least pretty, to warrant such a good showing. Icing-sticky, Laurel adjusted her binoculars to make a better assessment. One boy had dark hair buzzed short, a round doughy face, dimples in his cheeks. Laurel smashed the binoculars to her eyes until her eyelashes bent against the glass, trying to prove to herself what she'd known right away: it was Charlie. He *was* real. Laurel followed him like a sniper, pleading in her head for him to break away to use the restrooms attached to the barn. If she could get his attention somehow, maybe they could talk again. . . .

He moved behind trees and Laurel held her breath until he reappeared. He jumped and caught a twiggy branch, twisting until it ripped from the tree, and methodically stripped every leaf until it was a bare, blank stick. He walked the perimeter of the party, slashing at the air with his homemade sword. After almost an hour, Laurel realized he hadn't spoken to a single person.

The party moved through its phases. Athena shifted a ladder from tree to tree, climbing up and down with a lit taper, leaving a glow in the lanterns. Just as everyone was collecting to watch Katarina unwrap presents, Laurel saw Charlie get up from his seat, walk toward the bathrooms, check over his shoulder, turn sharply toward the back of the orchard, and disappear into the dark.

Laurel waited two minutes, then three, but Charlie didn't return. With a quick kiss and apology, Laurel closed Clover into the room and crept downstairs.

The door to the root cellar leaned against the foundation of the house and sagged in the middle. Laurel heaved it up and over, pulled a flashlight from her bag, and descended into the cool damp. Every time she went down there she got the spooks. Bookshelves full of jars threw back the shine of the flashlight as she made her way through the rows of picklings. Barrels of potatoes and squashes lined the inside wall. She didn't need any provisions; she needed the old service tunnel, connecting the house to the garden shed in the lower half of the cemetery. It was the only way for her to get out into the orchard without being seen: she had to walk under the graves.

Laurel hummed, trying to fill the space. She'd been down in the cellar hundreds of times, and dozens of times on her own, but she still couldn't shake the feeling that she shouldn't be there. It felt like trespassing. She thought of the wooden signs she'd helped her father nail to trees along the trails in their woods after she and Clover found spent shells, a meaty pile of guts: PRIVATE PROPERTY. NO HUNTING. NO TRESPASSING. POACHERS KEEP OUT.

This is my house, she reminded herself. *I belong here.*

She unlatched the door to the tunnel and a blast of dank air hit her face. She shone the flashlight as far down the tunnel as it would go, which wasn't far. Silvery flecks of dirt, lifted by the gust from the door, swirled in the spotlight. Laurel pulled the door shut behind her and set off into the dark.

At the end of the tunnel, Laurel climbed a short staircase and shouldered her way through the trap door into the shed, then out into the orchard. She had never been this close to a client's grave opening. Her experience was limited to Athena's and a couple of her cousins' ceremonies, and her own, of course. From ground level, Katarina's party filled itself in with all five senses, not just the one Laurel was confined to with her binoculars.

A long table held silver trays with fancy lids, like props from *Beauty and the Beast*. Under the trays, little blue flames sputtered from tiny jars. She paused behind a tree, watching one of the dads go back for seconds. Each time he lifted a lid, wafts of garlic chicken, or parsley-flecked lasagna, or fresh baked rolls unfurled in the air. Laurel's taste buds tingled.

The greedy dad's wife came over and put her hand on his back. "Did you say hello to Richard and Lynn yet? They're over at the Lowes' table."

The man sighed. "No, I haven't. I've been trying to have a nice time. Why do we have to stay friends with them?"

"Lynn is on the school board, for one. Plus the kids are friends, you know, so it's important for us to stay civil. For their sake."

"All right, if there's a free seat I'll take my plate over."

They turned back to the party and Greedy's wife said, "Looks like the Windhams beat you to it."

Laurel scanned the tables until she found her father pulling out a seat for her mother, who was talking animatedly with her hands.

"Guess I'm off the hook," he said, tearing a mini cheeseburger in half with his teeth. "You know, I almost feel sorry for them."

"Who, the Windhams? Are they still having trouble—?"

"No, Lynn and Richard! For having to talk to the Windhams."

"Shhh," his wife scolded, "not so loud!" But she was laughing.

Laurel wanted to mash their faces into the scalding lasagna until they gasped for air and forgiveness. She watched her parents chuckle along with the woman Laurel assumed was Lynn of the school board. Everyone seemed at ease, sipping drinks, dabbing mouths with napkins, smoothing wrinkles from the tablecloth, but the longer she looked, the more she saw. All the other parents at that table looked expensive. There was no other word for it. The women all had actual haircuts, with layers and highlights and things Athena was always talking about. Most had manicures and rings and glinting watches. The men, too, had tie clips and colorful silk peeking out of their jacket pockets. Next to the town parents, her mom and dad looked tired. More than that: they looked old. And they were. Laurel was the baby, the caboose in a very long family train.

Out of nowhere she thought, *Please don't die*, and then, *That's ridiculous. They're not going to die.* But the more she watched, the more it became a plea: *Please don't die. Please don't die.*

Shaking off the party, she tried to get as far out into the dark as she could before hanging a left for the old quad. Laurel stuck to the shadows, weaving between headstones and ducking tree branches. She had to find Charlie, wherever he was—and he could've been anywhere by then, watching the party from an apple tree, hitchhiking his way home. Laurel had no idea where to begin. There were no breadcrumbs to follow. But then she remembered: the unsealed grave. The jacket, not quite adult-sized, hanging from a tree.

As the music and light from the party grew fainter, the noise of crickets and owls took its place. Lightning bugs blinked in code. She swatted a mosquito from her neck and scratched until skin came up under her nails. Voices, loud voices, hit her in the back. At first she thought, *Ghost!* But her fear quickly switched gears—the voices belonged to real, flesh-and-blood people, people who could see her, who would scream and get her caught. If she ran, they would hear her. If she froze, they would run smack into her. There was only one option left: Laurel hitched her leg over a branch of the nearest tree and climbed.

"So what's it like, you know, living here? In a graveyard?" Roxanna held her phone up and a white flash erupted down the length of a row.

"Well, I don't technically live in the graveyard. I live in a house." Roxanna didn't get the joke. "Over there."

"Yeah, but I mean essentially the house is in a graveyard. Your neighbors are graves and dead people."

"You say it like it's dangerous."

"Not dangerous, just—creepy. Doesn't it bother you to have to see people visiting their graves and, like, every time someone dies they end up right in your backyard?"

"I guess I'm just used to it."

"What's the weirdest thing that's ever happened to you in the graveyard?"

"Um, I have to think . . ."

"Have you ever, like, seen a ghost?" She looked at Athena expectantly.

"Nope, never seen one." She thought of Lucy, banging through their house, leaving an entire tube of toothpaste squeezed in elegant ribbons across her pillows. "One time I was raking leaves and a windstorm came and picked up the pile of leaves, swirled them around like a twister, and dropped them right back into place. That freaked me out."

"Huh." Roxanna's eyes cut to the ground. "Weird."

Athena blushed and itched her nose nervously.

"There really isn't a ghost here?" Roxanna asked.

"I hate to disappoint you, but the cemetery isn't haunted." Athena knew not to talk about Lucy. How would it look? A grave keeper's daughter restless and bucking the whole system, not resting eternally in her grave?

"Have you ever found an unlocked door?"

Athena laughed. "No way." When she realized Roxanna was serious she said, "I mean, I haven't even looked. That's someone else's *grave*."

"Who would find out?" Her smile was conspiratorial. Athena had never been on this side of the conspiracy before, and she felt like she was being backed out onto a plank, blindfolded. "You're a good girl, aren't you?" Roxanna said it as if it were the name for a particularly low caste. "You get, like, straight As, right? Never late for class? Never grounded or in detention?"

"Sort of. I mean, yeah, I try."

Roxanna stopped walking. "It's cool, Athena, you can go. If you don't want to do this, you don't have to."

"No, I do. I'm fine."

"You sure?"

Athena nodded. "Positive."

"Awesome. I'll check this side, you check that side. If you find one, text me. Here's my number, ready?"

"I don't actually have a cell phone."

"Oh. Okay, so whistle or something. Ha, how *Hunger Games* is that? I want to get some pictures." Roxanna ran up the row, tugging on doorknobs. For a second Athena watched, thinking, *Great. This is just great. That whistling girl in* The Hunger Games *gets killed.* And then she found the nearest doorknob and turned. Locked. *Phew.* Down the row she went, barely testing the doors in case one was actually unlocked. The orchard was eerily quiet, far from the party noise. At each door she thought, *I'm sorry. Thank you for being locked. I'm sorry. Thank you. I'm sorry.*

After a dozen dead ends, Athena headed back. Roxanna jogged up to her at the end of the row. "I checked two whole rows, no luck. What about you?"

"No luck either." She sighed. "We could be here all night. I doubt we'd find anything."

"Shit. That sucks." Roxanna thought for a minute. "Why don't you show me your house?"

"My house?" Athena immediately took inventory of all the embarrassing things in her house: the cornucopia-printed wallpaper peeling in the dining room, the pink stains growing in the bowl of every leaky sink, the sticky-bottomed recycling bin in the kitchen fireplace, the dog hair nests in floor corners, the cobweb wisps in ceiling corners, the mulchy throw pillows on the couch. "Why do you want to see my house?"

"I'm just curious. People say—I mean, I've been to the cemetery loads of times, but I've never been into your house."

"It's kind of my dad's rule, don't take it personally. I'd love to show you around, but . . ." She shrugged exaggeratedly.

"Hey, what about your grave? Could I see it?"

"Seriously?"

"Yeah, seriously. I won't tell anyone, obviously."

Athena said nothing.

"And I won't take pictures." Roxanna laughed and pocketed her phone. "I'll leave my camera up top. Cross my heart and hope to die." She swung the camera strap over her head and made a big X over her chest, then hiked up her strapless bra. "I'd really love to get to know you better, Athena, and I mean, how much better can you know a person after you've seen their grave, right?"

A breeze lifted the ends of Athena's hair. "All right. I guess."

Laurel watched the top of Athena's head follow Roxanna toward the house. Despite the clear coast, Laurel sat hunter-still, her brain chewing through the conversation she'd just overheard.

Athena is taking a stranger into her grave.

My sister, the queen grave keeper, is about to break the biggest tenet of grave keeping.

She can't know that I know. I'd have to explain what I was doing out in the orchard during a party.

But sneaking out is not the same, not by a long shot.

The trees around Laurel shifted nervously. She scooted down from her perch and set off double time. Too many things were happening that night that shouldn't have been happening at all, and she felt the scales tipping toward disaster. Too many people out in the orchard tonight. Too much weirdness.

The first firework shot up from the road with a rocket shriek and burst over the house. In the brief pink blaze, Laurel counted three rows to where she had found Clover and the lunch bag and turned left.

"Holy hell!" she said, and slapped a hand over her mouth. The cracks around the door of the unsealed grave glowed. Yellow light shone up from all four sides and through the keyhole. Moths and mosquito hawks fluttered through the beams and beat their dusty bodies against the cracked wood. In the shadows, the carving on the headstone stood out starkly:

HERE LYES Ye BODY

Laurel screwed her courage into her fist and knocked.

Chapter 12

ATHENA'S MIND WAS A BLANK CHALKBOARD, BLACK AND cold, as she led Roxanna through the orchard. They zigzagged between headstones to steer clear of the party while more fireworks shot up in red-and-blue starbursts, gold weeping willows, green curlicues that spun and swam like koi fish. With each terrific boom, Athena felt the vibrations shudder down her rib cage.

"So your parents are, like, super strict, huh?" Roxanna asked.

"No. What makes you say that?"

"I don't know; it's just what I've heard."

"Oh. What else have you heard?"

"Nothing much. Just that, like, your family got really . . .

tight after the accident, and your brother works here, and your mom is pretty, like, devout. Don't you have a little sister?"

"Yeah."

"She's homeschooled?"

"Uh-huh."

The silence from Roxanna seemed to say, *I rest my case.*

They had learned about inflection in French class, how changing where the accent fell altered the meaning of a word. Roxanna was a master accent manipulator. Every positive became a negative: *close family, brother works here, devout, homeschooled.* Athena heard: *insular, abnormal, narrow-minded*, felt each description like a wasp sting.

"Has your dad ever kicked anyone out for breaking a Tenet?"

"Kicked them out of the cemetery?"

"Yeah."

Athena tried to laugh casually, but it came out as a choke. "No, of course not. He's not the grave-keeper police. Why, are you nervous you're going to be banished for going into my grave?"

"Ha, no-o-o. We'll never get caught. No sweat."

Liar.

"Does your dad have a skeleton key for the doors?"

"Yeah, somewhere. People lose their keys all the time."

"Shut up! Do you know where it is?"

Athena's stomach lurched. "No clue. His office is not exactly, like, organized." She took a deep breath, tried to clear the haze from her head. She felt adrift, but why? She was hanging out with Roxanna, who was strangely fascinated by her, so why wasn't it framed in Times Square lights: The Best Night of Athena Windham's Life?

Roxanna said nothing, snap-clapping her fingers in a rhythm that sounded like a galloping horse.

"This way." Athena drew Roxanna toward the silhouette of her canopy. Glancing past it at the house, she scanned the lit windows, but they were empty, curtains drawn. The mirrored window frame hanging on the back of the house was bright with movement of the reflected party. Athena's sundress felt flimsy and weak against the cooling night. *There's a sweater in my grave*, she reminded herself.

At the canopy, Roxanna hesitated. She carefully wrapped the chain around her camera and laid it in the grass. She took the curtains between her fingers, testing the limits. "This is a nice touch."

"It's weatherproofing, you know? Like a tent."

Roxanna nodded. "Smart. That's your sister's grave?" She gestured to the conspicuous patch of grass beside them.

"Yeah, that's Lucy." *But she's not really there*, she didn't say. "One sec, wait here." Athena stepped between the curtains, unclasped her necklace, and unlocked the door. She had performed this ritual thousands of times, locking and unlocking without thought, but this time she felt the teeth of the key catch in the lock and scratch around the grooves. The click seemed magnified, loud as a gunshot. Turning the doorknob, drawing the door up and over, she felt every muscle in her back contract individually. "Okay, come in."

Roxanna ducked under the canopy and looked down into the grave. "Awesome."

Athena pointed to the ladder. "After you."

Roxanna climbed down, and Athena waited for her to reach the bottom before following. Standing at the foot of the ladder, her grave felt miniaturized. With two people there was hardly room to sit down, and if you wanted to move past each other, you had to turn sideways. *A grave is for the keeper alone.*

Roxanna stumbled in the dark. "Is there a light somewhere?"

"We had to use it for the party. Sorry."

"No worries. I'll manage." She slid her cell phone out of her pocket and held the glowing screen over her head. "No pictures, I promise." She smiled. "Just for a light."

Athena nodded.

"You spend a lot of time down here, huh?" The phone spotlighted her dishwater-soaked shirt from last night still balled up on the newspaper, a stained pillow and natty blanket smashed permanently into the corner. Tattered magazines and weeks' worth of papers unfurled across the yoga mat, their clippings climbing the corkboard walls.

"Nah, not really." Her answer sounded hollow and fake even to her. She stepped on something soft—a sweater sleeve—and picked it up and put it on.

Roxanna held her phone up to each clipping, skimming for a few seconds before losing interest and moving on. "I didn't take you for someone so interested in fashion and makeup," she said, skimming a page about applying a flawless liquid line.

"Thanks?"

Roxanna moved around a stack of shoeboxes filled with what Athena knew to be the most embarrassing collection of things imaginable: gluesticks and glitter, costume cat's-eye glasses, lace gloves that had belonged to her great-aunt, blue glass marbles, goldfinch feathers, a plastic baggie of marigold seeds. The only acceptable secret was the shoebox full of forbidden makeup, mascara and shimmery eyeshadow and false lashes all still in their packaging.

"Your grave is awesome. It has such a lived-in feel."

"It does?"

"Yeah, you've never felt that?"

"Well, it's my grave. It's the only grave I've ever been in."

"Fair point. But still, you're like a true-blue grave keeper."

Athena couldn't tell if this was meant as a compliment or just another check on the list of "good girl" attributes.

Roxanna turned in place, her back to Athena. "I almost never spend time in my grave. My dad gets on my case about it every summer, but I don't think he means it. He just feels like he has to say that stuff. You know, be a parent."

Athena saw it all through Roxanna's eyes, the countless hours spent propped in the corner, air still, barely moving except to blink or sip ginger ale. It was a lived-in grave, as lived-in as an old sneaker, and it was weird. Virtuous, devout, yes, admirable even, but not something to be jealous of, not something attractive. Her grave had turned her into a carnival attraction, freaky as a bearded lady.

"Roxanna, I think we should go now."

When the phone glow found Athena's face her jaw was set, eyebrows tensed. "Yeah, I should probably get back to the party anyway." Roxanna adjusted her earring. "God, I need to find my shoes!"

After they climbed up, Athena locked the door and slid the necklace under her dress. Roxanna hadn't bothered to wait. When she emerged from the curtains, Athena could barely catch Roxanna's silhouette fading into the dusk. She wound her hair into a topknot, pushed up her sleeves, and set off for the party and cleanup duty and the last few hours of summer.

Shit, she thought. *Fuck fuck fuck.*

Chapter 13

LAUREL HEARD MUFFLED SCRAMBLING, A THUD, AND A short "Ow!"

"Hello?" she said, then louder, "Hello?"

Footsteps scuffed up the ladder and the door opened an inch. "Who's there?"

"Laurel. I live here."

"I thought you said you were only visiting." The door opened wide and Charlie's head appeared.

"What the hell! What are you doing in there?"

He slowly climbed out, letting the door fall to the side with a bang. He actually looked sheepish. A smear of frosting had dried at the corner of his mouth. "It's a long story."

"I bet."

"I ran away."

"When?"

"Just now."

"Why?"

He sighed. "I told you, it's a long story."

"I'll be patient."

"All right, but can we go back inside first? It makes me nervous to stand out here in the cemetery at night."

Laurel did not point out that the cemetery was nothing compared to the fact that he was sitting in someone else's grave; she simply followed him to the ladder and looked down. Candle stubs in old jelly jars covered the floor; she could feel the heat even from ground level.

"C'mon, hurry. You're letting the bugs in."

Laurel closed the door behind her. She sank to her heels at the foot of the ladder and wrapped both arms around her legs.

"Beef jerky?" Charlie offered her a plastic-wrapped stick.

Ugh, pipe cleaner meat. "I'm good."

Warped gray planks lined the walls. Laurel was afraid she would accidentally touch one and send the whole grave crumbling. In the candlelight, Charlie's eyes looked huge and inky, like a rabbit's.

"Are you going to tell your parents that I'm here?"

She thought for a second. "No."

"Do you promise?"

"Promise. But why did you run away?"

Charlie took a slug from his canteen and wiped his mouth. "I ran away because I couldn't stay at home anymore."

"That's like saying, 'I ate because I was hungry.'"

"It's the truth, though." Charlie's voice was heading toward a shout. "I couldn't stay there."

Laurel took a different tack. "Are you really from Albany?"

"No."

"So you're from Greene Falls?"

Charlie nodded. "My mom dropped me off at the party. She thinks I'm sleeping over at my buddy Josh's house so we can go to the first day of school together tomorrow. She won't realize I've run away until I don't get off the bus at three thirty—if she even realizes then."

"You're going to miss school?"

Charlie looked at her like she was either dumb or luring him into a trap. "Yes, obviously. It's no big deal. The school will assume I'm absent because—I've been absent a lot in the last year. They won't care."

"What grade are you in?"

"Eighth, or at least I would have been if I were going."

"Me too! Except I don't go to school."

"Hang on, first you said you were just visiting, then you said you lived here. Now you're in eighth grade, but you don't go to school?"

"Not exactly, no. It's kind of"—*lame*, she thought, *stupid*—"kind of weird."

"Who am I going to tell? I'm in hiding, remember?"

"I've found you twice now, so clearly you're not that good at it. Swear you won't tell?"

"I swear, I swear."

"I don't go to school because I'm homeschooled, because my sister died when she was little and . . ." How could she put it? She'd never had to explain it before.

"Oh man, you're Laurel Windham!"

Laurel nodded, picking a hangnail with undivided attention.

"I thought the name Laurel sounded familiar. Don't worry, I won't tell anyone that you're actually perfectly normal. Your secret's safe with me."

Laurel ripped off the hangnail with her teeth. "So how long do you plan on staying here?"

"A while. I have some money saved from allowance, but I need to find a way to make a little more. Bus tickets to California are not cheap."

"California, wow." The candlelight bobbed and flickered. One wick hissed as the flame consumed it. "How did you know about this grave? How did you know it was empty—I mean, livable?"

"My grave is near here, and I haven't had an opening yet, so it's unfinished and my parents don't make me practice being in there for too long. I've had a lot of time to wander around while my parents were thinking in their graves. I found Tamsen's unsealed door two summers ago, and it doesn't have a lock, so."

"But just 'cause it's unsealed doesn't mean it's empty!"

"I know, I know, but I checked."

Laurel felt the hairs on her arms stand on end. "Wasn't it gross? I mean, I know the door was closed, but hundreds of years without cleaning can turn any grave into a pit."

"Yeah, it was pretty much one giant spider web." Charlie gestured from one side of the grave to the other. "And dirty. Some bugs, a lot of weeds, actually, trying to grow up near the door. But I cleaned it all out. No biggie."

He spruced a grave. He spruced someone else's grave for himself. Right under our noses. "And what are you planning to do now?"

"Hang out. Explore the woods. Live off the land."

Laurel inventoried Charlie's pleated khakis, his thin nylon jacket, the kid-sized Harry Potter sleeping bag, the books poking out of his backpack, three open bags of Halloween candy. No canned food, no compass, no knife, no fishing tackle, no gun.

"Okay." Laurel stood. "All right. I need to get home before they realize I'm gone."

"Maybe I'll see you around?" Charlie looked worried, unsure about whether he should let her go or beg her to stay. Laurel heard what he wasn't saying: he was alone. He was lonely. She knew a little bit about being lonely.

"Definitely. I'll come back tomorrow."

YOUR EVERLASTING HOME MUST BE READY TO RECEIVE YOU, JUST AS YOU MUST BE PREPARED TO GO

For a long time after my death, I didn't understand what I was still doing there. My great-nieces and -nephews had mostly moved west, but a few lived in the village still; some even resembled my siblings, which just about cracked my heart. They couldn't see or hear me; all I could do was hang back and watch them as they harvested another crop, forgot the old generations, had babies, grew old, and died. Every time a family member died, I waited by each body for days, hoping they'd wake up the way I had, but it never happened.

I was the only ghost. It felt like punishment. I tried to reframe it: how could being forced to stay in the mountains that I loved so much ever be considered a punishment? But that line of thinking didn't always work. I missed my brothers and sisters, my parents. I lost interest in the new generations; the orchard aged and wilted before my eyes. I hardly noticed.

Clover snapped me out of it. Dogs don't dwell; they simply grow tired of one thing and move on to the next, which is exactly what I needed to do. I was tired of being alone, so I joined Clover every chance I got. She reminded me what it felt like to take joy in the mountains I'd once loved so much. And she reminded me that I still had a family, if I wanted one. I followed her back to the Windham house, gradually getting closer and closer.

At first I was wind, a creaky floorboard if I wasn't careful. It was intoxicating to be among a family again. The girls, especially, were bottomless springs for me. I soaked up their feelings and opinions and tastes and fears like parched ground. Athena was easier to tap into; she split wide open when she turned thirteen. She made herself so vulnerable in her grave; I could curl up on the grass above her and absorb energy through her breath.

Athena kept an awful lot right below her skin. Anytime a character on TV opened the door to find a police officer, hat in hand, she worked up a five-alarm case of heartburn. She'd opened the floodgates of pop culture for me, masterful as she was at watching TV in secret and smuggling magazines into her grave. Her favorite show, which was often chronicled in her magazines, was *Graves Across Time*. "Hideous," her mother called it. "Despicable." But I loved it, too. Under the guise of education, historians, anthropologists, and biographers re-created what the graves of Marilyn Monroe, or Henry VIII, or Emily Dickinson reportedly looked like. Mediocre special effects created "the feel" of the grave, letting viewers see what it would be like to lie where Marilyn does. Athena's reactions taught me what was tasteful, what was outrageous. Truman Capote kept a guestbook in his grave, and Athena's mouth hung open for the rest of the episode. The next morning she googled "Truman Capote" and went down a Wikipedia rabbit hole. (And that's how I learned what Google and Wikipedia were.)

Laurel was harder to befriend. She was long on walks and short on talks. It was fascinating to watch her. She could spend an hour lifting pads of moss from the north side of a tree's roots, rearranging them into a house, then a tower, then a bed, and then abandon the game out of the blue. She could run a mile uphill through the woods and fall asleep the instant she sat down on the back steps. She reminded me a lot of myself—when I was alive, of course. Laurel would never know me that way, but I had hopes. Hopes and suspicions that began to form a plan—maybe Laurel would come to know me yet. Maybe I could find a way to take her for my own.

Laurel found me when she was six, picking her way down the cliff at the eastern edge of the woods, barefoot and messy-haired, chanting to herself, "Left foot, left foot. Grip, toes, grip! Now hand, now other hand," until she reached the narrow stone shelf. She sat with her back to the stone, dirty knees under her chin, and looked down into the notch between the mountains. She sat for a long, long time. I had never before seen a person watch the forest with such stillness, unless they were hunting. She watched with the stillness of the forest itself.

The ledge was barely visible from the cliff-top lookout point fifteen feet above. For centuries, people had cast their gaze across the valley and it hooked on something far—they never looked straight below them. Laurel had found the ledge years ago, shimmying to the edge on her belly so that her head hung over the precipice. It was right below her: a landing, a little balcony.

At first the ledge provided plenty of room for her, but as she grew, it turned out to be just wide enough for her to sit cross-legged, just long enough for her to stretch out with the side of her body pressed to the rock. She visited first thing in the morning, with Pop-Tarts in her back pocket, or she brought a book during the home stretch of the afternoon. During the winter, she trudged out in a pair of old snowshoes and looked out over the same valley; the same trees, now naked, offered peeks at rooftops and baseball diamonds, but it was the tourist view. Seventy-five cents for ninety seconds at the binoculars. The winter meant she couldn't get down to her ledge, and as January veered into February, she missed it something fierce.

In the beginning I tossed pebbles and twigs her way, crunched pinecones in my fists and rained them into her hair. She craned at first, searching for a nest, perhaps some babies. But there was no nest, no visible source, so she accepted me as a part of the place. I liked to test the membrane between life and afterlife. How far could I go when there were no consequences? I took rolls of toilet paper and unspooled them into the girls' beds, then replaced the covers. At night they stuck bare feet into tangles of paper snakeskins. (In the morning, they carefully rewound them.) On windy nights, I jammed the windows open and let the wind-blown curtains pull their rods crashing to the floor. I broke their pencil points, all of them. I hid their socks, and sometimes their underpants. I jumped on creaky floorboards, stuck my fingers into cracks in the ceiling plaster to make it snow.

"It's just the wind," their mother told them. Or, "It's Lucy, keeping us company."

"Old houses settle," their father explained.

Their parents were lying. I was the wind. I was Lucy. I was the gravity, pulling their house down around them.

Chapter 14

LAUREL JOLTED AWAKE WITH ONE THOUGHT: *CHARLIE.* He was in her backyard. In a grave. She had promised to go back.

Clover snored softly, curled up in the hollow made by Laurel's bent legs. Athena's digital clock was turned toward her bed, so Laurel couldn't see what time it was. She filled her lungs, let her belly collapse. No birds yet, so it was early. Low-grade cricket static invaded her head.

She thought of Charlie in his sleeping bag at the bottom of the grave, drooling blissfully (she hoped). Shifting to her back, shoving Clover toward the wall, Laurel closed her eyes and imagined away the time-softened sheets and the down pillows (made by Athena years ago). She was now stretched out in a grave—her grave—peacefully dead to the world. High walls. Stale air. A deep kind of darkness.

Blinking, her nose itched. Slowly, her covers slithered away from her chin. "Lucy," she whispered, "stop." The covers sheepishly pulled themselves back up to her eyes, and she scrunched them under her chin. She couldn't do it, couldn't even fake being dead in her own bed. She'd thought many times about what she'd do if stranded in the woods overnight. It wouldn't be pleasant, but there were guidelines: locate a source of water, scout around for wood, build a fire, grow the coals, make an A-frame or climb a tree to sleep. She could do it. If that ever happened, she could burn some greens for a smoke signal because people would be looking for her and she'd want to be found. But no one would come to save her from her grave. And Charlie—he didn't want to be found.

She shifted and stretched for what seemed like hours, new thoughts tumbling out of the stillness to rattle her just as she was drifting off. What if her grave locked her in? What if she got sick or hit her head and passed out and no one wanted to violate the Third Tenet by rescuing her? Rain softened the silence. She slunk down to the kitchen, took a chicken head and a couple of fish tails from the freezer. Her animal cemetery beside the barn was already prepped for an early morning burial. Laurel needed to be outside. She needed sky.

Of course the first day of school would be muggy and gross. Athena stood in the shower, letting the water dribble over her face and drum her shoulders like impatient fingers. With her eyes closed she could hear the rain pounding on the roof, and it was as if a hole had opened up, the clouds unloading directly onto her head. Rain meant she'd have to take the bus instead of her bike. Rain meant frizz. She smoothed a second helping of conditioner onto her hair.

I have homeroom with Mrs. Brennan. Athena tried to steer her thoughts. *And then first period, chemistry. Second period, chorus. Third period . . .* It was impossible. Roxanna's voice ran through her head like a broken record—*"It has such a lived-in feel"*—upsetting her sleep, roaring in her ears the instant she woke up, and distracting her even now. No one had passed judgment on her grave before.

Athena lathered up her loofah once more for first-day good luck. Laurel still used their father's hunter's soap; Athena could tell from the long dark hair wrapped around the bar of lye. *It's a wonder she doesn't peel raw,* she thought, examining its cracked, pebbly texture. The soap was supposed to neutralize a hunter's odor, sand off any trace of sweat or oil, so that prey couldn't catch your scent on the breeze and hightail it to the thickets.

It was yet another gulf between Athena and her sister. Athena had never in a million years considered the possibility of joining her dad on a hunt. It sounded terrible: waking up at the crack of dawn, in the cold, wearing layers of camouflage, those awful hats the color of traffic cones, and then sitting still for hours waiting for an animal dumb enough to walk into your crosshairs. And that was just the start of it! Having to slice and dice the bodies? No, thank you. One time she had the misfortune of running into them right when they got back from a hunt. Walt had turkey fluff clinging to his coat sleeve, and Laurel had thrown her bloodstained gloves on the doormat in the kitchen.

"Gross! Don't just leave them there! People eat in here." Athena was horrified.

"Oh, my apologies." Laurel bowed and snatched the gloves, chasing Athena through the house shouting, "Bloody gloves! Bloody, bloody gloves!"

It still amazed her that weenie Laurel, who was too scared to call in a takeout order to the Chinese restaurant, who barely made a peep at holiday dinners with her own extended family, was brave enough to walk into the woods with her rifle (and her dad) and blow a hole through a living creature in the name of dinner. *Oh God, am I turning into one of those eco-freaks from Environmental Club?* She remembered the handful of kids distributing leaflets in the cafeteria: *Fun Facts about Alternative Protein!* or *Packing Peanuts: Earth's Deadliest Allergy*. Maude Gelwick, from the library, with her bandannas and clashing plaid shirts—she was in that group somehow. They wore sandals with socks in the winter.

Maybe I'll go wild and join a club this year. An entire migrating swarm of butterflies churned through her stomach. *"It has such a lived-in feel."*

What will she do when she sees me?

Dread. Dread was the only word for what Athena felt.

✧ ✧ ✧

She got her answer at lunch. Despite Simon's threatening advice, Athena fully intended to spend the first lunch period in the art room, listening to classical music on the paint-splattered radio with Mrs. Adelaide. Instead, an electric blue note waited for her, taped to the door:

BUSY AS A !
WILL BE OPEN DURING LUNCH TOMORROW!

So Athena walked as slowly as she could manage to the cafeteria.

Her lunch table wasn't really "hers" at all. It belonged to the remainders—World of Warcraft kids, a Mormon girl, a couple loners with seemingly no hobbies or interests whatsoever—who simply allowed Athena to take up space there. As she crossed the lunchroom to their table in the corner, she noticed Roxanna sipping a CapriSun, shoulder to shoulder with the most popular girls in the school. Her best friend (and the cheerleading captain, of course), Lindsay Nathan, nudged Roxanna and nodded in Athena's direction.

Roxanna took the straw from her mouth and waved. "Athena, come sit!"

She stopped herself from saying "Really?" and walked carefully to the empty chair beside Roxanna.

She tried not to smile showing her teeth. Relief washed through her. She suddenly felt more awake than she had in months. "Hi," she said to the blank faces around the table. "I'm Athena."

Jordan, who held the school record in the mile track event, said, "Yeah, we know."

"How's your first day going?" Roxanna had a package of Gushers open in front of her; she alternated gummies with picking nibbles from a wedge of brie with her fingertip.

"So far, so good." Athena peeled back the wax paper from her cream-cheese-and-jelly sandwich. "I was planning to do some work in the art room during lunch, but Mrs. Adelaide is cleaning." She glanced across the table at Nicole, who had been in her drawing class last year, expecting her to nod in sympathy, but Nicole was zeroed in on her phone and didn't look up. Athena tried for a save. "Do you ever work in the darkroom during lunch, Roxanna?" Remind the rest of the table what her connection was, why she was there, even though she already knew the answer.

"Not really, no."

"Athena"—Lindsay leaned around Roxanna—"Rox was just telling us how much fun she had with you at her sister's grave opening." Nicole looked up from her phone. Jordan put her apple down without taking a bite. "She said it was the most interesting grave opening she'd ever been to. Right?" She elbowed Roxanna, who started laughing with a cheesy finger in her mouth.

"It's too bad the season's over," Jordan said.

"Hey, guys." Maude Gelwick perched a bucket of candy on the edge of the table. "We're selling lollipops for the Green

Summit, which is a three-day event we'll be hosting in—"

"How much are they?" Nicole asked, once again looking at her phone.

"Fifty cents each. Three for five dollars."

"What? That doesn't make any sense."

"Can you break a twenty?" Lindsay asked.

"Prices just went up. Dollar-fifty each, three for fifteen."

"You're funny," Roxanna said.

"Are you touched? Or are you just really bad at fund-raising?" Lindsay snapped her wallet closed. "I could give you some pointers, since the cheerleaders raised over two thousand dollars last year."

"No takers? Okay, later, dudes." Maude swung the bucket off the table and walked to the next. "Hey guys, we're selling lollipops."

Jordan said, "What a psycho."

Nicole said, "I'm tweeting about this immediately."

"So, Athena." Lindsay turned back to her as if nothing had interrupted their conversation. "We should hang out."

Athena snuck a glance at Roxanna, who was absentmindedly sucking her CapriSun dry. "Yeah? I mean, yeah. That would be great. What do you guys like to do?"

"Oh, this and that." Lindsay flapped her hand.

Roxanna let go of her juice pouch with a slurp. "You're always begging to go to Burger King." She turned to Athena. "We spend an inordinate amount of time at Burger King."

"Do not!" Lindsay actually seemed embarrassed. Look at

how much Athena was finding out already! "We hang out at the mountain"—Jordan's family owned the ski slope, Athena knew that—"and we take semi-regular trips to the Phoenicia Diner. They have the best black-and-whites." She slapped Roxanna's arm. "Like we even hang out all that much anyway. Roxanna is literally unreachable ninety-five percent of the time, and she won't tell us where she is or what she's doing."

"Who she's doing." Nicole smirked. "My money's still on Andy Wentworth." Athena's locker was next to Andy Wentworth's. She had never in the history of the alphabet ever noticed Andy talking to Roxanna.

Roxanna squirmed out of Lindsay's reach and said, "Ugh, not this again. What do you do, Athena?"

"Where do I hang out?" She couldn't just say home. Truth was out of the question. "I have a babysitting job, so that takes up a lot of my time. I think I've seen every single episode of *Phineas and Ferb*." She rolled her eyes. Truthfully, she loved *Phineas and Ferb*, and her babysitting job was morphing to strictly Saturday nights now that school was back on. She knew Roxanna knew the truth about what she did, and where. "I've never been to the diner—it looks awesome, though, from what I've seen online."

"We'll go sometime," Roxanna said, and Athena smiled.

"Whoa, Athena," Jordan piped up from across the table. "I think that's the first time I've ever seen you smile. You look so different." Was that a compliment?

"Yeah, but maybe sometime we could come over and just hang out." Lindsay's smile was crocodile-sincere.

"Come over to my house?"

"Of course! We don't need to be at a grave opening to hang out, right?"

Athena looked across at Jordan, who was still studying her with a blank face. "I try not to smile because I hate my teeth." It was the first honest statement she'd made.

"Ugh, don't get me started," Nicole said to her phone. For a split second, Athena thought Nicole shared her hatred for Athena's teeth.

"Yes, please, don't get her started," Roxanna said.

"Nicole's obsessed with her slight overbite," Jordan explained.

"I had braces for four years! Four! Years! That's a lot of my life thus far, a pretty big percentage. Plus, they hurt. You're lucky you didn't have braces."

Athena was the only one at the table without impeccably straight teeth, so she assumed that was directed at her.

"Irregardless—" Nicole continued.

"That's not a word," Roxanna said.

"Shut up. Irregardless, you should smile more. It's good for your mental health."

"I heard on the news the other day that Botox is now being used to treat depression, because if you can't frown"—Athena pulled her face into a tragedy mask—"you don't feel sad as much."

"That's bonkers."

"I would never get Botox," Jordan said. "No matter what. You can always tell with the New Yorkers at the mountain—you can see plastic surgery from a mile away. Especially in the cold. That shit freezes."

"I would totally get my chin shaved down," Nicole said.

"What!"

"Ugh, I'm eating."

Athena found out more than she'd ever wanted to know.

Laurel walked the rows that rainy morning without seeing the ground in front of her, or her own two feet kicking along. Zigzagging through the orchard, she took a rabbit's path to Charlie, meandering and recrossing her trail to confuse those in pursuit. Doubt needled her, as though she couldn't trust her own memory from the night before, sitting in the grave with him, having a conversation. She half expected to find the grave abandoned and untouched, the logical conclusion of which would be: Charlie was a ghost.

But as she came upon the grave, its door closed and quiet, she heard a faint clicking, like the keys of a computer. Charlie sat against the dry side of a tree trunk, baseball cap pulled low, wrestling with his DS. "You have got to be kidding me," he said to the screen.

"You're not very stealthy, you know."

Charlie flinched at the sound of her voice. "Why do you always have to sneak up on me?"

"If I were really trying to sneak up on you, you'd never know I was here."

Charlie got to his feet, brushed off his pants with his free hand. "So what's up? What do you want to do today?"

"What do I want to do?" This kid had no clue. "There are things I *have* to do."

"Okay. Like what?"

"Wash the milk bottles. Weed. Probably go to the dump with my dad to drop off the last of the party trash. But right now I have to check my traps."

"Can I go with you?"

"I don't know." Laurel tried to organize her thoughts. "You might not—it might not be pretty."

"I can handle it. I just want something to do."

"What if someone sees you?"

"In the woods off Roaring Kill Road? You're right, it's a bustling city street. I'd better not risk it." Charlie opened the grave door a crack and dropped his DS onto a pile of clothes. He lifted his hat and looked at Laurel. "Well?"

As he followed her into the trees for the long, chilly walk down the creek, Laurel finally caught up with her thoughts. She wanted a friend more than anything. It looked like that friend was going to be Charlie.

Snares and traps were Laurel's preferred hunting technique, and she was good at it, too. Setting a good snare is skill, but reading the paths is talent. Laurel could spot the holes in the hedges growing up along clearings, track the shade to make sure her wire didn't glint in the sun.

There was nothing to rush for, but she jogged uphill

toward the clearing near the cliff, shooting out a finger to warn Charlie of a tree root or animal hole. Each time she held back a branch, she half expected empty air to follow, but there he was, sweating and panting. He had brought his backpack. Something inside clanged as they ran. *At least he'll warn any bears away*, she thought. They made it to the clearing, the very edge of the forest. Dirt gave over to rock near the cliff, but where Laurel had set her snares, long grasses grew in tufts. Sure enough, two out of three snares held one rabbit each.

Charlie stood a good six feet back from the action as Laurel pulled on a pair of her mom's old gardening gloves. "It's not much, but it does help if they try to scratch me." Charlie silently took his notebook from his backpack and jotted a reminder. The rabbit clawed at the dirt, trying to escape even as Laurel lifted it with one hand around its neck and the other around its hind legs.

She turned back to Charlie with the rabbit in her hands. "You may not want to see this." The rabbit's black eyes stared.

"No," he said to the rabbit. "I want to see."

Laurel tightened her grip around the animal. With a small pop, like a knuckle cracking, she broke its neck, and laid the rabbit in the grass before she moved on to the second. Charlie tucked his notebook into his backpack.

By the time she'd bound the rabbits' feet, Charlie had wandered into the sun on the cliff. She made sure he was out of earshot before telling her catch, "Thank you. You've done a great job as rabbits. My family will be glad to have you for dinner." She smoothed one finger over each of their ears and then stripped off her gloves. She'd return to reset the snares in the evening, alone.

Leaving the rabbits and her bag in the shade of the clearing, she walked to the cliff edge, where Charlie sat cross-legged. He had collected every rock and pebble and twig within his reach and was chucking them as hard as he could into the sky over the notch. He didn't look up when her shadow covered his rock pile. "Ready to go?" she asked.

"In a minute."

"I have to get the rabbits back to my mom. She needs to dress them."

"Go ahead if you need to."

Laurel, so used to taking orders, turned to go before she thought about the consequences of leaving Charlie alone, tossing forest junk off a cliff. "But how will you—what if you get lost? Coming home, I mean."

"Runaway? Lost? What does it matter?"

"I said you didn't have to watch. I don't know why you're mad at me now." Laurel had wanted to scare him off, or at least test him. She kept waiting for him to stop to catch his breath or beg off on account of a cramp. He knew nothing about the forest, nothing about what he was getting himself into. Laurel could tell after five minutes with him.

He chucked another rock. "I'm not mad at you."

"Some people can go to the grocery store, other people go hunting or fishing. It's really no different. I'm sorry if that offends you or something."

"I said I'm not mad at you, but now you're getting mad at me." Charlie shielded his eyes to look up at her. "Sit down."

Laurel squatted on her heels.

"This view is amazing. There's the Rip Van Winkle Bridge, and down there is Saugerties. And over there"—he pointed into the far distance—"those are the Green Mountains in Vermont."

"How do you know all that?"

"The view from the Mountain House site is similar. I used to hike up there with my dad and the dogs pretty often, when I was little."

Laurel didn't say it, but she was thinking, *I've never been up here with anyone.* Until now. She hadn't known what she'd been looking at. Just below them, camouflaged by a carefully placed branch at the cliff's edge, Laurel's secret ledge beckoned.

"Did you ever hear about the skeleton they found down in Mary's Glen? It happened right before we were born."

Laurel had to wrench her focus back to the cliff top. "No."

"Well anyway, these two hikers were off trail in the park and they saw a leg bone or something coming through the dirt and they called the rangers and the rangers called the archaeologists and it was an old skeleton. Well, part of a skeleton. The head was missing."

Laurel thought of her turkey carcass, buried headless.

"They did an excavation, like dusting with tiny brushes and all that, and studied the bones and estimated them to be hundreds of years old. It could've been part of a Native American

burial mound, even. You really never heard of this?"

"My parents don't tell me anything interesting."

Charlie brushed his hands against his shins. "I don't know what made me think of that. I like it up here. Do you spend a lot of time here?"

Laurel hadn't seen the snare. Charlie didn't know he'd tied one. "Not really," she lied. "Every few days I guess. For my snares. Speaking of." Laurel stood, and pins and needles shot up and down the backs of her legs. "I should get home with the groceries."

Charlie stood, too. "I'll go with you. I'd be lost in thirty seconds by myself; I don't know who I was kidding."

When they got to the creek, instead of turning to follow it back to the orchard, Laurel said to Charlie, "Want to see something?"

And Charlie said, "Always."

She took him along the creek in the opposite direction. They walked for a few minutes until they came to a dead tree bridge. "Shoes off," Laurel said, shifting her pack from her hip to her back and sliding one Ked onto each hand. "Watch your step."

"Yeah," Charlie said as he stepped gingerly onto the bark-stripped log. "There should really be a sign."

On the other side, shoving their sweaty feet back into their shoes, Charlie admitted, "I saw myself going headfirst off that log, one hundred percent."

Laurel didn't reply.

The ground changed from rocky creek bed to mossy underbrush to dense forest as they moved away from the water. Charlie's backpack clanged along. They waded through ferns and backtracked to avoid pricker bushes.

"Where are we going?" Charlie whined.

"Here." Laurel stopped and Charlie walked into her shoulder. "Look."

It was barely a clearing. The house looked abandoned, maybe haunted. Pine boughs hovered right above the chimney, and a sapling grew out from under the porch steps. Bald two-by-fours propped up the porch roof of the house like the opening of a trap. Moss grew over the shingles. Broken windows sported cardboard eye patches ripped from Genesee cases. A single lawn chair, rusted permanently open, sat next to the door.

Charlie couldn't disguise the wonder in his voice, even in a whisper. "Where the hell are we?"

"That's Mr. Vandeveer's house. Van. Do you know him?" They stood shoulder to shoulder behind a tree.

"I know who he is. Do you know him, like know him for real?"

She shook her head. "I've never even seen him. I keep thinking I'll run into him at some point. Unless he's dead in there. Want to go check?"

"Are you crazy?" Charlie stepped back and his foot slid on pine needles. He flailed until he regained his balance. Laurel snickered. "Shut up."

"Come on." She stepped nimbly around him. "These rabbits won't stay fresh forever."

Chapter 15

ATHENA KEPT HER HEAD DOWN THE REST OF THE DAY, terrified of looking up and meeting Roxanna's, or any of Roxanna's friends', eyes. She'd managed to dodge Lindsay's pestering for the rest of lunch, making excuses about babysitting and openly lying about going away with her family on the weekend for a post-opening-season getaway, but now the dread had returned full force. Even through the sheer joy of sitting at their table, of catching people noticing her there as they passed by on the way to the garbage bin, Athena felt like a mouse at a table of cats. That hunted feeling fogged her head all day.

In French class Madame Karpinski asked, "Athena, *dormez-vous?*"

In algebra Mrs. Brennan said, "I realize it's the first day back, and some of us, ahem"—she stopped by Athena's desk—"are still getting into the swing of things, but we're going to hit the ground running, so pay attention. Ready for this proof? Don't blink." Athena sleepwalked through the entire day and even missed the bus home because she forgot that she hadn't ridden her bike that morning.

Somewhere around sixth period the sun had asserted itself, layering heat over the humidity. As she walked down Main Street toward the traffic light, blisters bubbled on the backs of her heels. *Walking up the hill is going to kill.* She smashed down the backs of her Keds and wore them like clogs, picturing Shirley Temple's ringlets bobbing as she danced around in her wooden shoes. She and Laurel would always join in and dance around the living room with kitchen towels tied around their waists like aprons. *I'm a little Dutch girl dressed in blue, and these are the things I like to do.*

At the corner, waiting for the crosswalk's red hand to change to a boxy person, which always looked to Athena like a chalk outline at a crime scene—not an inviting signal—she remembered the book her mom had asked her to pick up for Laurel. Across the street from the library, the forbidden antiques shop's OPEN flag hung over the sidewalk. It snapped and strutted in the breeze, flirting with her. It had been a shitty, shitty day. She looked over her shoulder. Ghost town.

As casually as she could, she pushed the door open, and sleigh bells glittered the air. A middle-aged man behind the desk looked over his reading glasses. "Welcome to Sally's. Anything I can help you with today?" His hands broke the spine of a spy novel—all the O's in the title were bullet holes.

"No, thank you." Athena's voice was an octave higher than normal. "Just looking."

He returned to his paperback. "Let me know if you need anything."

The store wasn't nearly as big as Athena had pictured it, basically a square room cluttered with tables and shelves. A large ceiling fan clicked away over her head. Athena turned a rack of postcards with glamorized pictures of places she knew: Plateau Mountain, Compass Lake, the ski lift running like a zipper up the slope.

She walked along the glass jewelry cases, poring over tarnished brooches and lumpy turquoise set in wide silver cuffs, old brass keys and silverware. She stopped in front of a set with dogwood flowers etched into their handles—forks and knives, tea- and tablespoons, even a silver gravy boat and ladle. The note card said, *Mostly complete set, circa 1880. Originally sold by Chester Jewelers in Kingston, NY*, but Athena knew more: it was a wedding gift to her great-great-grandparents. The last few pieces were still in the drawer in her kitchen, reserved for her mother and father at mealtimes. She put both hands on the glass. They had been selling Granny Lawrence's silver.

Mostly complete, the card said. Even the buyer knew it was only a matter of time.

She wandered away from the display case, absentmindedly

chewing her thumbnail. She'd always thought her family had it figured out; they managed. Her mother grew vegetables. Her father hunted turkey and deer. They had chickens for eggs, and sold the extras to the deli in the village. The hens had been laying better, lately, come to think of it. That was something. Laurel fished and trapped. Athena helped her mother can and pickle. They followed the sales circulars, and their freezer was always full of half-price specials. But what was she missing? How delicate was that balance?

By lunch that day Laurel's mosquito bites were big as quarters: four on her arms, six on her legs—two dollars and fifty cents' worth of misery. She shook an ice cube from the tray and held it to the welts.

"How'd you get so bitten up?" Walt half turned from the sink where he was filling his glass.

"Um." Laurel thought back to sneaking through the orchard. "Checking my traps by the creek"—not a total lie—"they chewed me up pretty bad."

Claudia screwed the cap back onto the mayo. "It's 'cause they know you're sweet."

Their empty sandwich plates lay on the table. Simon had gone into town for the chili special at the deli, and Athena was almost halfway through her first day of eleventh grade. *She can complain all she wants about going to school, but she took extra-long getting ready this morning. For someone who doesn't care about school, she sure puts in a lot of effort.* Laurel looked up to find both her parents staring at her. "What?"

"Laurel, we need to have a little chat."

They know.

"Okay." She dropped the melting ice cube in the sink. "About what?" *How could I think they wouldn't find out? Now I'll never go to school. They'll keep me here indefinitely.*

"It's about your grave, sweetie." Claudia patted her hand reassuringly. "Have you been thinking in it much recently?"

"Oh." Laurel tried to recover from her genuine surprise. "My grave, I—no, I haven't really—I mean, yes! Yeah, I've been thinking in it a lot. Recently."

"That's great," her dad boomed. "I knew you'd be invested in it. How could you spend all day walking rows without becoming more interested, right?" Walt shot a glance at Claudia, but she deflected it with one of her own.

"What's going on?" Laurel asked.

"Honey bee, we need to talk to you outside."

"Outside?"

"Just for a minute. It's important."

"Okay." Laurel slid into her shoes. *Did I leave something behind last night? Do they have evidence?*

The trio headed out into the damp heat, and everything looked the same: same tilting woodpile, same gray clothesline with its dangling basket of pins, no sign of disruption or disobedience whatsoever. Walt led them into the orchard, going slow on account of his wife's labored breathing. By the time they made it to their row, Laurel was thoroughly confused.

I haven't been in my grave in weeks—what do they expect to see? Her yellow door waited, glinting in the sun.

"Well, honey"—Claudia caught her breath—"open it!"

The key is in my jewelry box, she thought, but it was too late to argue. She turned the brass knob and heaved the door up and over. Her grave glowed like a jar of lightning bugs. A new purple ladder descended from the foot of the doorway. She could smell the fresh paint. As her eyes adjusted, she saw that one of her dad's old green camp lanterns had been set up on the floor, and her mom had sewed the cushions that reclined in the far corner. The wood floor gleamed in the lantern light. The simple sprucing her grave had gotten for her opening had amounted to a throw pillow, a flashlight, and a good scrubbing. This was above and beyond.

"Oh, wow" was all she could say. And then it came to her: "Thank you!" She hugged her father around his middle, kissed her mother on her doughy cheek. "Thank you so much."

Walt chuckled in relief, and Claudia's smile squeezed out tears. "Here you go." She handed Laurel her grave key. "Sorry I had to borrow that, for the surprise and all."

Laurel said, "It's okay," but she was thinking, *How did they know where to look?*

"It's the sprucing we wanted to give you at your opening."

Her dad stuck his hands deep into his pockets. "It just took us longer than we wanted to get things ready."

"If you want to, go on down." Her mom motioned to the ladder. "Go right ahead."

She wanted to be in the sun, but she knew that was the wrong answer. Halfway down the ladder, Laurel looked up. "Leave the door open, okay?"

"Sure thing, sweet bay." Her father gave a little wave and then walked her mother back down the hill.

It wasn't the first time she'd been down in her grave, but the surprise of the grave redesign left her feeling out of place and out of practice. For a few seconds Laurel didn't know what to do; she just stood numbly, staring up the ladder at the fringe of apple leaves framing blue sky. When she was sure her parents weren't coming back, she picked up the lantern to have a better look around. The walls were made of salvaged mirrors, dotted black with tarnish and ghostly white nicks. Here and there, her mother had taped up photos: Laurel and Athena climbing on the tractor; Peanut, their old beagle, asleep in his basket; her mom in the rocking chair, feeding baby Laurel a bottle.

She sat down in the pillow pile. Tenet number one: A grave is to think. Athena liked to recite this whenever Laurel asked her to walk the rows or play chess. "I can't, Laurel," she'd say. "A grave is to think." And she'd stuff her book bag full of magazines and disappear into the orchard.

How long do I have to stay down here? Laurel's sneakers bent over the rungs as she climbed toward the sky; the temperature warmed after only a few feet. Like a stunt harness, something grabbed her around the middle and yanked. She flew back into the pillows and her head met stone. "Lucy! Not cool!" One hand massaged the back of her head. "What the heck?" She crawled over to the lantern and dragged it closer. Under the pillows, in the very corner of the grave, there was a little door, also painted yellow. The key hung from the tiny doorknob by a piece of yarn. She unlocked the door and peered down into a perfect doll-sized replica of her grave. They'd thought of everything.

Chapter 16

NORMA BLACKISTONE PRACTICED THE ORGAN EVERY afternoon at three thirty, a fact well-known to the town's regular library patrons, which accounted for the emptiness of the place when Athena walked in after her detour to Sally's. Strained chords blared through the rafters over the stacks, just as they had when the rows were carved wooden pews. While Norma practiced, her sister, Noreen, manned the due-date stamp.

Noreen was dozing delicately, her chin nestled in her silk scarf. *How can she sleep through—oh my God, is she dead?* Athena leaned in, thinking, *Am I looking at a body or a person? Please be a person.* She had to stay very still to see it, but Noreen's chest rose and fell. Athena hurried past the reference desk before Noreen changed her mind and expired.

She wandered through a few stacks until she found the right section. Athena walked her fingers along the spines beside the stained-glass window of St. Gregory in his red hood. Below, a stand of offertory candles burned low in their glass holders. A shout broke Athena's concentration. She looked up into the face of Maude Gelwick.

"Sorry, what?" Athena shouted back.

"Can I help you find something?" Maude had an OLMPL name tag pinned to her thrifted bowling shirt above the name *Roger*, embroidered in navy thread.

"No, thanks. Just looking." Athena turned back to the shelf.

"Looks like you're looking for something specific. I can save you some time, point it out?" The organ trilled at the top of a scale.

"That's okay." *Why is she being so nice? It's not like her boss is going to see—or hear.*

"Isn't it early to be starting in on your research paper? Day one of school? Kudos, dude."

"The book isn't for me; it's for my sister. I think the author is Geoffrey Crayon?"

"Let's see." Maude dipped into a grand plié and returned with a book from the bottom shelf. "*The Sketch-Book of Geoffrey Crayon*? Washington Irving is the author, though." Maude's nails were painted dark blue, almost black, with a coat of glitter on top. They looked like little galaxies.

Self-conscious of her bare, close-bitten nails, Athena took

the book quickly. "That's the one. Thanks for the help." Her sweaty fingers stuck to the book's plastic raincoat as she rounded the corner and headed down the side aisle toward the potentially deceased Miss Blackistone. Much to her dismay, Maude followed.

"Listen, if your sister's interested in Washington Irving, I can request a few more books from interlibrary loan. We don't have much of a selection here—of anything. I'm working on getting the DVDs cataloged, though! Pretty soon people will be able to rent movies—isn't that nuts? Kind of sad that libraries have to cater to everything besides books, but foot traffic is key. If they come in for DVDs, I'm hoping maybe they'll stay for the books. Of course, this doesn't help." She pointed overhead, gesturing at the invisible organ noise that surrounded them. "It's kind of cute, though—she takes her shoes off. Sometimes I sneak up and watch her. Do you want to see?"

For a librarian in training, this girl sure talks a lot. "That's okay. I have to get home. I'll check back, though, about the DVDs." *Even though we don't have a DVD player.* Athena started walking again, but Maude touched her shoulder.

"What are you interested in, Athena?"

"Um," Athena fumbled, flummoxed. No one had ever asked her. "I guess I like . . . history? English is okay, too. French is my worst subject; I'm awful."

Maude smiled, and a wad of neon green gum peeked out of the corner of her mouth. "I don't mean in school, I mean in life! What catches your attention?"

Athena zeroed in on a water stain where the carpet met the wall, speechless. "I'm not really sure."

"It's cool. Get back to me when you figure it out. See ya in chorus." Maude touched her arm again as she swept past, trailing a scent like cedar.

What was that? Athena felt like she'd failed a pop quiz and a job interview in the same breath. Athena looked at the spot on her arm where Maude had touched her, as if she would find a mark there.

That night at dinner, Walt had news: the September grave opening was off. Despite Athena's prodding, he wouldn't say much. "Chickee, I've told you all I know. I got a call this afternoon, very apologetic, saying that they didn't know when they'd be able to have the ceremony, so it was best to call it off for now. Family illness, he said. I'm not in the gossip business."

"Good. One less thing to think about." If Claudia felt relieved, she wasn't showing it.

"May I be excused?" Laurel held her crossed fingers under the table.

"Honey, you hardly put a dent in. You feeling okay?" Her mother held the back of her hand to Laurel's forehead. "You feel a little warm to me."

"Yeah, I've been feeling not quite one hundred percent today."

Laurel put on a tired face for her mom, who said, "Well, okay. But take it easy tonight. Bedtime on the early side."

"Okay." Laurel carried her plate into the dining room, where Clover's bowl waited for scraps. Instead of scraping the entire plate into her tin, Laurel broke off a hunk of hamburger and fed Clover from her fork. Clover swallowed it in one chomp and sat politely, asking, *More please? Please, some more?* Laurel held a finger to her lips and pulled a folded square of tinfoil out of her back pocket. She transferred the rest of the leftovers into the foil and tucked it into her waistband. Back through the kitchen without stopping, plate into sink, Clover hot on her heels, she said, "I'm taking Clover for her night walk," and was out the door before anyone could say a word.

Charlie ate straight from the foil package, practically inhaling the mash of burger and potatoes and boiled carrots.

"So how's living off the land going for you?"

He ignored her.

She watched him plow through, trying hard not to address the question that nagged at her every time she thought about Charlie hiding out in her backyard.

"Charlie? Aren't your parents worried about you?"

Mouth full, he shrugged and nodded.

"Won't they call the police?"

"They probably haven't realized I'm gone yet. Whatever. I'll mail a postcard tomorrow."

"A postcard? From the grave? What will it say? *Having a swell time, wish you were here*?"

"Shut up, no. I packed a bunch of prestamped postcards

from places we've been together, so they'll know it's really me. I'll tell them not to send out any search parties or I'll take off for real, where they won't be able to find me so easily."

"And they're just going to buy that? They'll take you at your word?"

"I'm sure they think I'll give up and come home by tomorrow. I'm not exactly what you'd call"—he paused briefly—"an outdoorsy person."

"I kind of got that impression earlier. Have you ever been camping?"

"No."

"Ever been fishing?"

"No."

"Hunting?"

"Hell, no."

"So you just went to school and, like, played video games?"

"No, I did—stuff. My dad and I used to go hiking, sometimes, when I was little. I told you that. The things I've done aren't really helpful at the moment. I've been the captain of the robotics team. We built a remote-control car using K'Nex and wiring from an old computer. I've been to thirteen countries. I did a genealogy project and traced my family roots all the way back to Charlemagne."

Laurel didn't know what Charlemagne was—an ancient city, like Carthage?—but it sounded impressive. But it still wasn't something that would help him in the woods. "Wow," she said. "That's really something. And after all that, what you most want to do is live in a grave?"

Charlie had gone back to eating, his eyes focused on things that weren't there. Running away had been Laurel's favorite threat when she was little. One day, after a particularly hideous fight with Athena and punishment from her mom, she'd packed her dress-up handbag with Tic Tacs and clean socks and snuck out without anyone seeing her. She'd made it to the end of their road before giving up. She hadn't had anywhere to run to.

"I could show you a few things in the woods if you want. Tricks and, uh, pointers." The candles, burning low in the coffee cans, suddenly popped and sparked.

"Really?" He swallowed. "When can we start?"

They decided to start the next day after breakfast. Laurel tucked a peanut butter sandwich into her shoulder bag, along with her compass and a pack of playing cards, which Charlie had requested. She walked quickly down the Champs, too quickly to seem nonchalant. Glancing back at her house, she saw two police cruisers parked beside the barn, her father unlocking a grave door for a pair of big-bellied cops. Another officer walked slowly down the Dovers' row, following a German shepherd on a long leash. Over her shoulder, she watched Walt slide the skeleton key into his breast pocket and squint off into the sun while one cop stepped down onto the first ladder rung. She hustled toward Tamsen's unsealed grave.

✧ ✧ ✧

Charlie walked behind her, stepping where she stepped. "I have a question."

"Already?"

"How do you know where to go in the woods?"

"Okay, so. First thing is the trail markings. You'll get to know them the more you use them, but if you need help remembering how to get back to the orchard, you need to break a stick, like this." Laurel snapped a pine branch at eye level. "Or else pile some twigs and rocks in a little sculpture, to show you where to turn on your way back." Laurel didn't need these tricks anymore, but Charlie scribbled furiously on his notepad. Laurel thought, but didn't mention, all the times she'd done that, only to be misdirected by a rogue stone pile she hadn't made, or a snapped branch that led her farther into the woods. She'd always thought it was a poltergeist or a fairy, a backward Hansel and Gretel situation.

"There are some landmarks I'll show you that'll really help, but if you get super-duper lost, just find the creek. Follow it downstream until you get to the dam, and then you can follow the road back. If you stay in the trees, no one will see you."

Charlie scratched his hairline with the pencil eraser. "Um, just wondering: bears? Mountain lions? Any—any sightings?"

"Oh sure, bears are around, but they're only looking for food."

"Shit monkeys."

"Not you—you're not the food. They want human food, so just be careful with your trash—I'll take it up to the house—

and don't, like, wear cologne. Also, if you come across a bear, remember to run downhill, not up. Bears have a hard time running downhill. And don't make eye contact."

"What about mountain lions?"

"Nah, they're endangered. My dad is the only person I know who's seen one, and that was ages and ages ago. And probably he was lying anyway."

They tramped through the woods, Laurel in the lead, swinging around saplings and hopscotching mushroom colonies. She pointed out the lightning-struck oak at a fork in the trail—down went to the creek, up went to Name Rock, two boulders stacked like a gaping alligator mouth by a glacier millennia ago. Laurel paused at Name Rock like a tour guide. "This is a choice spot if you find yourself stuck in a downpour."

Charlie stuck his head into the small cave and frowned at the lichen pocking the edge of the entrance. "Lovely."

"And up top is a great lookout point. Let's check it out."

Charlie followed, scrambling on all fours up the crevasse. He brushed his hands off on the back of his pants. "What am I supposed to be looking for?"

Laurel hadn't realized it until now, but she was bursting to have an audience, someone to show her everyday life to. She pointed down into the creek notch. "Well, you can't see it because of the leaves, but over there is the best swimming hole, and down there is a really good spot for fishing—that's where I met you. Remember, you fell in?"

Charlie dropped his head and gave her a look that clearly

said, *Go ahead, remind me.*

"And then up that way the creek goes pretty close to the tennis courts at the country club, so be careful if you go up that far. Sometimes kids hit the ball over the fence and come looking for it."

Charlie had turned his notepad sideways and was drawing a snaking creek from left to right, labeling it with landmarks that he wasn't sure he would recognize when he saw them.

"Why did you run away?" she asked suddenly.

"Why do you care so much?"

"Not telling me is making me care more than I ever normally would." When Charlie didn't answer, Laurel went on. "Cops were in the cemetery when I left this morning."

Charlie looked up at her. "Where?"

"In the Dovers' row. Near where the grave opening was."

"Maybe someone lost a diamond earring at the party." Charlie laughed nervously.

"I'm sure that's what the search dog was for."

He started to say something, then thought better of it. "Just forget it," he said, and went back to his notepad. Laurel saw him glance over the edge of the paper at an infinity sign peeking out from under his shoe. Not an infinity sign, an eight, carved deep into the rock. "William 1918," he read. "Who's that?"

Laurel followed his pointed finger to the name and date. "Oh, that's my great-great-uncle or somebody. All these people used to live in my house at one time or another." She waved her hand over the boulder, and Charlie noticed for the first time: the entire rock face was tattooed with names and years, sometimes whole dates, like *July 4, 1876*, and sometimes love proclamations, like *Owen + Patricia*.

"All these people are related to you?"

"Yup."

Leopard spots of sun shifted over the stone as a breeze came through. Charlie sat on his heels, brushing dirt and brown needles out of the etchings. Some were washing away, just gray ghosts of words, while others looked like they'd been carved last week, they were so elegant and precise. "How'd they do this?" He traced a letter *E*, which was as crisp as if a typewriter had punched it into the rock.

"They carried chisels with them when they came out here, I guess. And hammers."

Scuttling like a crab, Charlie found Felix, Ian, Edwin, Hugh, Mary, John, and various years, both with and without names attached: 1821, 1943, 1907, 1896, 1865. "How come there are only men's names here?"

"There are a few women. See? Patricia, and there's Mary."

"But they're with men's names. Owen plus Patricia. Mary plus John. Why not any girls on their own?"

"Probably the men were the ones who could carve. Plus, I don't know if the girls had time to come out here and sit around and tap at a rock all afternoon. The girls made other things." After a moment, Laurel said, "Want to see something?"

"Okay."

She scuttled down the boulder and disappeared from sight.

"Wait! Where are you going?"

She belly-slid, headfirst, into the narrow cave under Name Rock. It felt prehistoric cold, and her hands searched out the plastic bag protecting her waterproof matches. Folding her shoulders, she flipped onto her back. Her shoulders were almost too wide for that maneuver. Pretty soon she'd have to get herself one of those skateboards they used to work under cars. She struck a match and waited for the rust-colored outlines to surface. There—the humped outline of a bear, head lowered, his back in soft peaks like a mountain. Another shape that could be a pinecone or an ear of corn.

Charlie's voice filled the cave. "What are you doing?"

"C'mere."

"It's gross in there."

"Oh my God." Laurel blew out the match before it burned her fingers. "Come here!"

Charlie inched his way into the space beside Laurel, refusing to lie down until the absolute last minute.

"You have to relax," she told him. "Let your eyes adjust." Shoulder to shoulder, hip to hip, the cave fit tight as a coffin around them.

"I'm trying. It's too dark."

"Just wait. You'll see them."

"Does it feel colder in here to you all of a sudden?"

The whoosh of the match igniting sounded like a small explosion so close to his face. He felt its feeble heat fighting through the chill. "Is that—?" Charlie reached a finger, Laurel batted it away.

"Don't touch. Are you crazy?"

"I wasn't going to! I was just going to point." He pointed, slower this time. "Is that the moon?" Concentric circles hovered over the bear.

"I always thought it was the sun." They were close enough for Laurel to smell Charlie's unbrushed teeth. She supposed that meant he could smell hers.

Someone from another age had traced their hand onto the rock. Charlie held his hand a few inches below it. With one finger, he touched the blank space of the palm. "Amazing."

"I thought you'd like it." And she thought but didn't say, *I'm running out of secrets.*

Chapter 17

As Athena sat at Roxanna and her friends' lunch table over the next couple days, she still felt wary of their sudden interest in her. Roxanna sent up a timid flare just before math, though Athena could have hallucinated it. Stress was high that day thanks to rumors about a pop quiz in math. (*A pop quiz the first week of school!*) Athena sat at her desk, nervously chewing her ring fingernail, restraining herself from biting all the way through. In walked Roxanna, just as the bell went off. Across the heads of people kneeling in their chairs, exchanging homework pages, while Dana Andrek sharpened not one but three pencils, Roxanna crossed the room and ever so casually jutted her chin toward Athena. If Athena hadn't already been looking at her, she would've missed it. She raised her hand and dropped it without waving, as though someone had called her name for attendance.

The official invitation had come at lunch that day—the third consecutive lunch period Athena had spent at that table, not that she was counting (but she was). While the other three were deep in conversation about the rumor that Katie Somerset was hooking up with the girls' lacrosse coach, Roxanna turned to Athena and said, "We usually get something to eat right after school. You busy today? I know it's a school night."

Slowly, like the opposite of a stammer, Athena replied, "I'm not busy." She regained consciousness enough to stipulate, "I have to be home by six, though. My parents' friends are coming over for dinner." It was a solid-gold lie. Roxanna bought it, with sympathy, so Athena put her plan into action. Step one: call her mom from Roxanna's cell phone with an excuse about volunteering to help Mrs. Adelaide paint the new mural in the science wing. Step two: meet Roxanna at her locker after the last bell. Step three, much later: get dropped back off at school to pick up her bike and head home as if it were the most ordinary Thursday and not in fact the first time she would be riding around in Roxanna Dover's car along with Roxanna's closest friends.

And so, come 2:35 p.m., Athena and the four girls walked the long hallway toward the chorus room and the exit to the student parking lot. Athena had to keep ducking behind them to allow oncoming traffic to pass by, but she was still very much *with* them. It was obvious, she was sure. Athena's backpack weighed forty pounds between her math and history books alone. Roxanna breezed into the warm afternoon with only her oversized leather shoulder bag; Lindsay carried an iridescent clutch. Jordan and Nicole each had a backpack that seemed more for appearances than actual function; they looked practically empty.

At Roxanna's car, Lindsay opened the passenger door and flipped the seat up for access to the backseat, so casual, like it was second nature to her. Nicole climbed in behind the driver, then Jordan waved Athena on. She sat with her feet up on the raised center of the floor, her gigantic backpack lumped on her lap like a lead beach ball. She could barely see over it. "So do you guys, like—are you coming back for the books you need? For homework?"

"Nah," Lindsay said as she buckled her seat belt. "I can get it all done in homeroom and study hall tomorrow."

Beside Athena, Jordan let out a long *pffffffff*. "Keep telling yourself that, Linds." Roxanna turned the car out of the school parking lot and began the long coast down Main Street, past Maude waiting at the crosswalk, past the library, past Sally's Antiques. Athena kept her eyes straight ahead.

On the other side of Athena, Nicole said, "It's the first week of the school year. Teachers don't expect you to do your homework. Not yet."

That was news to Athena. "So where are we going?" She spoke to Roxanna's eyes and nose, the slice of her face she could see in the rearview mirror, but Lindsay answered.

"Wendy's!"

Athena laughed, thinking it was a joke, but Roxanna said, "Finally you see reason. Wendy's is five thousand times better than Burger King."

"And it's way nicer to hang out there," Nicole agreed.

"Whatever." Lindsay picked at the chipped nail polish on her thumb. "I just feel like a Frosty."

"Are you, like, the events coordinator?" Athena said to Lindsay, who twisted painfully over her shoulder to look at her.

"Huh?"

Roxanna raised her eyes to the rearview mirror.

"I just mean," Athena fumbled, "you seem to"—*not dictate, too negative*—"shape the day's plans. So, events coordinator, you know?"

Lindsay smiled. "I like that. Events coordinator. I'd like to think so."

Jordan moaned. "Oh, brother."

"Don't encourage her," Nicole said.

Roxanna slid the tape adapter into her car's cassette player and thumbed around on her phone. The car slowly edged over the double yellow lines, then overcorrected by kissing the white line at the shoulder. Athena scratched her nose and reminded herself to take even breaths. Blondie burst into the car loud enough that conversation stopped. "Hanging on the Telephone" segued into "Call Your Girlfriend."

"This one's too obvious," Jordan shouted. "Telephones."

Roxanna turned the stereo down ever so slightly and shouted back. "It's my telephone-slash-badass-babes-with-questionable-haircuts playlist."

"You didn't go with 'Call Me'?" Athena asked. Roxanna turned the volume down more. "Isn't that the song Blondie is really known for?"

"Exactly, too predictable."

"My favorite of your playlists was the uncrackable mix," Jordan said.

"That was a good one, if I do say so myself. The guessing got annoying, but I really got my money's worth. It took you guys almost a month of listening to it over and over."

"See if Athena can guess it," Nicole piped up.

"The first song was 'Free Falling.' Then there was 'A Case of You,' I think." Jordan grabbed her head. "I've heard it thousands of times, why can't I remember?"

"'Tiny Dancer' was another one," Nicole chimed in.

"A seventies theme?" Athena guessed.

"No." They all shot her down gleefully.

"'Bohemian Rhapsody' was the grand finale," Jordan said, looking at her expectantly. "That was the one that tipped us off, finally."

"Uhhh." Athena shook her head. "I'm stumped."

Roxanna met her eyes in the mirror. "Songs that people sing in cars in movies."

Jordan ticked off the examples on her fingers. "*Jerry Maguire. Practical Magic. Almost Famous. Wayne's World*!"

"And I haven't seen a single one of those movies," Athena laughed.

Nicole grabbed her arm. "You haven't seen *Wayne's World*? Oh, I'm so excited to show it to you. You have so much goodness ahead of you." Athena felt her stomach flutter; Nicole had just seconded Roxanna's vote of confidence in her.

"Can we skip to 'Call Me Maybe'? If this is a telephone-slash-whatever mix, it's gotta be on here somewhere." Lindsay grabbed for Roxanna's phone, but Roxanna nabbed it off the dashboard and tucked it under her leg.

"Off limits."

"Nice try, Linds." Jordan patted her on the shoulder. "Almost had it."

"We get it, okay?" Lindsay said to Roxanna. "You have secrets. You're mysterious. Now will you get over yourself for three minutes and let me listen to Carly Rae?" Lindsay held her hand out.

Roxanna kept her eyes on the road. "New playlists deserve the respect of one full listen before you make any requests to the DJ."

The song changed to a creepy chipmunk voice repeating, "Used to be one of the rotten ones and I liked you for that." Roxanna turned up the volume.

When Nicole had said that Wendy's was "way nicer" than Burger King, she must have been referring to the single tree planted next to the Dumpster at the very back of the parking lot. Roxanna parked her car in the minuscule shade and the girls sat with the top down, dipping French fries into Frosties. Athena only had the $4.50 she had been planning to spend on the September *Nylon*, so she ordered a small fries and orange soda, insisting she was still full from lunch. She propped the paper bag up on her backpack and fished the crispy stragglers out of the bottom while Jordan plowed through a ten-piece chicken nuggets and Nicole shook another salt packet onto her large fries. "Halfway down you have to reseason," she said.

Roxanna had left the keys in so they could keep listening to her playlist, but no one was paying any attention.

"You know what I was thinking?" Lindsay had turned all the way around in the front seat so that her legs were against the seatback and her back was resting against the glove compartment. "It's a beautiful day—"

"It's a beautiful daaaaaay!" Roxanna sang.

"Shut up." Lindsay laughed. "As I was saying, it's a—lovely day, perfect for being outside in the fresh air. Why don't we take this picnic to the cemetery at Athena's?"

Athena looked up from the paper bag in a panic.

"Sounds like a great idea to me," Jordan said with her mouth full of nuggets.

"Not today, guys." Athena tried to sound bummed. "My dad is fertilizing and it smells like shit. I mean it *is* shit, so . . ."

"We could hang out inside then, couldn't we?" Lindsay asked.

"But you just said that it's a good day for fresh air—"

"Her parents are having a dinner party tonight," Roxanna interjected.

"So what? It's barely four o'clock now. When is the dinner party?"

Athena, suddenly self-conscious of any food in her teeth, spoke without moving her lips. "People are coming over at six."

"Plenty of time!" Jordan crowed. "We'll leave before the dinner party. I know what those are like."

"Or maybe we'll be invited to stay!" Lindsay clapped her hands. "There's always too much food, right? We can be the extra mouths to help clean the plates."

"Ew, you make it sound like we're going to eat the scraps," Roxanna said.

"Oh please, I was speaking metaphorically." Lindsay spun around in her seat. "Driver? To Athena's!"

Roxanna looked at Athena in the mirror for the briefest second before sliding on her aviators and turning the ignition.

The music was loud. No one was talking. Athena's worries crisscrossed like shot-off fireworks. As one exploded, another burst right behind it. The orchard was one thing, but the house? The wallpaper peeling up at the seams and the mildew smell in the entryway and the fridge so old it shook the window glass whenever it rumbled into cooling mode. And Lucy! Her knuckles whitened. The only people who ever came into the house were people who knew about Lucy, and people who Lucy had known, like Suze. And Lucy was a jerk to them! What fresh hell would she cook up for strangers?

"I really don't think we should go to my house. It's so boring. I don't even have Netflix," Athena yelled over the music. "Plus my bike! Roxanna, you were supposed to drop me off at the school to get my bike, remember?"

Roxanna turned down the music to say, "No worries, I'll bring you back to the school in time for you to ride home for the dinner party. Or else you can leave it there overnight and I'll pick you up in the morning for school."

This offer should've thrilled Athena, but she steamrolled ahead with her self-preservation campaign. "I really don't think we should go to my house."

"What's the big deal?" Lindsay said nonchalantly. "Don't you trust us to behave ourselves?"

No, I don't, Athena thought, but she said, "It's not that. My mom will be rushing around getting the dinner ready and she'll want me to straighten up and she'll be so mad if she has to entertain new guests before her invited guests even arrive."

No one responded. They had turned onto the long serpentine asphalt of Orchard Hill.

YOUR GRAVE KEY IS YOUR KEY TO LIFE

Before the car had pulled onto the dirt road, I could feel Athena's miserable energy rolling ahead of her like the gusts that bring a storm. Generally, I didn't like people traipsing through the orchard cemetery, which is what I expected the carful of girls to be doing. Grave-opening season rattled me the same way it did Laurel. My natural instinct was to meddle and scare, but too many new people made me shy in a way that I never was when I was alive. And that made me mad. But as long as I could spend those days and nights with Laurel in the house, I was calm. I was content to wait for everyone to leave or die, whichever they preferred. When Roxanna's car parked alongside Walt's truck and two doors opened to let the five girls out, Laurel wasn't home to be my company. My instincts roared back to life.

Athena chattered without pause. "Guys, please? My house is the worst. It's so dull. My sister is probably out running around in the woods with the dog, so you won't even get to meet Clover Honey. She's the best member of my family. You should come back when you can meet Clover."

The girls walked slowly. One stopped to pick a pebble out of the bottom of her flip-flop. Each one wanted the other to go first. Each one wanted to see inside desperately.

"Roxanna, why don't we go to your house? Don't you have, like, a whole entertainment system in your basement? And your darkroom! I'd love to see your darkroom!"

"Try a different tack, my friend," the athletic one said, sounding distinctly unfriendlike. "Roxanna never lets anyone into her room, much less her darkroom. She's probably hiding bodies up there."

"Well, that's okay." Athena soldiered on. "We could go to your house, Jordan."

Jordan ignored the suggestion altogether. They made it to the front steps and Athena thought, *Oh God, the peeling paint all over the steps, the broken bird bath lying behind the bush there*, while she said, "It doesn't smell so bad after all. Let's take a walk in the orchard while the sun's still out. Guys, come on."

One girl had her hand on the screen door handle, the other one was holding a sparkly bag. Athena thought, *If I let them into my grave they won't see my house. That's probably what they really want, anyway.* She opened her mouth and started saying, "Lindsay—" And that was my cue.

I lifted the cell phone right out of the shortest one's hand and sent it flying into the nearest tree. She screamed.

"Nicole, what the hell?" Jordan asked.

"I didn't do that! I didn't—"

Lindsay let the screen door go with a slam and hunched over her wounded hand. "I think it shocked me!" Fine hairs on her head floated in midair.

Jordan's eyes grew wide and she rubbed the goose bumps rising along her arms. Her teeth chattered. "Why am I freezing all of a sudden? What the hell is happening? Athena?" I waited until her nails turned blue, and then I went for Roxanna, who was looking at Lindsay's hand with concern. I recognized her by her short dark hair. I knew which grave was hers.

"My ears are ringing." Roxanna looked at Lindsay. "Why can't I hear you?" she said louder. "My ears are ringing!" I took Roxanna and I pushed her so hard she caught some air and landed on her back. She couldn't scream because I had knocked the wind out of her.

Athena said quietly, "Lucy, that's enough."

I must admit, even though I am not Lucy, and even though I don't need to take orders from anyone, I took *huge* satisfaction from the stricken looks on all their faces as they processed what Athena had just said.

Nicole crouched over Roxanna, helping her to sit up. Jordan got on the other side of her, still shivering, and they lifted her under her arms. As if I had broken Roxanna's legs! By then she had gotten her breath back, too, because she had started to cry.

"Roxanna, are you okay?" Athena started toward her and she cried louder, choking and shaking her head, both hands out in front of her as if walking in the dark.

Lindsay said, "She'll be okay. We should go." Holding each other, they hurried across the lawn to the car. Lindsay took Roxanna's bag and got into the driver's seat. The car turned around in the driveway, leaving a cloud of dust behind it.

Athena went inside and locked the door behind her. She went straight upstairs into the bathroom and locked that door, too. "Athena?" Claudia yelled from downstairs.

"I'm taking a shower!" she yelled back, and turned on the hot water until steam fogged the mirror. She sat on the closed toilet lid, hugging her legs and hiding her face in her knees.

"Lucy," she said. "You have made a gigantic mistake."

I turned off the lights.

"Thank you for protecting me."

I turned them on.

Chapter 18

LAUREL STILL HAD CHARLIE ON FRIENDSHIP PROBATION when she suggested they put their sitting-around time to good use and stake out Van's house. Charlie, who was desperate to fill his day, agreed. It was the time Laurel would've spent on her ledge, watching the valley change as the clouds and their shadows moved from west to east. As far as things to show Charlie, the ledge was at the absolute bottom of the list, below her own grave. Staking out Van's house was probably the closest she could bring herself (and Charlie) to the ledge without actually going there.

She led them through the woods on the house side of the creek, so Charlie wouldn't have to attempt the log bridge again.

He had packed like they would be gone for a weekend instead of a few hours: bag of mini Snickers, pack of cards, full canteen plus an empty one just in case, Slim Jims, his DS, and his pristine solar-powered flashlight that looked like it had never seen sun. Laurel brought binoculars.

The house looked just like they'd left it: untouched and forgotten. Laurel noticed things she hadn't before, like the heap of trash in the side yard—rusted, broken, wheel-less things. She noticed the compost barrel, down the road a bit from the house, and the lack of a porch light, the lack of a mailbox, the lack of telephone poles. In a Grimm story, it was the house at the end of a trail of ashes, with a caged bird that sang, "Turn back, turn back, my pretty young bride. In a house of murderers you've arrived."

"How often have you done this?" Charlie asked when they'd settled themselves against two neighboring trees.

"Spied on Van? Never."

"You seem like kind of an expert." He gestured to her binoculars, which she held in both hands.

"Don't get me wrong—I've done lots of spying. I've never been allowed to play on the playground, or go to the community pool, or—"

"Or really be out in public in general?"

"Yeah, so I figured out ways to spy on my sister when *she* would go out."

Before the silence got awkward Charlie said, "Interesting." He fished around in his backpack and held up the playing cards.

"Do you know how to play poker?"

Laurel kept her eyes on the house. "Nope."

"Good, then I'm going to win." He shuffled the cards. "Okay, so poker. You start with five each. The object is to make the best hand by getting different pairs, or straights or flushes." He pulled examples out to show Laurel, but she was back to watching the house. "Hey."

"Hey yourself." Laurel turned to look at the cards. "Got it. But you realize that in order to stake out a house we have to actually *watch* the house."

"I am." Charlie shuffled, watching the house. "I'm only going to be here for a little while longer, you know. Then it's off to the west coast. So take advantage of the time you have with me before it's too late."

Laurel sighed loudly behind her binoculars.

"Do you happen to have a charger?" he asked.

"On me? No."

"I mean at home. Could you plug it in for me? My DS died."

"Already? How are you going to get to California when you can't see two days into your future?"

"Whoa, never mind. Forget I asked." He dealt them each five cards, his eyes trained on the front door. "Okay, we'll use this as an example round. I have"—he turned his cards over—"two of hearts, seven of diamonds, queen of diamonds, two of clubs, and two of spades. Wow, I really didn't shuffle well at all. Okay, what do you have?"

Laurel flipped her cards over one by one: five of hearts, ace of clubs, ace of spades, eight of clubs, eight of spades.

"Holy hell, you got the dead man's hand."

Laurel said sharply, "The what?"

"Black aces and black eights. That's the hand that Wild Bill Hickok was holding when they shot him dead."

"Wild who? When who shot who? When was this?"

"Eighteen hundreds, the Wild West. That's a really unlucky hand."

"Unlucky how?"

"I think it means you're going to die."

"Don't be ridiculous. Everyone is going to die. That prediction is never wrong."

Charlie gasped so sharply that his breath caught in his throat and he started coughing as he scrambled to stand. Laurel looked over her shoulder and there, two trees away, stood an old man with heavy white stubble all over his face, except for his mustache, which hung over his mouth so only his lower lip showed. He held a nicked hatchet in his hand. The Red Sox cap on his head had salty white sweat stains edging out from the brim like tree rings. His watery red eyes moved from Charlie to Laurel, but no other part of him flinched. Charlie grabbed his backpack and went crashing through the trees toward the creek.

Van stared at Laurel. She stammered, "I—we weren't—" as she got to her feet. Van didn't move except to blink. Laurel looked at the fist curled around the hatchet. The other hand, she noticed, held a bundle of kindling and twigs. She couldn't wait any longer for him to shout or reply or invite her in. She tore after Charlie, through the pricker bushes and over fallen tree limbs, running too hard to look back.

They stopped to catch their breath half a mile down the creek, long after they were sure he hadn't followed them. "You jerk!" Laurel huffed. "You took off without me!"

"When you meet a crazy man in the woods and he's holding an ax"—Charlie clutched the stitch in his side—"it's every man for himself."

"We left all the cards."

"Oh, who cares. Dead man's hand and he shows up? You're lucky to be alive."

Laurel was spooked by how easily he'd snuck up on them, how she hadn't heard him at all. He didn't seem mad to find them parked outside his house—at least, he didn't express anything with his face. Did he recognize her? Did he know she was a Windham? When was the last time he'd seen another person?

Athena only had to make it through one more day of school after the fiasco with Roxanna and her friends, and then hopefully a weekend's worth of amnesia would wash over them all. She had taken the bus that morning because Roxanna hadn't driven her back to school to pick up her bike like she'd said she would. (Shocking.) Things with Roxanna were complicated—and also tense, confusing, and humiliating. She and her friends avoided Athena in the hall and in class, smirking behind their sunglasses in the parking lot like rich-kid villains in an eighties movie. They held on to the secret of Lucy, ready at any moment to open up their mouths and free it.

Athena committed herself to ignoring them with the drive and ambition of an Oscar-striving actress. Their encounter with Lucy, if they talked about it, was enough to crumble the already cracking foundation of the Windhams' business. Ghosts went against everything the grave keepers believed in: eternal rest in a nicely sealed grave, peace and comfort to those left alive. That combined with Roxanna's foray into Athena's grave would send the townsfolk up Orchard Hill with pitchforks. For over two centuries her family had lived on the orchard property, and now in the span of one week, Athena had basically pulled the pin holding it all together.

When a small crowd had gathered in front of a poster taped to the main office window that morning, Athena hadn't paused to read the fine print. Jordan's topknot stood above the clustered heads like a hair-sprayed red flag. Athena returned to her pre-Roxanna rituals: she ate lunch in Mrs. Adelaide's art room; she doodled with undivided attention during class; and she beelined for her bike at the final bell.

Athena walked her bike down Main Street, her helmet dangling from the handlebars. She hated the possibility that anyone would see her in a helmet, but she was too scared of tempting fate not to wear it when she rode. She walked without seeing anything in front of her until she found herself locking her bike to the rack beside the library. The organ music sounded faint and almost pretty from outside.

Maude was shelving in the children's corner below a statue

of the Infant of Prague. His round baby face looked bizarre floating between his green satin robe and bejeweled crown. He held up two fingers and Athena thought, *Peace, Baby Jesus. Peace, dude.*

"I've been thinking about what you asked me," she shouted at Maude's back.

"Oh, hey, Athena! You scared me." Maude smiled. "What did I ask you?"

"I'm interested in lots of things, I just blanked when you asked. I'm interested in grave keeping and wildlife preservation and cosmetics"—she thought it sounded more respectable than *makeup*—"and Paris, even though I hate French class, and psychology, like, for example, why do we make the choices we do? Why do we have the traditions we do? Why do we mean one thing, but say another?"

"Wow. Whoa. Okay, where to start? Are you looking for books on all of these subjects, or do you have a particular focus for right now? I can get you started with—"

"Oh, no no no. Sorry. Miscommunication." Athena's eyes darted from the floor to the windowsill to a picture book with a ragged, gnawed cover. "I'm not looking for any books. I'm not researching any of these things. You just asked me what I was interested in, in life, and I thought about it and these are some of those things. That I'm interested in. In life."

"That's really cool. Wildlife preservation, huh?"

"What are you interested in?"

Maude checked her watch. "How much time do you have?"

Athena laughed. "Actually," she said, "I have an hour before I need to be home. Want some help with those books?"

"Sure! Thank you so much. It's great that we can count on little kids to use the library, but they destroy it—I mean, *destroy it*—every Monday, Wednesday, and Friday at story time. One time I found a diaper shoved in at the end of a shelf."

"Dirty?"

Maude raised her eyebrows. "I didn't investigate. Half the time I just want to throw these books out."

Athena picked up a book cover in one hand and its innards in the other. "I see what you mean."

"But I was joking; I would never throw out books. 'Repair, donate, recycle' is the library motto. Or at least my motto. The Blackistones' motto is 'Let Maude take care of it.'"

"How did you get this job?" To Athena, any job that came with a name tag seemed far more official and impressive than babysitting. It meant a scheduled paycheck, clocking in and out, paying taxes. Taxes!

"I needed a summer job last year, so I went into every store on Main Street, and also down in Brewer, but that was mostly as a backup 'cause I'm not trying to ride my bike down Route 23 every day in August, you know? But I talked to everyone. Most people said no thanks right away, but when I got to the library, Norma just said okay."

"You were like, 'Are you hiring?' and she was like, 'Okay'?"

"Pretty much, yup. They can't keep up with this place. And there are volunteers, but they come and go when they please. So I get $8.75 an hour to shelve books and set out ant traps and order new books when the budget has the room. The Blackistones are actually really good at what they do. They read all the major papers and book reviews and keep a running list of books for me to order, but they also like their naps."

"Who doesn't?"

Athena and Maude hung out for the rest of her shift, exchanging magazine recs and history notes, concocting plans to dip-dye Athena's hair purple and teach Maude how to bake cinnamon bread. When Athena left she thought, *Damn it, Simon was right.*

That evening, Laurel brought leftovers and a book out to Charlie. "I couldn't find a charger," she said, "but Athena brought me this from the library, so if you're ever really bored . . ." She handed over *Geoffrey Crayon* and the foil packet.

"Thanks," he said. "What's for dinner?"

"Squash casserole."

Charlie wrinkled his nose and said, "Good thing I'm starving."

"It's another way of saying squash with lots of cheese sauce. It's good."

"Let's go down to Name Rock to eat. What's for dessert?"

Laurel threw up her hands. "You would make a horrible prisoner!" She put on a haughty voice. "Oh, what kind of bread is it? Is it mineral water?"

"I'm not that picky, come on."

They teased each other all the way to Name Rock. Laurel went headfirst into the cave to retrieve the bagged box of matches, the stash of kindling and dried leaves they left last time. Handing the matches to Charlie, she bundled the kindling against her chest and followed him up the rock. At the very top, he froze.

"Beep, beep. Keep going there, buddy." She pushed on his knees until he stepped aside and she could see around his legs. In the middle of Name Rock, tied neatly with twine, sat the playing cards they had left scattered all over the ground outside Van's.

Charlie set the matches down. "How did they get here?"

Laurel stood beside Charlie, arms full of twigs. "I guess Van brought them back for us."

"We should count them."

"Go ahead, they're not booby-trapped."

Charlie slid the twine off and shifted cards from one had to the other, counting in his head. Laurel scanned the trees slowly, wondering.

"Fifty-two," he said. "They're all here."

Chapter 19

Several nights later, down in her grave, Athena kicked up into a handstand, her heels scratching against the corkboard as she shifted for balance. It wasn't yoga, and it wasn't graceful, but it helped her think. Blood and thoughts settled in her head. She un-shrugged her shoulders, fingertips digging into the foam mat, and her body lengthened up the wall toward the canopy. When the artery in her neck (Was it the aorta? She took bio last year, but summer had performed its memory charm.) felt like a dam about to burst, she flipped down onto hands and knees, tiny sparks of light popping before her eyes. As the blood flowed back into her body, this was the thought remaining: *Maude is my friend.* Or at least, they were on their way to being friends. It made her feel like a kindergartner. *I have a friend.*

There had been a few times over the last several days, sitting on the steps of the altar in the library, or waiting for Maude's dad to pick them up, when Athena was gripped by a sudden urge to run. To make some excuse about family or babysitting and hightail it home before Maude could realize that she had better things to do than hang out with her. And then as soon as it passed, Athena wanted to confess, "You are my first friend. Ever." As if that would explain something. Because that's how she thought of her: First Friend Maude.

Athena gathered her hair in front of her face to study her split ends. She imagined the tips as a deep bluey-purple, the color of a mallard's wing stripe. "You're so lucky," Maude had said. "Your hair will take on any color you want, it's so light. I'd have to do something red on mine. Any other color would come out looking brown." Athena had laughed, delighted by the fact that someone with a purse made out of duct tape could be so conscientious about dyeing the ends of her hair.

Before this school year, Athena's only conversation partner was Laurel, and Athena would never share the same things with her little sister as she did with Maude. For instance, she had confessed earlier that week, "I feel terrible saying this, but Olivia Helms has the worst breath. She sits behind me in Mrs. Bair's class and fire-breathes all over the place."

Laurel would not have said, "We need to get you a gas mask, stat!" and cracked up the way that Maude did. She would have said, "What do you do in English? Do you get to choose where you sit? Why don't you just move? Why don't you give Olivia Helms a piece of gum? Are you allowed to chew gum?"

Or, for instance, had Athena told Laurel about the reverse wedgie she'd gotten when leaving the bathroom that day—her skirt, unknowingly pinched in her underwear, yanked out by an invisible hand before she could embarrass herself—Laurel would not have given her big round eyes and a trout-out-of-water gaping mouth and said, "A ghost, do you think?" She would have shrugged and said, "Ghost. Duh."

Funny thing was, Athena, for the first time, had experienced a school day the way that Laurel imagined it. Well, maybe not completely—Laurel had a mental collage of *Saved by the Bell*, *Arthur*, and *Gilmore Girls* filling the space where a regular kid's memories would be. Athena was no Kelly Kapowski; changing for gym would always make her squirm, and reading aloud in French class would always make her blush. But the prospect of eating lunch with Maude (and the Environmental Club), walking to the library after school, having these slivers of fun to train her sights on as she lip-synced her way through chorus made Athena understand: *This is what Laurel wants so badly. I get it.*

Over the weekend, while collecting water samples with Maude at different spots around Compass Lake, Athena had shared the worst of the worst—the truth about Roxanna and Lucy. She'd felt the confession coming on like a bad cold. She waited until they were in the reeds, dipping test tubes labeled with the exact coordinates of their location, until she said, "You know Roxanna Dover, right?"

"Personally? No." Maude capped her test tube and climbed onto the bank.

"But I mean, you know who she is."

"Of course."

"Well, I'm avoiding her at the moment, and she's avoiding me, because my sister's ghost attacked her last week."

Maude reached down to help Athena out of the water and said, "Okay, say that again on dry land."

Athena rewound the tape and told her everything, starting with Katarina's grave opening and Athena's hopes of getting to talk to Roxanna. Every embarrassing detail, every snippet of conversation, she relayed to Maude, who nodded attentively and never interrupted.

When Athena finished, Maude said, "You've had more going on in the last week than I've had going on in the last five years."

"I'm not a drama queen," Athena said quickly. "I'm not enjoying—I don't go looking—"

"No, no, no, don't listen to me. I'm just speechless. Those girls are so, so awful, for doing that to you. Forcing themselves uninvited—trying to get into your grave—even more awful than I already thought they were."

Athena was stunned. She had never thought of it in terms of what happened to her or what those girls did to her, it was what she did. "But Maude, I broke a Tenet. A big one."

Maude smiled. "What are there, nine more? No big deal."

Athena, for the first time in days, grinned. "My mother would faint if she heard you say that."

She smiled again remembering it now. Sitting in the middle of her yoga mat, looking up at the walls covered in clippings meticulously arranged like a game of Tetris, Athena no longer recognized her grave. Carefully, because she might one day want to read them again, she unpinned all the articles from the corkboard walls and folded them into a shoebox. Her shadow grew to gigantic proportions as she moved closer to the floor lamp. Profiles of Olympic divers, new research on the correlation between running and memory, a long article about elephants with post-traumatic stress disorder—she could hardly remember why she'd saved them in the first place.

She worked until the walls were bare, gathering the papers into a blanket and bundling it up. A pillow under one arm, blanket bundle hanging from her fist, she kicked her grave door shut and didn't bother to lock it.

Laurel brought a stopwatch, her green book, and Stephanie, her doll, out to her grave after dinner. Athena was already mooning around in the bottom of hers. She stepped carefully, testing each rung and gripping the ladder sides with both hands. Without a canopy, Laurel could see straight up into the darkening sky. *When the stopwatch says 30:00:00, I'll go inside.* Clover army-crawled to the edge and stuck her snout in, her two paws hanging over into the grave. "You're breaking so many rules right now, nosy. I'm sorry I can't let you in—I could get you down here, but we'd be stuck. You've got to stay."

She unlocked the doll's door and sat Stephanie inside. Better than being completely alone, sure, but she felt silly, making the doll do something because she had to. She opened to her bookmark and read: *She walked almost all day long until she got to the middle of the forest, where it was really gloomy. There she saw a house standing all by itself, and she didn't like the look of it because it seemed dark and spooky.* She thought about Van way out in the woods, without a car or a plow, without electricity or heat.

Van had lived out there in the woods for longer than Laurel knew—her whole life, at least. He was related to Suze somehow, a distant cousin of her husband's. He'd been a forest ranger—how did she know that? She had always known about him, but she had never worried about him until now. A slamming door made her jump. Athena's footsteps hurried away. The stopwatch read 13:28:40. Clover's paws were gone from the doorway. But she had to stay.

Later that night, her grave now blank and empty out in the orchard, Athena sat in the living room watching *Real World* with the volume on two and one finger on the Previous Channel button. Technically, she wasn't allowed to watch it at all. Her parents thought "those kids" were "terrible role models."

A camera sat beside her on the sofa, borrowed from school for her first photography assignment. The developed photos were due in eight days, and she hadn't even touched the lens cap yet. She stared at it as if waiting for it to speak and tell her what images it wanted to capture. The assignment was to photograph your home, "the very essence of it," Mrs. Adelaide had said. "You must communicate to the rest of the class what your home feels like to you, not just what it looks like." Athena had walked around the orchard for an hour with the camera in her hands, weighing the possible subjects: apple trees, clouds, the roofline, the barn. Photographing the interior of the house was out of the question. Roxanna and her evil friends had tipped her off to how novel it would be to see inside, and she didn't want to give anyone the satisfaction. Besides, no one needed to see the ratty, punched-in furniture or the legions of black-and-white portraits ascending the wall along the stairs. She might as well photograph her family's underwear drying on the clothesline.

The commercial break ended, and Athena slowly inched the volume up. She didn't really need to hear what was going on; it was enough just to see it. Half the cast was in the hot tub, snapping bikini strings and letting their hands get lost below the bubbles. It was hard to believe that "those kids" were only a few years older than she was, barely out of high school. There was one girl on the show, a nineteen-year-old from Minnesota, who was so gravesick she cried in the confessional nearly every episode, completely distraught over whether to stick it out and hope for the best or listen to her feelings and go home to her family and her grave. *Poor Michelle. At least she tried—at least she moved to Puerto Rico with the intention of being gone six months.* Athena imagined a grave cam, a tiny eye installed in the wall that she could talk to the way the kids on TV talked to a camera alone in a soundproof room. She'd heard about a few different grave tape scandals, the girls who'd recorded themselves dorking around in their graves and the videos that somehow ended up on the internet, much to their and their family's humiliation. She'd never seen one of them herself, though. A deep vein of fear ran through Athena, a certainty that she'd be tracked down and fined for watching illegal content. There were grave selfies—much less incriminating, but still slightly illicit. People did that with cameras long before Instagram.

As if on cue, Michelle's wet face filled the TV screen. "I guess [sniffle] I just don't [sniff] understand why it's so hard for me [sob] and so easy for everyone else." Athena tipped a handful of popcorn into her mouth, watching Michelle's black tears roll down her cheeks. *Someone get that girl some waterproof mascara.*

Claudia and Walt creaked up the stairs and in the back door with empty teacups for the sink. Athena, quick on the draw, hit Previous Channel. The screen jumped to reruns of *The Big Bang Theory*. Her parents continued their conversation without missing a beat, clearly unaware of the TV at all. She flicked back to *Real World* just as Walt said, "I wouldn't have brought this up if I hadn't given it a lot of thought already."

"I'm sure you did, and that's not what I'm saying. I just think that advertising is a cost we can't afford at the moment."

"If we get that September grave opening back, we'll be able to afford it."

"So we rob Peter to pay Paul."

"Well, not exactly. I'm telling you, the skiers, the weekenders, they're an untapped market. People are constantly upgrading graves these days, moving to better cemeteries in better locations. Just because it's a foreign concept to us doesn't mean it doesn't exist in the world. Just because we would never do it, doesn't mean we should pass judgment on people who want to."

Silence from Claudia.

Athena strained to hear.

Her father continued. "It's win-win. The most those new clients would be up here is every weekend, and we know that they won't visit their graves every time because really they'll be up here for the skiing or the casino. Upkeep will be minimum; there won't be that much more traffic, plus most clients will be older anyway, so we'll fill plots without having to deal with the openings."

"That's true," Claudia said slowly. Athena knew she was rubbing her temple below the strap of her eye patch. It was her thinking habit. "But as far as upkeep goes, you'll be doing way more of it, not less."

"How do you figure?"

"City folks have higher expectations, Walt. They're going to want pristine grass, dazzling trees, landscape design, basically no sign of real nature whatsoever."

Emily Dickinson, the cat, who had snuck in the back door between Claudia's and Walt's legs, jumped onto Athena's lap.

"We can do that, to a degree. I'm not replanting perfectly good trees, though. There's gotta be a line somewhere."

"You'll need extra help from Laurel and Simon either way. Probably Athena, too."

Athena knew what that meant: Laurel wouldn't be going to real school then, at least not for another couple of years. *And we can both kiss free time good-bye.* Laurel was constantly off in the woods these days, some new spy route or experiment, who knew. Athena was already noticing the changes in her little sister, how strong and knobby her hands were getting, how her cheekbones seemed to be flaring out under her baby pudge. Athena even caught a glimpse of a pale pink bra strap peeking through the stretched-out neck of Laurel's T-shirt.

"It's a moot point unless the September grave opening is back on." Claudia sighed. "Which I hope doesn't happen anyway. I'll think about it. In the meantime, get the orchard straightened up and we'll see."

"Trust me," Walt said, and Athena heard him kiss her mother's cheek. "This will give us the break we need. I'm sure of it." His shadow reached the doorway. Athena flicked back to *How I Met Your Mother* and tossed the clicker to the end of the couch to cover her tracks.

"Oh hey, 'Thena. Didn't realize you were in here." He crash-landed in his favorite seat. "You got the clicker?"

"You're sitting on it."

"Dang it, am I?" He felt around behind his back and between the seat cushions until he came up with the remote. The batteries were held in by a feathered strip of tape, and all the markings had been worn off the front; Walt punched buttons by feel and reached a giant hand into the bowl of popcorn. "The Bills game is on."

"I forgot they were playing tonight. Does Simon know?"

"He's the one who reminded me."

"Well, he's late. We should make him run sprints."

"Right?" Walt laughed. "'Thena, do me a favor? Jump up and get me a Buddy?"

Athena unfolded herself from the couch, dropped Emily Dickinson to the floor.

"Thanks, sweets. I'm just so beat." Her father worked the bridge of his nose between his fingers. It was rare to see him like this in the off-season. Usually only grave openings could elicit jaw-clenching, shoulder-stiffening stress in her father. Athena thought about Granny's silver, wondered how much her parents kept from her and Laurel, even from Simon.

Athena pulled a can from the six-pack on the bottom shelf of the fridge and returned to her end of the couch. "Dad, what were you and Mom talking about a minute ago? Advertising or something?"

Walt punched through the can top and said, "Oh, we're just talking. You know me—the off-season makes me jumpy. I hate sitting still. I was just thinking out loud is all."

The back door slammed and Simon jogged into the living room. "What'd I miss?"

"Nothing, the first kickoff. You'd better get those filthy boots off."

"You've got some dirt on your face," Athena said when her

brother came back into the room in his socks.

"Dirt? Please. I'm growing out my beard for good luck. The Bills are gonna go all the way this year; I really think so."

"Solidarity." Walt raised his beer.

"Fear the beard!" Simon collapsed in the recliner and pulled a mushy pillow from behind his back, dumped it on the floor. "Any update on that missing kid?"

"Nothing new. They're still interested in the orchard as a crime scene, since that's the last place the kid was seen, at the Dover grave opening." The unspoken hung in the air.

Simon grew quieter. "But they don't suspect us of anything, do they?"

Walt snorted and took a long pull from his beer. "No one has said as much, but I think that's mostly because Johnny and I are friends. They'll be back again tomorrow, not suspecting us."

Athena remembered the poster at school, the crowd of kids snapping pictures to post and tweet, their version of community action. "Who is the kid again?"

Simon shrugged. "Charlie St. James is his name. I don't know his family at all. Must be new."

"Not new—returned. Up in their great-grandparents' house, young family. He's about Laurel's age, I think." Walt glanced out the window at the orchard. He took a slow, overly casual drink.

"That's kind of young to be running away, isn't it?" Athena thought about being twelve or thirteen, in the mountains, bored as hell but pretty much stuck. Could a twelve-year-old really escape? Where would you even go?

"What the hell? Interference! Come on, ref!"

Athena crossed her arms and tried to focus on the game. She tried to follow the ball from shotgun snap to quarterback pump to interception, which had Simon roaring, but her mind dangled mid-conversation with her dad.

Chapter 20

From dawn until dinner, Charlie, Laurel, and Clover crisscrossed the woods, dissecting owl droppings with sticks, digging for bait and stones to skip across the glassy pool at the dam. They stayed far away from Van's house and only went up that way to check the snares.

In the creek they strung their shoelaces between two sticks and netted crayfish. Laurel found likely hiding spots and lifted the rocks. Charlie pounced with the net and flipped the scrabbling crayfish into a blue pail. The creatures settled at the bottom, "Like baby lobsters," Laurel said.

"No way, they look like alien bugs."

"People eat them, boil them and put them in stews and

stuff. I've had them—they're good." There were some days when Laurel was expected to bring home at least a dozen, if she couldn't manage a few trout.

Charlie looked at her as though she'd just admitted to cannibalism. "You better not expect me to eat those things. They'll come ripping out of your stomach like in *Alien*, brraawwww!" His hand scurried around under his shirt and he thrashed in its death grip. After they'd found five crayfish aliens, they dumped them back into the stream and watched as they clawed into hiding again. Laurel felt a little guilty, but her mom hadn't asked for dinner help that day.

"Citizens of Earth, we are being invaded!"

"Some invasion—they're gone already."

"That's what makes them so dangerous." Charlie dropped his voice to a sinister level. "They live among us, completely undetected, until they invade your body and destroy you from the inside out, taking over your organs one by one." And then he got a strange, zoned-out look on his face, as if he'd tasted something awful. Without saying a word, he walked upstream toward the fishing spot and their backpacks.

Laurel followed. When Charlie shut down, he really shut down.

At their fish camp, Charlie sat against a skinny pine tree. "Want to play cards?" While Laurel had been teaching Charlie the rules of fishing and tracking, Charlie had been teaching Laurel the rules of rummy, spit, and seven-card stud. Ever since getting the cards back from Van, he carried them everywhere.

"Sure."

He dealt seven cards each and brushed away pine needles before setting down the remainder of the stack. Their fishing poles were a few yards behind them, wedged between rocks at the edge of the creek, lines swirling in the current. Laurel arranged her hand and drew a card from the deck. *Let it be a king; I need a king; come onnnnnn, king!* It was a four of diamonds. "Damn!" She rearranged her hand, keeping the jack and queen at the end, ready to slap them down in victory, if victory ever came. A few yellow sugar maple leaves pinwheeled on a breeze into the middle of their game. "How are you doing out here at night? Are you warm enough?" Night temperatures were dipping lower and lower, threatening frost.

"Hell, yeah. That sleeping bag you gave me is awesome!"

"Quiet, the fish!"

"Sorry. That sleeping bag you gave me is awesome. I am toasty."

Charlie's hair was especially bonkers that day, sticking up at angles from his head. He looked younger with a halo of hair; his face looked smaller. His fingernails were jagged and packed with dirt. Laurel approved. In the evening, downstream, he brushed his teeth and washed with a special bar of soap she'd given him, to cut his scent and make him untrackable. *I'll have to figure out a way to sneak him into the house. Pretty soon it's going to be way too cold for him to stay out all night.*

"I'm down to three cards. How many you got?"

Laurel counted her hand. "Nine."

"Ohhh baby, another win, I can feel it."

"Don't count chickens. What do you want to bet?"

"I'll bet you a Snickers and a truth that I'll get out first and win."

"Make it two Snickers and a truth."

"Deal." Charlie picked up five cards from the discard pile and laid down one with a pair of cards he'd already had in his hand.

"Bold move. How many cards do you have left again?"

"Just go already."

After five more turns, Laurel and Charlie were dead even and casting off cards one at a time, rummying on the other person's triplets and straights. Instead of the king of clubs, Laurel drew a ten and lay down her ten-jack-queen with a flourish. "Well, look at that!" She waved the card in front of Charlie's nose. "I have only one card left. Looks like I'll have to discard it, and then . . . I WIN!"

"The fish! Be quiet!"

"The fish are long gone; Clover scared them away ages ago. You can pay me the Snickers when we get back to the grave, but you'd better be ready to tell the truth right now, Charles."

Tapping cards into a pile, he said, "Yeah, whatever."

"Don't be a grump. This is the first time I've beaten you. Hmmm, let me think a minute." Laurel stood and stretched. *I could ask about his house, or his family. What does he write in his postcards? I could ask about the thirteen countries he's been to, like what's his favorite and describe it in detail. I could ask him why he really ran away, like why he "couldn't stay at home" or whatever. He'd probably refuse to tell me.* Clover came to observe as Laurel inspected the empty fishing lines. Laurel scratched down her dog's spine. "Your coat is really filling in there, Clo. Good work."

Handing a pole to Charlie, Laurel emptied the bait can onto the ground and swung her backpack onto one shoulder. Charlie led the way back to Name Rock, plodding along slowly, head down, fishing pole resting on his shoulder. *So dramatic. It's like he's being led to his execution.* They stowed their gear in the cleft below the rock and climbed up top to build a twig fire. Laurel had traded Athena a week's worth of dishes duty in exchange for marshmallows, graham crackers, and a couple of Hershey's bars, smuggled into the house in Athena's bookbag. Charlie propped twigs into a small pile on the rock and snapped pine boughs into bite-sized pieces to feed the fire.

"Okay, I have my question."

"Finally."

She was embarrassed, but she made herself look him in the eye. "What's school like?"

Tension evaporated from Charlie's face. "Seriously? I thought you were going to ask—never mind. School is—I dunno—school is okay for the most part. If you get a good teacher or a good class, then it's awesome. Last year we started doing experiments in science. We learned how to explode dough with baking soda and stuff; that was cool. Um, what do you want to know, exactly?"

"I want to know, well, it's hard to know what I want to know because I've never been in a school before. What's the best part and worst part? What's lunch like, and recess? Do you bring or buy? Do you play an instrument in the band? Do you—"

"Okay, okay, let me answer those first before I forget." Charlie struck a match and held it to the nest of twigs, just as Laurel had taught him. "The best part of school is the last week before summer. There's spirit day, where we have a water balloon toss and eat as many Popsicles as we want, plus then every day becomes a class party. Homework stops and we just do art projects and watch movies and hang out. The worst part is definitely gym."

"What do you do in gym?"

"Depends. Sometimes we do drills for different sports, like layups and dribbling contests. Sometimes we play soccer or flag football, which I hate. I hate running, and I can't catch a football for my life. It always just hits me in the gut and I drop it. And sometimes they'll peg me on purpose, like for extra points."

"Who?"

"Some boys in my grade, Greg DiNapoli and Alex Portman. It's like, five points if they hit me in the stomach, three points in the legs, and an extra point if it trips me and I fall."

"They get away with that? Where's the teacher?"

"He's around, but sometimes he doesn't notice for a little while. Anyway. Second half of last year I got a doctor's note to sit out gym. That was sweet. I could do my math homework for the next day, and then I didn't even have to bring the book home."

"What's lunch like?"

"Lunch is great."

Laurel nodded, as if she did, in fact, know it was great.

"Mostly I bring my lunch; my mom still makes it for me, which is embarrassing I guess, but she puts in the good snacks, Fritos and Golden Grahams. I only ever buy on pizza day, but sometimes I'll get tater tots if I feel like it."

Describe it, Laurel wanted to say. *Tell me about the lunch ladies and the cafeteria trays and your table. Have you ever been in a food fight? Have you ever seen someone throw up? How true*, she wanted to ask, *is the cafeteria in* High School Musical *on a scale from one to ten?* But she didn't want to get sidetracked—there was so much more school to cover. "And recess?"

"Recess used to be awesome. Everyone played on the jungle gym, or in kickball tournaments, but now it's all about impressing other people." He glanced sideways at Laurel. "Girls, mostly. The boys all play football or soccer like tough guys and the girls all do gymnastics or, like, cheerleading dances."

"All the girls do cheerleading?" Laurel could not for the life of her picture Athena participating in such shenanigans.

"Well, not all of them. The quieter kids, like me, we mostly sit on the bleachers behind the backstop and read or play cards. Some girls do each other's hair; some jump rope." He shrugged. "I'm not totally sure, I don't keep tabs on everyone."

"No, yeah, I know. So, what was your favorite teacher like?"

Charlie answered all thirty-four of Laurel's questions, despite her technically winning only one truth from him. He didn't mind. No one had ever taken such an interest in the details of his life before. It made him feel like a celebrity being interviewed before a live studio audience.

Laurel's curiosity burned brightest for school. Elizabeth and Jessica had Sweet Valley High; Matilda had Crunchem Hall; Harry had Hogwarts; even Laura, way out on the prairie, had a slate and a bench in the one-room schoolhouse. But Laurel had nothing. She lay back on Name Rock and listened to Charlie recount the time Mallory Glover ran for class president. (She taped posters of her school picture up and down the halls, and the next day they were defaced with mustaches and blacked-out teeth and cartoon penises and boobs where she didn't have any.) Laurel's imagination filled in the colors of the lockers (bright blue) and Mallory's reaction to the graffiti (tearing down the posters one by one, red-faced and fighting back tears). It was better than books, better than TV, because these people were real and these things really happened. They happened right down the road in town, in the three-story school building up on the hill. She knew its exterior by heart—the chipped flagpole, the tall windows that cranked open, the great double doors at the top of the steps—but this was the first time she'd ever been given a glimpse inside.

Chapter 21

On this particular Wednesday, Athena had the art classroom to herself, exactly as she'd hoped. Of course Athena was delighted to finally have a real lunch table to belong to in the cafeteria. Maude saved her a seat and never made her sell lollipops, but after an entire lunch period of discussing the ethics—or lack thereof—of meatpacking plants while she choked down a bologna sandwich, Athena needed a break.

She tossed her lunch bag into the garbage can labeled *GENERAL SQUALOR* (in smaller font below, the sign read, *NO OIL PAINT DEBRIS OR WASTE. DEPOSIT ALL OIL PAINT–CONTAMINATED ITEMS INTO THE FIREPROOF BIN. THINNING AGENTS ARE HIGHLY FLAMMABLE!!!)*, threaded her headphones through the neck of her shirt, and ducked behind the folding door of the darkroom, which had once been a broom closet.

Her first self-developed photos were hanging from the clothesline, drip-drying after her morning photo class. In one close-up, Clover regarded the camera with a suspicious look, not bothering to lift her head from the braided rug on the kitchen floor. In another, a ladybug crawled across the black button at the center of a coneflower. On that afternoon, the shiny red back of the ladybug had stood out like a sequin, but in black and white, the little beetle disappeared into the gray scale. The images in her head didn't align with the images trapped by the lens, and she felt silly for thinking they would, for thinking she understood how it worked. *It's something, though.* She touched the corner of the thick photo paper with one finger. *I chose it. I let the light in around this image.*

Earlier that day in class, Mrs. Adelaide had talked about the frame of a photograph. "It isn't simply what you choose to take a picture of," she'd said, perched on the corner of her desk, earrings swinging wildly, "it's also what you choose to leave out. Each frame captures one thing and leaves countless other things to languish in the forgotten, unaddressed." *What had been left out of this frame?* she thought now, turning back to Clover.

The kitchen in lamplight. Dishes slick with grease stacked in the sink. Laurel at the table beside Clover, poring over that green book of hers, one hand in her knotty hair, twirling, twirling. Brittle fly corpses swaying on the strand of flypaper taped to the ceiling fan. Smudges on the wallpaper from resting heads. Toast crumbs in the butter. Hot waves of dust curling out from the bottom of the refrigerator.

The longer she inventoried the beyond-the-frame, the harder her teeth dug into her lip.

When she pushed through the folding door back into the classroom, Maude was sitting at a drafting table pulling long strands from her string cheese. "Yo."

"Uh, yo. Why didn't you knock?"

"Didn't want to ruin your photo making. Want some?" She held out the frayed cheese.

"I'm good."

"Is anyone else here?"

"No, why?"

"I have some slightly bad news. Minor, really. Hardly anything, but I thought you'd like to hear it kind of immediately, if not sooner." She dangled a line of cheese over her open mouth.

"Spit it out, Maude."

"Okay, so I was doing my rounds at lunch, selling lollipops for the State Park Conservation Association because they're making a big push for reforestation this year—"

"Uh-huh." Athena gestured for Maude to fast-forward.

"And I was by Roxanna's table and the other girls were bugging her, like, 'Tell us whose grave it was, c'mon!' And she was being so fake-humble, like, 'I'm not saying anything more. I gave my word, naming no names.' It was about something she wrote on her blog, so I checked on my phone."

Athena felt like she could be washed down the sink with the developing fluids. "What did she say?"

"Nothing much." Maude looked away, sniffed. "I just wanted to tell you to read it later."

"Maude. Tell me now."

Maude sighed. "It shouldn't matter, she's just doing it for attention."

"Please, I really need to know."

"Fine, but we have to go to the library. We should see the whole enchilada."

"Wait, I think I've seen Mrs. Adelaide get passes from that drawer."

Under a cluster of Cray-Pas stubs she found the yellow hall pass pad and tore off the top sheet before carefully replacing everything in the drawer. She pulled the slip up her sleeve. "Let's go. We can fill it out in the bathroom."

The classroom door opened with a gust of wind. "Hello, girls." Mrs. Adelaide glided in with a Styrofoam cup of chicken noodle soup in one hand. "You look like you're plotting something sinister."

"Oh no, we were just talking—"

"It's nice to see you back here during your lunch period, Athena. I haven't heard about your summer yet. I don't believe we've met"—Mrs. Adelaide turned to Maude—"but I'm infatuated with your earrings."

Maude and Mrs. Adelaide took turns complimenting each other's jewelry, comparing notes on estate sale finds. "But does your nose ring ever get in the way?" Mrs. Adelaide asked. "How do you blow your nose?"

"Honestly, most of the time I forget it's there," Maude replied.

She didn't take any pictures, so she must've written about my grave. At least she hasn't attached my name to it—yet. Athena's head throbbed. "I don't mean to interrupt, but Maude and I were just about to head to the library." The hall pass crinkled in her sleeve.

"Well, come back to see me soon, Athena. Do you need a hall pass?"

"No," said Athena, at the same time that Maude said, "Yes."

"We'll be fine." Athena laughed.

"All right, girls. I'll leave you to it, then." With a wave she and her soup swept into her office at the back of the classroom. Sounds of a swelling symphony came from behind the closed door.

Athena and Maude stared at each other for a moment before Athena burst out laughing. "What's so funny?" Maude looked aghast. "That was close! I can't get detention—I have to work!"

"You should see your face. C'mon." Athena pushed her out the door, still laughing. By the time she forged Mrs. Adelaide's signature against the bathroom wall, tears were leaking down her cheeks. The entire scenario was crazy: Stealing a hall pass? Sneaking around the school during lunch? This was someone else's normal. True, it wasn't the most wild adventure they could've gone on—at that very moment, some seniors were probably out in the parking lot hotboxing Joey Stanfords's Buick—but it was an adventure nonetheless. Athena had a partner, and now she had a crime.

"If you keep laughing like that, it won't matter that we have a hall pass. Mr. Neilson will think we're up to something immediately."

Athena snorted and laughed even harder.

"Oh my God. You're hopeless."

"I can't help it," she gasped. The line between laughing and crying was thinner than an eyelash. Athena knew she was headed for devastation, scuffing down the hallway in her clogs (borrowed from Maude). She knew Maude was going to show her Roxanna's blog and an entry linking her to the breaking of a Tenet. She knew that by now most of the school had read it, that in true Athena fashion, she was the last to be in on the secret. Did that explain why Lou Hernandez had said, "What's up, Athena?" when she came out of the locker room after gym, or why she'd caught Tim Reynolds staring at her, twice, during chorus? Had she done the impossible? Had she turned out to be even more of a freak than people already believed?

Maude took the computer at the end of the row, farthest from Mr. Neilson and his online poker addiction.

A gray screen with red lettering. *Rox Talks* in calligraphic font across the header. An entry titled "Beyond the Grave."

"Here." Maude highlighted a section and scooched over so Athena could share the chair. "Read this."

So, dear readers, I've been holding out on you. Originally I decided that I wasn't going to share this juicy tidbit, but life has been pretty zzzzzz lately, so for your benefit, I'm willing to bend the rules.

It was a dark and stormy night. JK JK, it was dark (all nights are), but the weather was fine. My life's exasperation (aka my little sister) was having her grave opening and I was still grounded for piercing my ear cartilage without permission, so my parents forbade me from inviting any friends to the party. LAME. I resigned myself to the reality that I would be forced to waste the last night of summer sitting around with my parents and their awful friends (no offense if said friends are your parents) and eating seven slices of grave cake and then feeling fat (that always happens).

But THEN! Action! Adventure! Intrigue! I ditched Snoozefest 2017 and found my way into an open grave. But not just any grave—a real grave keeper's grave, one that was more like a bedroom than a grave. I mean, truly. Extra clothes and food, mountains of reading material—it was super lived-in. Like you wouldn't believe. I didn't even know graves could be like that.

Now, before you get the wrong impression, I didn't break in. I was let in, by the grave keeper herself. Second only to being in someone else's grave is the weirdness of being in a grave with somebody else. I wouldn't recommend it, kids.

Unfortunately, I couldn't snap any pics for you, dear readers, but here are a few that I took beforehand of the party. BAR.

"Bar?" Athena asked.

"It means 'burn after reading.'"

Athena's hands went to her forehead, palms over eyes. "Shit, shit, shit."

"You're not in any of the pictures—they're just of the cemetery, which is not news to anyone. Obviously that's where she was. She didn't mention you specifically."

"Yeah, 'cause she didn't have to." Athena bit the inside of her cheek until she tasted metal. She felt chilly, as if she'd swum through a cold spot in the lake. The new reality—her new celebrity—dawned on her slowly. She looked at Maude, who seemed to be biting back words. "Thank you for telling me."

Maude shrugged. "I'd want to know if someone were talking shit about me. Now the question is, how are we going to shut her up?"

"We can't. She'd just laugh in my face; all those girls would. Plus, how could we get her to shut up without making it more public than it already is? I mean, anyone could read this. My parents . . ." Athena swallowed quickly.

"I could accidentally elbow her in the face during gym."

"But you're a pacifist!"

“There’s a time and a place for everything.”

“Gandhi said that, right?”

“Okay, look. I’m not saying that you need to pull a *Mean Girls* and push her in front of a bus, but you do need to do something. This isn’t going away.” She dropped her voice. “What if she or one of those creatures tells about what happened with Lucy? It could get worse before it gets better.”

“You’d think they’d have something more going on in their lives.”

“Those girls seem so sophisticated and important, but they’re just as bored as we are.” Maude scoffed. “What an idiot. She’ll get in just as much trouble as you.”

And when she does, the whole school—the whole town!—will know that my grave is not only the most pathetic place in the world, but also that I’m desperate enough to let a complete stranger in to see it. And if Mom and Dad find out . . . if she spills about Lucy . . . How would it look for the daughter of a cemetery owner to show complete disregard for the Tenets of Grave Keeping?

Ironic, Athena thought. *After all this, the only thing I’ll have left is my grave.*

“Hey.” Maude nudged her with her sandal. “You okay?”

“I’m fine, just tired. Had a stupid French quiz today. *Quel désastre.*”

“You know what? We should go to the Goodwill. That always makes me feel better.”

Athena had been to the Goodwill down in Catskill for every growth spurt and every back-to-school spree. It was synonymous with punishment, not fun. "I've never been," she lied.

"What? We have to fix that." Maude stood and swung the long strap of her bag over one shoulder. "I'll ask my mom if I can borrow the car after the library today."

"I think I should probably go home right after school, but I could go to Goodwill later probably."

"Okay, I'll call ya."

"Okay, and hey—watch those elbows in gym."

Maude put her hands up. "No promises, man."

A soft rain pattered on the door of Tamsen's grave. Charlie slammed cards hand over hand into the discard pile and slapped the empty space a split second before Laurel. Her palm came down hard on the back of his hand.

"Jesus." He shook out his hand. "It's almost like you'd rather hurt me than beat me."

"Isn't that funny," Laurel said dryly. "I beat you either way."

"Har, har, har." Charlie gathered the cards in rough piles and tapped them in line. "Want a rematch?"

"I'm sick of spit." Laurel leaned back and pointed a flashlight up at the door. "If the rain starts leaking in here . . ." She was going to say *come up to the house*, but the follow-up questions popped up all at once: *How? When? Where?*

"It won't," Charlie said. "These walls would be completely rotted out if it had been leaking for the last three hundred years."

"More."

"Exactly my point."

"Want to play poker?"

"I'm kind of tired of poker."

"Rummy?"

"Nah."

"Well, I don't know what else there is then. Old maid? Slapjack? War? Those games suck with two people."

"Can I see the cards for a sec?" Charlie handed over the deck, and Laurel thumbed through them face-up. "One summer I spent six weeks at my gran's in Pennsylvania." She paused as a queen of clubs went by.

"Uh-huh," Charlie prompted her.

"My mom was taking care of her dad at the nursing home, and my sister and I were alone with Gran a lot. There wasn't much to do—no TV. Some books, but none for kids. We played cards, and at some point every afternoon she would tell our fortunes with them."

"Like, *you will be very rich and famous and live in a mansion*, that kind of thing?"

"Kind of." Laurel studied the cards, flashing meanings they hadn't had a few minutes ago when all she'd wanted was to get rid of her hand and slap the empty space where the pile had just been.

"Or like, *you will suffer, but your enemy will suffer more.*"

"It's not—you sound like Professor Trelawney. It's not a prediction. It's not something you tell in complete sentences. It's like clues—pieces that you fit together. Want to try?"

"Abso*lute*ly."

Laurel handed back the cards. "Shuffle them and think of a question you want to ask the universe. It could be big and general, like about the distant future, or very specifically about now. Concentrate on the question and send it into the cards."

Charlie shuffled over and over. His jaw muscles clenched and released nervously. Finally he held the deck in both hands for a moment, then said, "And now?"

"Cut the deck three times toward yourself."

Charlie made three uneven piles between them.

Laurel picked the piles up in reverse order, keeping what had been the bottom pile on top. "I really don't know what I'm doing here," she said.

"That doesn't matter. Just go with it."

Laurel laid out cards one by one, facedown and with purpose, the second lying across the first, then the third, fourth, fifth, sixth in a ring around them. A line of cards bordered them to her left, starting near Charlie and ending near her knee.

The camping lantern flared and Charlie turned the flame lower. "This is a little spooky," he said, pulling on his sweatshirt.

Laurel slid the first card out from under its cross-card and flipped it over. "King of clubs. This is supposed to be you, I think. Or where you are right now. But you're a little young to be a king."

"Speak for yourself."

"I mean you would probably show up as a jack. Anyway, this card represents you and your present. Maybe yourself or someone close to you, probably an older man."

Charlie folded his arms. "Okay."

Laurel turned over the second card that had been on top of the first. "This is what's on your mind, or what your obstacle is. Ace of spades."

"That would be a killer poker hand."

"I think this one means bad luck. Misfortune—my gran would say something like that. Misfortune is on your mind, or a trouble from your past hasn't cleared up yet. She was much better at spinning it all into a story."

"Misfortune, like an illness?"

"I guess, sure. That's one form of misfortune." She turned the next card. "This is your past, I think. Nine of hearts. That's your wish! Whatever you wished for came true."

"In my past."

"Well, I guess in that spot it represents a happy past, but anytime the nine of hearts shows up anywhere it means you got your wish. I used to pray for the nine of hearts like nobody's business."

"I didn't know to wish for anything."

"Come on, everyone wishes for something, even if they don't mean to." A clap of thunder broke right over their heads, and Laurel let out a little "Ah!" and was immediately embarrassed. The rain strengthened from patter to pour.

Charlie turned the lantern up again. "Let's keep going," he said determinedly.

Laurel turned over the fourth card. "I can't remember what this one is. Let's say it's your present—it tells us something more about your current circumstances."

"And what does an ace of hearts say?"

"I think . . ." Laurel put her hand into her hair nervously. "I could be wrong, but I think it means your heart, like your home or something close to you, but that seems too obvious. I do remember my gran saying, 'Pair of aces, change of places.'" Laurel tapped the ace of spades and ace of hearts. "Which we know to be true for you, right?" She gestured at the grave around them. Lightning illuminated the doorframe and thunder boomed immediately.

"The storm is right over us," Charlie said, looking toward the door.

"It'll go by in a minute," Laurel said, and the lantern went out. She shouted, "What did you do?" at the same time that Charlie screamed.

"Nothing! I didn't touch it! The gas is still going, I can hear it."

"Well shut it off or we'll keel over! Didn't I just put new little socks on the burners? They shouldn't be out already."

Charlie reached out, grabbing blindly until he felt Laurel's sneaker. "Laurel," he said slowly, "are you playing with the hood of my sweatshirt?"

"No, I'm way over here in front of you."

"What the *hell*?! Someone just pulled my hood over my eyes."

"Stop it," Laurel said to her ghost. "That's not nice."

"I'm not playing a joke on you!" Charlie said, and the lantern flashed on, brighter than ever. Charlie turned the burner down and thunder rumbled, more distant this time.

"Look." Laurel stared at the half-finished reading. The jack and king of spades were side by side near Charlie. The queen of clubs and queen of diamonds lay directly in front of Laurel, so close to each other they overlapped. The rest of the face cards in the deck lay end-to-end with the ace of spades bisecting their parade. All the remaining cards were flung to the far walls of the grave.

"Misfortune for those poor dummies, huh?" Charlie said, peering over the line of face cards.

"But not for these two pairs." Laurel held hers up. She remembered her gran had told her she would be the queen of clubs in a reading, but who was the queen of diamonds?

"Someone really did pull my hood over my eyes," Charlie said, glancing behind him.

"Tamsen?" Laurel said teasingly, but at that word all the cards jumped a few inches straight into the air and landed right where they had been.

"Well," Charlie said. "I'm not going to get any sleep tonight. How about you?"

A KEY IS UNIQUE TO THE INDIVIDUAL; AS THERE IS NO SECOND YOU, THERE CAN BE NO SECOND KEY

Here is one thing that happens when you die: you get to keep your memories. All of them. They return to you, sharper than when you were alive. I could lift the tiniest corner of a memory and find the entire scene, cast and crew, waiting in their places.

The final summer, when I fell on the ledge, my long hair wrapped my face like a shroud. I waited and waited for someone to peer over the cliff and see my leg bent where there was no joint. I focused on the pinkie of my left hand, willing it to twitch, but then it turned gray. When the ravens came, I watched them bring my rib cage into the light. Eventually I realized that I didn't have to stay with my body, so I wandered home. The village was empty, search parties gone into the woods, but it wasn't quiet. I tried to match my mother's wails, to let her know I was there, but she couldn't hear or see me. I screamed until my throat shredded. I tore through houses and sent dirt spraying into eyes. The trees flung their birds from my path. Without a voice I sat in the corner of our house and waited. And waited.

I tried whispering in ears, pulling and pinching and shrieking. Tried leading a searcher to where I fell. But it was no use. I was alone. When my mother announced her pregnancy, I knew it was time to go. I couldn't stay and watch another child sleep in my place, or follow my brother to the river, their arms hugging empty pots. While my mother slept, I pressed my cheek to her cheek. She shivered and drew her blanket up, but she didn't wake.

For a long time after that, I lived in the treetops, hoping to die or stop dying, whichever would bring me rest. I was sixteen when I lost my body, not that it matters anymore. Some days I feel older than the wind, as dull and used as rocks in the riverbed.

Laurel was tipping from childhood into adulthood. All these words they have for it now! Tween, teenager, young adult—but no mistaking, it's a departure from life as a kid. Laurel was beginning to inventory the childhood things she couldn't do anymore, like swing around at the end of her brother's arms until her feet left the ground, or sit in her mother's lap after dinner. She couldn't entertain herself the way she used to, either. Instead of playing pretend, she needed distractions. Blowing the gray heads of dandelions used to thrill her. But now the idea never crossed her mind.

She had always dealt in the teenaged currency of secrets. Spying on the town playground, on Athena, ducking into graves, even her visits to the cliff ledge were all classified activities. But she stayed younger because she was on her own so much—no classmate comparisons to be made, no one to make her feel left behind or embarrassed. Peer pressure is much harder to come by when you have no peers. Slowly, she was changing that. She'd already found one friend in the orchard, and she was closer to finding me.

Chapter 22

"Laurel, have you seen the can opener?" Her mother was rummaging in the utensils drawer, piling unwanted gadgets on the counter: the egg slicer and melon baller and box grater. Four orange cans waited behind the growing heap of utensils; she was making pumpkin bread for the back-to-school bake sale.

Laurel knew exactly where the can opener was—with Charlie—but she said, "Nope, haven't seen it."

Over the past two weeks that he'd been hiding in the orchard cemetery, Charlie had turned Laurel into a thief. She swiped food, towels, blankets, dishes, can openers—anything he needed—when her mother's back was turned and smuggled them to Tamsen's grave, the bottom of which was no longer covered with candles in jars. It looked like a dry goods store.

"I bet Simon took it and left it in the barn. I'll get it later." Claudia returned to her chair, her fingers busying with the ledger before she could even settle down and get comfortable. "You about ready to head out?"

"Yup." Laurel rinsed her cereal bowl in the sink and took a clean jam jar from the cupboard. At the pantry, she glanced over her shoulder to make sure her mother was occupied with her record keeping before shaking extra raisins into her jar. She quickly tucked it away in her bag.

The coffeemaker burbled and spit. The smell of it made the whole kitchen warm. "Hey, Mom?"

"Hey, Laurel?"

"I was thinking maybe I could go to the library and look for another book for my report. I still have questions . . . about my topic."

"Athena will pick up anything you need. Just remember to tell her."

"Yeah, but I was actually hoping to do it myself. I think it would be a good learning experience, like firsthand research or something."

Claudia held her pen between two fingers, as if weighing it. "I'll think about it."

Laurel had never gained so much ground before. Anything other than a flat "no" was major progress. She hurried to fix the tray for her mother: coffee in the carafe, sugar bowl, pitcher of cream, and a mug.

"If this is the treatment I get while I think it over, I may never make up my mind." Her mom winked, or maybe she blinked—Laurel could never tell. "What do you need at the library?"

"Nothing in particular. I mean, I don't know yet. I'm going to look through the books when I get there." It was the honest truth—Laurel didn't need anything in particular, and she didn't know what she would find there. Claudia stirred her coffee.

A soft tapping came from the front hall. They looked at each other.

"Probably just birds in the feeder." Her mother went back to her ledger, but the tapping came again, this time distinctly from the paint-chipped front door. Claudia lumbered down the hall, muttering, "No peace anymore, no privacy. If that's the police again, Johnny Curran's getting a piece of my mind." The deadbolt turned with a loud crack.

Laurel peeked around the corner. A petite woman with huge owlish glasses stood on the front porch beside Clover, who was wiggling and panting like, *Look who I found!*

"Can I help you?" Claudia asked.

"Yes, hello. I'm—my name is Marie St. James. My brother, Herb, came to see your husband about my son's grave opening, which we were hoping to have in September?"

"Oh, right, well, you should really talk to my husband about that. He'll be in the barn," Claudia said, and began to close the door.

"No, wait! That's not why I came. My son, Charlie, he's run away."

Claudia waited with her hand on the doorknob. Laurel's heart took off running. "Yes." Claudia shifted her weight to her back foot. "I heard about that."

"Well anyway, I've been going door-to-door, hoping to find someone who may have seen him." She held a wallet-sized school portrait up to the screen door.

"Mrs. St. James—"

"Please, it's Marie."

"Marie, I'm awful sorry about your boy, but I haven't seen him."

"Oh, well, it's taken me a while to make it all the way out to you folks." Marie looked down at her blocky white sneakers, and Laurel translated in her head: *I've been working up the nerve to come all the way out here to this strange house on the edge of the known world.*

"The police have been out here since day one, as far as I know." As she spoke, Claudia's voice softened.

Marie nodded, eyes on the floor. "So they tell me. I realize it's a strange thing for a kid to do, but I had this nagging feeling that he might have come to his grave. He hasn't had his opening yet, so the door isn't locked."

The screen door screeched. "Why don't you come in? I've just made coffee."

Laurel couldn't believe her ears. *There is no way Mom just invited a perfect stranger into her house for coffee with her. The only person she ever has over is Suze, and that's more like Suze inviting herself. What will Lucy do?* Clover barreled down the hallway ahead of the new guest and into Laurel's waiting hands.

"Marie, this is my youngest daughter, Laurel. Laurel, this is Mrs. St. James."

"Hello," Laurel said. *That is Charlie's mom. Charlie's mom is in my kitchen. Charlie is in my backyard.*

"Hi there. How old are you, about twelve?"

"Thirteen."

"Same age as Charlie. Well, his birthday is at the end of the month." Her red-rimmed eyes spilled over effortlessly. She'd reached a new level of crying, her eyes leaking uncontrollably.

"Here now." Claudia pulled a handkerchief from her pocket. "Sit down. Take a breath."

"I'm sorry, I'm just—it feels so hopeless. The police have been helping, but they don't have any leads whatsoever, except they're treating me like a suspect—they call and check in on me day and night—and my husband has been sick, so a lot of the time I have to choose between taking care of him or going out to look for Charlie." She took a deep breath. "But now we have a hospice nurse, so I can get some rest at night—not that I'm sleeping anyway, but . . ." She trailed off as Claudia set a mug down in front of her.

Laurel watched Charlie's mother's thin fingers working over the crumpled handkerchief. Her wedding band hung loose between her knuckles. A chilly thread looped itself around Laurel's waist and knotted at her back. She could feel it tugging her toward the door. *Lucy, be good.*

"I can't imagine—" Claudia stopped and started again. "If you don't mind my asking, what is your husband sick with?"

Marie cleared her throat, sat straighter. "Bone cancer. It's not responding to treatment anymore, so we're just waiting. That's why we wanted the grave opening to be in September—I know we should do it next summer, but it was so important to Alan to be there for it. I know it's hard for Charlie to see his father like this, and I think that's why he ran away, but he needs to be here. He will regret it his entire life if he misses out on his dad's last few weeks, and I can't let that happen. I've got to find him."

"I wish I could do more for you. As I said, the police have been out here . . ." Claudia trailed off.

"I checked his grave, but the police have it roped off. It was silly of me to think this is where he'd come. He doesn't have a spruced grave yet, or his key, and how could he stay in a grave anyway? What would he eat? He's a very picky eater."

"What does he like to eat?" Laurel couldn't help herself.

"Laurel, that's not a polite question to ask."

"No, it's okay. He likes chicken nuggets, pizza, Boston cream doughnuts. His list of dislikes is much longer: spaghetti, mayonnaise, any kind of soup."

"He doesn't like soup?" Laurel had seen him eat soup. She'd showed him how to heat a can over a campfire.

"Never has. He's stubborn."

"What does he like to do for fun?" Laurel's fingers still held tight to Clover's thick fur at her neck.

Marie thought for a moment, turned her wedding ring around and around. "You know, I . . . he likes building things. I know he likes reading—I'm forever paying overdue fines at the library—but I couldn't tell you what books he reads." Her face scrunched up in that terrible silence before a sob.

Laurel's mother nudged her. "Get the box of tissues from the bathroom." When Laurel came back, Claudia had her arm around Marie's shoulders, her cheek against Marie's hair.

"I don't even know my own son," Marie was saying. "I'm his mother and I don't even know him. He slinks around the house and hardly ever comes out of his room. It took us thirty-six hours to even realize he was gone. No wonder the police suspect me!"

"Twelve is a difficult age. He doesn't know himself, either, or he's just starting to. But he'll be back. You'll see. He'll come home." Claudia rocked gently back and forth. "Laurel"—Laurel's head snapped up—"you haven't seen anyone who might be Charlie when you've been out on your walks, have you?"

Marie slid the school portrait across the tablecloth. Charlie looked up at Laurel from the tiny square, his face rounder, hair cut and combed, a hole in his smile where a tooth now was. Laurel shook her head. "I haven't seen him."

Later that afternoon, after rushing through the FOILs of her binomial equations, Laurel took her Spanish CD for a walk in her Discman. As soon as enough trees had closed in the view between her and the house, she took off running, straight up the Champs and into the woods. The voice in her headphones droned on. *"¿Cómo te gusta la sopa?"*

She found Charlie sitting on Name Rock playing solitaire. "Your mom," she huffed, peeling off her headphones. "Your mom came to my house. This morning. Looking for you."

"What?"

"She's going door-to-door." Laurel sat on the stone across from Charlie, ladders of cards strung between them. "She really misses you."

"Yeah, well, she seems busy enough—I'm surprised she noticed I'm gone."

"I don't believe that."

"What did she say?" Charlie played on, rearranging cards.

"Your dad is really sick."

He looked up, startled by how casually Laurel said it. "Uh-huh," he said.

"No, but like, really sick. She said the medicine wasn't working anymore. I think he's dying."

"He's been dying for a long time."

"Well, it's for real now. She said he only has a few more weeks."

Charlie turned a card over, lay red on black.

"Listen, you have to go home. This has been fun, but—"

"I'm not going home, Laurel."

"But what if your dad dies? What if he dies and you're out here and you don't find out about it for days and you miss the whole grave sealing and everything? You miss saying good-bye to him, you miss being there for your mom?"

"I won't miss the grave sealing. I'm already here, remember?"

Laurel sighed and stretched out on the rock. "She was right; you are stubborn." *How can he just not care?* She pictured her own father, whittled and weak, in bed, inside, the year-round tan draining from his face and forearms. "If I were losing my dad, I'd want to spend every possible minute with him."

"No you wouldn't. He wouldn't be the same dad anymore. It's like spending time with a stranger."

"Then do it for your mom. She's worried sick about you."

"No. If they really wanted me back, they would've found me by now. It's not like I'm on Mars or something. I've been sending the postcards."

Laurel sat up. "Charlie, you didn't see your mom today. She looked awful. She burst into tears when she heard I was the same age as you. I already lied to her once. If you don't go home by Monday, I'm going to tell."

"What! You can't do that!"

"Actually, I can. It gives you plenty of time, a long weekend to enjoy in the grave."

"Laurel, you have no idea what you're talking about. You don't know what it's like at my house. Everything stopped for my dad's cancer. It's like time stands still there, waiting for him to die. I just want it to be as close to normal as possible. I want to go to school and fight with my mom about cutting my hair, and have my grave opening next summer, when I'm thirteen, like a normal kid. I hate all this waiting. I can't wait for him to die."

"You don't mean that."

"I do! I can't wait for him to die because then everything will have to go back to normal. There won't be a hospital bed in our living room. My cats won't have to stay at my aunt's house because their dander makes my dad's breathing worse. I can have my house and my life back."

"And do you really think your mom will forgive you? Do you really think your life will be just"—*snap*—"like it was before?"

Charlie shrugged. "Who knows. Who cares."

Laurel lunged across the rock and punched him in the shoulder. Cards scattered under her knees.

Charlie lost his balance and turtled onto his back. "Ow! What the hell?" He covered his head with his arms.

Laurel scraped up handfuls of cards and threw them at him. "You're a real idiot, Charles. On Monday I'm telling my mom where you are. Whether or not you're home by then; doesn't matter to me."

She ran all the way back to the house and took the back steps in two leaps. Her mom had found a backup can opener and was scooping spoonfuls of orange slop into a mixing bowl. "Don't slam—" she said, as the glass rattled in the door. Laurel didn't stop to apologize; she thundered up the stairs and into the study.

"Laurel Windham, what in the world?" Claudia yelled behind her. "You and your sister slam every door in this house!"

The oversized books were stacked horizontally on the bottom shelf, and though the paper cover had fallen off long ago, she knew the one she wanted by its navy spine. She pulled the battered parenting book from its resting place and shoved it up under her shirt. Back down the stairs, through the kitchen, she didn't bother closing the back door at all this time. Ignoring Clover, who was crawling under the porch for her afternoon nap, she charged up the hill to her grave. With her yellow door open wide to the sky, Laurel collapsed into her pillow corner and peeled the book from her sticky skin.

The Grave Keeper's Guide to Parenting had seen her parents through Simon, Lucy, and Athena, and the margins were filled with her mother's tight cursive notes and reminders to herself, connections to points in other chapters, ideas for further research. The names of Simon and Lucy were most common, by virtue of their being the oldest. Laurel's name, on the other hand, was nowhere to be found, but she knew that her mom still referenced her parenting book whenever she had a Laurel issue. For years she used to sleep with it next to her bed, which was where Laurel found it when she was six and hungry to read everything.

She'd read it in secret. She'd found the other team's playbook; Laurel knew exactly how her parents would react no matter what she did: cool indifference when she whined, a curt talking-to when she talked back. With the book open on her lap, Laurel scanned the table of contents until she found "Grieving and Death: What Your Child Needs to Know." The chapter was dog-eared, tattooed with ballpoint underlines.

Laurel ran her finger down the page, skimming for any

insights into how older kids might deal with death. "Grieving is best dealt with in your grave. If your child is too small to be on his own in his grave, invite him into yours. If the child is mature enough to think on his own, encourage him to work through his feelings of loss in his grave." *Okay, but what if the grieving kid is already living in a grave? What then?*

Laurel kept flipping through the chapter, scanning the headings: Death of a Pet (*Don't want to think about it*); Death of a Sibling or Friend (a few pages in this section were water-warped); Death of a Parent (*Bingo*).

> *The sealing ceremony of a child's parent is perhaps the most important event of his young life. It represents the culmination of a life spent grave keeping. It is both a departure and a return home. For a child to understand the importance of grave keeping, he must also understand the importance of the sealing ceremony. What follows is a simple definition of a sealing ceremony, which you may want to use to open a dialogue with your child.*
>
> *A grave sealing happens when the grave keeper has died and is ready for everlasting rest. His coffin is placed in his everlasting home, after a life of tending it in preparation for precisely this moment. The grave keeper's family locks the door and drops the key through the mail slot, so that the grave keeper's rest will be unbroken. Then, the family seals the door by covering it with dirt and grass. Some people like to plant flowers or small shrubs as well. By covering the door*

with earth, the grave keeper's family is tucking him in for his everlasting rest.

After the sealing is finished, the family and all the guests sit together at one table in the grave keeper's row and share a meal in his honor.

Laurel slammed the book shut. *What is this,* Grave Keeping for Dummies*? I already know all this!* It wasn't a matter of explaining tradition. Charlie knew what was happening, what was at stake. He knew the importance of his dad's sealing ceremony, and he didn't care.

Chapter 23

"God, I'm starving," Athena complained. "I don't know how you can eat a salad for lunch every day and not get hungry by seventh period." She handed books up to Maude, who was standing on a step stool in the Mystery/Thriller section. Both girls had orange foam earplugs in, which Athena had stolen from her dad's stash by the power tools in the barn, to mute the sound of Norma Blackistone at the organ. They talked exaggeratedly, reading each other's lips.

"You picked all the tofu out of your salad. You're missing the protein."

"Ugh, tofu. You couldn't pay me to eat tofu."

"I have some nuts in the back. You want?"

Athena nodded vigorously.

"I have to say, I really appreciate the former first lady's campaign for better school lunches. The Enviro Club tried to get tofu on the menu the last two years and we got laughed at, but then it magically appeared this year, like poof! Tofu! Thank you, Michelle."

"You should send her a card."

"I should."

"I was kidding," Athena said when Maude's back was turned, following Maude down the narrow hall behind the altar that led to the exit for the rectory.

"I'm not sure you're supposed to be back here, but we'll be quick." Maude opened the door leading into a storage room. Stained-glass windows the size of notebook paper were the only sources of light. It was the backstage area, the dressing room where priests put on their vestments and altar servers prepared the chalice and the host. Instead of robes and wine, though, the storage room held two narrow cots, sheets in crisp hospital corners, parallel to each other. Cloth-bound hardbacks with tattered spines were gathered in clusters and piles. Maude turned sideways down the narrow walkway between Jenga towers of books and shuffled to the mini-fridge in the corner.

The more Athena looked, the more she wished she hadn't seen: a hot plate rested on twin pillars of encyclopedias. A pair of knee-highs hung limp over a heating pipe. A tarnished silver frame displayed a yellowed picture of two little girls in pinafores standing beside a seated woman with a cameo pinned at her throat. "The Blackistones live here?"

"Yeah. I assumed you knew." Maude shook the Tupperware full of almonds.

"But this is where they live?" Even though there were two of them, it seemed achingly lonely, like orphanage lonely. *What will happen when one of them dies? What will the other one do?* It broke Athena's heart to think about it.

"They had to sell their family home ages ago. It was way too much for them to maintain. Don't you remember it, overlooking the lake with the big porch? It used to be so dark and viney, but the new family redid everything, and now it looks like Martha Stewart lives there."

"What's with all these books?"

"I used to think that they were overflow, books that didn't fit in the stacks but that they didn't want to get rid of. But I guess maybe"—she looked around at the dusty stacks along the walls—"they belonged to the Blackistones' family?"

"Maybe we should . . ." Athena pointed to the door.

"I'm right behind you."

The girls sat in the itchy armchairs on the altar, Athena tossing almonds into the air and catching them (half the time) in her mouth. Roxanna's blog post kept bobbing to the surface of her thoughts. No matter how she tried to distract herself, Athena couldn't keep the worry submerged. She second-guessed her tosses and almonds flew backward over her head, or bounced off her front teeth.

"Just make sure you pick all those up," Maude said. "The

church mice never got the memo about it being a public library now. They still run the joint."

Athena crawled around her chair on hands and knees, collecting the strays. "I can't stop thinking about that blog post," she said to the carpet.

"I've been thinking about it, too. We should egg her car."

"Too generic."

"Or, like, Margo Roth Spiegelman her and leave a giant dead catfish in her car. And then saran-wrap it shut."

"Interesting, but still—if we piss her off enough it might backfire. She might throw down her trump card."

"Lucy?"

Athena crawled back around the chair and sat on her heels. "Yeah." She sighed. "Lucy. And that would be one million times worse than what is out there on the World Wide Web right now."

"Worse than your parents finding out you let her into your grave?"

"Mmm, I dunno, but I think so. The grave thing is bad, but it mostly impacts me—my behavior, my grave. But Lucy is everyone's secret, not just mine."

"So what we need is leverage. We need a secret of Roxanna's to balance the secret she stole from you. We could follow her."

Athena shrugged. "We could try, but it seems like she's insanely private. Jordan told me she doesn't even let those girls into her room."

Maude leaned her forearms on her knees, drawing level with

Athena. "Why would anyone do that unless they had something to hide?"

The next evening, Laurel was on her belly, one arm dangling from the couch, watching a *Full House* rerun, when the phone rang. Laurel's eyes swiveled over to her dad. Walt continued reading his biography of JFK. The book was so big that Laurel sometimes used it as a step stool to reach the cookies in the pantry. The phone rang again.

"I got it!" Athena thundered down the stairs. "I got it, I got it, I got it."

"So get it," Walt said from his chair.

"Hello? Hey, it's me. Are you always so polite? You sound like you're trying to sell something." Athena's voice grew softer as she made her way back upstairs to their bedroom.

"Who could be calling Athena?" Laurel wondered.

Walt shrugged, continued reading. "Probably a friend."

"Athena doesn't have any friends." Unless . . . *That girl Roxanna? Did they bond down in Athena's grave?*

"Mmm," he said.

"You already know how that book is going to end," Laurel said. "What's the point?"

Her father looked up. "Just because you know how it's going to end doesn't mean you know the whole story."

"Can I have ice cream?"

"Only if you get me some, too."

Laurel stood in front of the open freezer door. The little

red light on the phone cradle burned bright in the dim room. Something was up. Last week, Athena had called from the pay phone at school to say she'd gotten a volunteer position at the library, re-shelving books after school. She came home with her hair in braids, with blue polish on her nails. New stuff turned up on the floor of their bedroom—brooches, fat paperbacks, a pair of sunglasses the size of saucers. Wooden-soled clogs materialized out of thin air; Athena now clacked all over the house. Laurel had been preoccupied with her own adventures, but she couldn't help but want to investigate her sister's new phase. Laurel closed the freezer and tiptoed upstairs, skipping the seventh step, which creaked loud enough to wake the dead.

Athena's muffled laugh reached her in the hallway at the bottom of their attic staircase. Laurel strained to hear more, but it was gobbledygook. "I know! Murphy idle snooze. Fishnet hoo ha." *I've gotta get closer.* Slowly, on all fours, she crept up the attic stairs to the landing outside their bedroom door. At the third step from the top, Athena's voice came into focus.

"Did you get the Keaney homework? Can you tell me the pages again?"

Silence. A stack of paper shuffled together.

"Okay, thanks. And for combustion, the product is always H_20 and CO_2, right? Okay, that's easy."

Leave it to Athena to have the most boring private phone conversation on the planet.

"Oh my God, did you see Teddy Hilman in gym today?"

Here we go. Finally.

"With that hot pink sweatband on? I thought I was going to pee myself. Yeah, I think it belongs to Kerry actually, but Teddy stole it or something."

False alarm. *Of course Athena befriended the second-most-boring person in the entire high school. It's like she has radar for boring. I expected more from Roxanna. I bet they talk about their graves, and how much they love brushing their hair. Roxanna is in her grave almost as often as Athena.*

"No, I think we're playing badminton tomorrow, too."

Laurel crabbed down the stairs in retreat. Switching on the lamp in the study, she flopped into the threadbare wing chair by the window. She looked out the window at Athena's grave canopy, ghostly in the growing dark. *Athena hasn't been in her grave much lately. And she's been wearing that weird sweater with all the different-color thread. Looks like she got it out of the Dumpster. Yesterday she went to school with her hair twisted into Princess Leia buns.* Laurel thought a moment longer. *And she hasn't been bringing her cream-cheese-and-jelly sandwich anymore. Didn't she tell Mom that she'd buy a salad at school? A salad?*

"Please tell me you have a plan."

"Hold on a sec." Athena put her palm over the receiver and whipped open her bedroom door to the empty staircase. "Okay, never mind. I thought my sister was snooping. Nope, I haven't got a plan, not since I saw you two hours ago."

"C'mon!"

"It's hard to plan revenge for something you don't want to think about."

"If you don't take action, *she* will."

"Not necessarily."

"She's interpreting your silence as complicity."

"Speak English."

"The fact that you haven't said anything to her only makes her think that what she's doing is okay. And it's not."

"So maybe I could just talk to her. Like, ask her to take down the blog post or something." Athena could picture it perfectly: her, short-breathed and stammering; Roxanna, amused and haughty, surprised that Athena would come up to her in the hall, in plain view of everyone.

"Oh yeah, I'm sure she'd be sympathetic. Are you kidding? Roxanna Dover?"

"Well, that was the only idea I had. What do you got?"

"We could *Carrie* her at prom."

"Ambitious, except we'd have to wait another, like, eight months to do anything."

"I knew you were going to say that. You never want to try anything risky."

Athena sighed. "What's Plan B?"

"Hack into her blog?"

"You can do that?"

"No, but I'm sure we could find someone who can. I bet Eric Larson could. He's always in the computer room after school."

"I don't know. We'd have to pay him to keep quiet. Do you trust him?"

"To be honest," Maude said, "I haven't spoken to him since we were in the same fourth-grade class."

"Great."

Maude chattered on about other ways to sabotage Roxanna into submission, but Athena wasn't listening. She was back in the orchard, in that stupid green dress, moving through the memory as if flipping through a photo album. Roxanna coming up to her out of nowhere. Roxanna goading her into looking for trouble. Her nerves humming just below the surface, overtaking the excitement of it all with a steady static of fear. The tension came back to her instantly, behind her eyes, up the back of her neck. Roxanna had said, "*I won't take pictures.*" Athena felt her face burn scarlet.

Pictures. Roxanna didn't take pictures, but I could.

"Maude, I just thought of something."

"It's about time!"

"I'm not sure if it's even possible, though. Let me call you back."

"I've got meditation tonight. Just call me tomorrow. Oh no, wait, I volunteered for the search for the missing boy. Do you want to come? It's at the crack of dawn tomorrow at the lake."

"Can't. Chores."

"Oh, right. Are we still on for Walgreens, though? Those lipsticks aren't going to test themselves."

"Totally. I'll be free by the afternoon."

"Cool, call me after lunch then."

"Okay. Later, gator."

She tossed the cordless phone into the rumpled sheets on her bed and pounded down the stairs.

Laurel glanced up from her book as Athena, phoneless, breezed by the study with her camera. No sound of creaky stairs. Laurel stuck her head around the doorframe. Athena's voice issued softly from Lucy's room at the end of the hallway. The door stood open so Laurel could see Lucy's desk lamp had been turned on. Athena was probably sitting on Lucy's bed, just out of view to the right of the door. Laurel crept slowly down the hallway, keeping close to the wall where Athena couldn't see her, and stepped into the open doorway of the room next to Lucy's.

"You saw how it ended, sort of," Athena whispered, "but it's still going on."

Who is she talking to?

"And the problem is," Athena continued, "now that they know about you, they could tell. I need to do something to stop them from telling. What do you think I should do?"

A loud bang made Laurel jump. The ghost must have knocked something over. Laurel heard Athena cross the room. "I'm not sure what knocking over a desk chair means"—she slid the chair back into place—"but it seems aggressive." She walked back to the bed and sat, making the springs squeak. Very quietly, almost scolding, she said, "Lucy."

Laurel stepped back into the hallway, just far enough that she could see Athena's legs hanging over the edge of the bed.

Lucy's doll-sized tea set was laid out midair on an invisible table. An invisible hand poised the teapot over each cup; the cups lifted to invisible lips. The teapot floated over to Athena and hovered in front of her. "Lucy, this isn't the time to play." But before Athena could finish, the cups fell one by one with a dull thud onto the braided rug.

Laurel counted three heartbeats before Athena whispered, "Are you saying poison them?" The teapot settled on the floor at her feet. "No, this was stupid." She rushed from the room, straight into her sister. Athena's shock lasted only a fraction of a second, then she took Laurel by the arm and yanked her back into Lucy's room. The door closed without anyone touching it. "What did you hear, you creep?" she hissed.

"Nothing, just—"

Athena shook her. "Tell me."

"I don't know what I heard! Except Lucy wants you to poison someone at a tea party, which is ridiculous." Laurel tried to laugh it off. "What is this, *Pretty Little Liars*?"

Athena let go of Laurel and paced over the rug and back. "Of course you close the door now! Why wouldn't you let me shut the door when I came in to talk to you?"

"I didn't know you talked to Lucy." Laurel sat tentatively on the bed, massaging the pinch marks in her shoulder.

"Well, generally I don't, so you haven't missed much."

"Who were you talking to on the phone?"

"Oh God, Laurel, get a life." Athena had her ponytail pulled over her shoulder and was wrapping it around her hand like a boxer taping up her fist.

"I have a life!" Laurel dammed her mouth before the rest could spill, but she wanted to scream, *I have a secret best friend, I'm the only person who knows where he is, and you have no idea what you're talking about.* "I bet I know who it was."

"Bet you don't."

"I bet it was Roxanna Dover."

Athena turned slowly toward the bed, dropping her ponytail. "Why would you think that?"

"I saw you. At the grave opening, I saw you together. I heard you talking."

"Yeah, and I saw you sneaking through the orchard, creep. And I kept *your* secret." Athena spoke softly, rage stamped on every word. "But maybe I'll just have to tell Mom after all."

"If you tell Mom I snuck out, then I'll tell her you took Roxanna Dover into your grave."

Athena burst across the room and pinned Laurel to the bed. Laurel struggled, but Athena clamped a hand over her mouth. "Please don't, Laurel," she whispered. "Please, please don't." Laurel stopped fighting and looked into her sister's face. Athena was crying. "Please, Laurel. Please don't tell on me." Her hand tasted salty and metallic against Laurel's mouth.

Slowly, Laurel nodded. When Athena finally sat back, Laurel found blood on her lips from her own teeth. "So you did, then."

Athena curled into a ball on the bedspread. Her breath made a muffled suction sound behind her hands, clapped tight over her whole face. Athena felt a hand pressing into her shoulder, all five fingers gripping. "I didn't think"—she paused for a breath—"I didn't think it would turn into such a big thing. I actually believed Roxanna would keep it a secret."

"You trusted her," Laurel said, without pity or accusation.

Athena let out a low chuckle. "I was dumb enough to trust her. And now she's written about it on her blog. And virtually everyone knows it was me, my grave."

"She wrote about it? Then she's the dummy. She would get in just as much trouble as you if anyone who mattered found out."

Athena dissolved back into tears, burying her face in the bed. Laurel sat with her, holding her shoulder. *The barn,* Athena thought. *I have to search the barn. I have to stop this from getting bigger than it already is.* After a minute Athena said, "I'm okay." When Laurel took her hand away, cold air replaced it. She heard her little sister pick up the tea set piece by piece and replace them on the doll table in the corner.

"These are actually really pretty," Laurel said, examining the rosebud pattern.

Athena wiped her nose on her sleeve. "Ugh, I need a tissue." She opened the door and headed down the hall to the bathroom.

Laurel straightened the bedspread and switched off Lucy's desk lamp. As she walked down the stairs, Laurel felt Athena behind her, moving like a ghost back down the hallway to Lucy's room.

In the living room, Walt called from his chair, "Where's my ice cream?"

Chapter 24

SATURDAYS AT THE ORCHARD MEANT WORK. ATHENA'S radio alarm clock glowed red, and Kelly Clarkson's voice blared into the shadowy attic, even earlier than on school days. Something soft landed on Athena's face, and she swatted it to the floor without opening her eyes.

"Your alarm has been going off for fifteen minutes," Laurel said from the other side of the room. "Mom will be mad if she has to climb up here to get you."

"I'll be there in a minute." Athena rolled toward the wall. She heard Clover's tags jingle, and then Laurel landed hard on her back.

"Smell-o-gram!" She puffed a lungful of morning breath

into Athena's face just as Clover jumped up to join the pile-on, snuffling and whining happily. "Double dose of dog breath!"

"Get off! Both of you!" Laurel retreated from the strike zone, but Clover kept playing, nosing Athena's face and neck, biting at the pillow. "Clover, go on!" Her tags hit Athena in the teeth. "Go!" She pushed, and Clover jumped down, thwacking Athena's face with her tail on the way.

"Clover, let's get breakfast. C'mon." Laurel clicked her tongue.

The sound of Clover's ticking nails faded down the stairs. Athena ground her palms into her eye sockets, sat up slowly. She pulled back the curtain next to her bed, the window Laurel watched grave openings from every summer. In the orchard, the grave doors lay lifeless; one of them belonged to Roxanna Dover. Athena's camera sat on her night table, lens cap on, a full roll of film inside. *The key is in the barn; it has to be.* Laurel would know. Maude would help her. Tonight—they could do it tonight.

The silver lining to the morning was the debut of her new old canvas jacket. Maude had driven them to Goodwill after the library earlier that week, and with Maude's help Athena had stocked up on vintage blouses, minimally scuffed saddle shoes, and home-sewn dresses. It was a totally different shopping experience. Where things once had seemed tired or worn, now they had potential. "This is like Zooey Deschanel on the prairie," Maude had said, holding up a cap-sleeved dress. "You're trying it on." When Athena had found the basket of ladies' handkerchiefs and tied one around her ponytail, Maude had clapped like a little kid. "So *Pleasantville*!" Later that day, after Athena was done with her chores, they were going to meet at Walgreens and test red lipsticks, and then hopefully Maude would sleep over at Athena's so she could outline her plan.

Athena and Laurel were still too small to use the leaf blowers—or so their dad said—so they raked the first leaves of the season by hand and broom-swept grave doors. The calluses that she tried to lotion into submission every other day of the week were actually appreciated on Saturday mornings. Athena could hardly feel the splintery handle as she dragged the rake across the root-gnarled lawn. Her new old jacket hung almost to her knees, but the canvas was faded and soft, and with the sleeves rolled, the plaid flannel lining stood out in neat cuffs.

"Where'd you get that dirty old jacket?" Laurel asked from her perch in a nearby apple tree.

"Get down and help. Quit being lazy."

"I'm not lazy. I do stuff like this all week long." It was true—Athena used to be a full-time employee, too, when she was still homeschooled.

"C'mon, this'll go way faster if we work together. Please?"

"Answer my question."

"I got it from the Goodwill."

"When did you go there?"

"The other day, with my friend."

"Awww, you have an imaginary friend, how cute. Is she here now? Hello, Athena's friend! Nice to meet you!"

"Shut up, she's not imaginary. And you should talk—she's not a dog, either."

Laurel swung down from the tree. "Oh, you got me. Right where it hurts."

"She's coming over later." Athena raised her voice to the whole orchard. "I'm inviting her." *Be nice, Lucy,* she said in her head.

"Okay, weirdo." Laurel picked up a broom and walked down the row.

"She's my friend, so be nice to her."

They worked in silence, each girl lost in thought. Laurel's drifted to Charlie, who was somewhere nearby, either in his borrowed grave or in the woods. Anxiety spread through her body, flooding her from ankles to eyelashes. *What if he doesn't leave and I have to tell Mom? What will she say when she finds out I've been helping someone live in an unsealed grave, and that I lied to Charlie's mom? I'll probably never set foot in school, much less college.* As she swept, the broom head whacked a tarnished doorknob and set it rattling. "Great." Laurel took a screwdriver from her pocket and dropped to her knees.

Down the row, Athena raked without seeing the leaves. Her mind was combing over Roxanna's blog yet again, swinging wildly from one desperate thought to the next. *What if someone shared it on Facebook—would Simon see it? He wouldn't tell. Should I ask him what to do? Should I tell him about what happened with*

Lucy? Lucy had always been a nuisance, hiding things, turning lights on and off, playing practical jokes on her and Laurel. But she had never done anything dangerous before. What she did to those girls—they had it coming, but did she really need to shove Roxanna like that?

Maude was right. Athena had to do something. All this worrying was getting her nowhere. *What did I used to think about before this nightmare? Probably being friends with Roxanna, how cool I'd be.* She snorted. *Delusional.* Over her shoulder, she saw Laurel bent close to the doorknob, tangled hair in her face, singing, "Adventure time, c'mon grab your friends. We're going to a ver-ry distant land." What had Athena thought about when she was Laurel's age, before she went to school?

I thought about how amazing it would be if I could go to school. By the time she was Laurel's age, though, she was in middle school. *Be careful what you wish for*, she thought. That year was one long, unbreaking wave of culture shock. It wasn't fair: how could she be branded weird when she didn't know the rules? She was an alien with her tube socks and plain white Keds, her liverwurst sandwiches in wax paper. Her bras were white or beige, barely better than training bras, and certainly not polka-dotted or lime green. Her favorite TV shows were on Cartoon Network, not HBO. She didn't even know what it meant to be "a Shoshanna."

With school a disappointing and confusing reality, Athena had turned to something else: graves.

Some people, like her mother, believed grave keeping helped

a person face her mortality, and thereby live a better life. Death was the permanent thing—life was just a prelude. Did eighth grade really seem like an eternity when compared to death?

Death still seemed preferable, most days, she thought.

Athena came to the end of a row and moved across the Champs into the next quadrant. Laurel watched, thinking, *Where's Charlie? What if Athena sees him by accident? She's getting too close to Tamsen's grave.* "Athena!" Laurel yelled down the row. "We should get these leaves onto a tarp before we do another row!"

Athena opened her mouth to protest, but Laurel was right. If a wind came through, all their raking would be undone. Better get the leaves down to the pit first. She dropped her pruning shears and dragged her rake to the leaf pile.

Laurel was stunned. No argument, no deal making—Athena just agreed. *Maybe things will be different now, after last night. Maybe Athena will actually show me some respect for a change.*

"Hold the corner down. No, *that* corner. God."

Maybe not.

Once it was full, the girls hauled the tarp to the pit on the far side of the house, out past the mailbox. A ring of stones marked the spot where they burned leaves and branches each fall and spring after mucking out the orchard. "Dad says he wants to burn them today," Laurel said. "So if you have anything else you want to burn, like old magazines or secret letters to your secret friend, don't forget."

Athena looked at Laurel. "What do you think I do all day at school? Work for the CIA?"

"How should I know? You never tell me anything." Laurel took a corner of the tarp and headed back for the rows, dragging the blue plastic like a giant blanket.

Athena jogged to catch up. "That's not true. You know my biggest secret now."

"I guess." She wiped her runny nose along her sleeve.

"My life really isn't that interesting, Laurel. You're not missing much."

"Well, if your life isn't interesting, then my life is deadly dull."

"That's not true. You were here when the police did the sweep for that lost boy, right?"

"No, I mean, yeah, but I was fishing most of the time. I didn't see anything."

"Aw, man, I was hoping you could tell me what went down. I haven't wanted to ask Mom and Dad, because, you know."

"Duh."

"They don't like thinking about police, much less having them at the house."

"I said *duh*."

"Yeah, well. Keep your ear to the ground. If you hear anything." Athena nudged Laurel with her elbow.

A gust of wind blew through the orchard rows, shaking leaves across the freshly raked lawn.

✧ ✧ ✧

That evening after dinner, Laurel toed open the door to her room and looked up from her book. Athena and another girl were sitting on Athena's bed with a plastic drugstore bag between them. Their lips were scarlet and shiny, as if they'd eaten ten cherry Tootsie Pops each.

"Laurel, this is my friend Maude."

Maude crossed the room and shook Laurel's hand. "Nice to finally meet you."

Laurel stared at the stud in her nose, a tiny green stone that winked in the light. Seeing Maude answered a lot of questions, like why Athena was suddenly bringing home dresses for their mom to hem and wearing thick wooden bangles stacked up her left arm. Maude was clearly the source of Athena's new used clothing, shoes, and accessories, with her overalls-shorts and patterned black tights.

"You're real. I mean, you really exist. Athena really has a friend—a friend named Maude."

"You make me sound like a phantom! God, I love this house. You never know what to expect. Little sisters and phantom friends—what's next?" She crash-landed on the bed.

Athena poured Skittles into her palm and ate the undesirables (orange, lemon) before getting to her favorites. "Maude's sleeping over, Sissy."

"Tonight?"

"Yeah, obviously." Athena pointed to an army green rucksack on the floor.

"Okay, I'll just take my pillow." Laurel tried not to feel guilty abandoning her dolls, leaving them sprawled on her bed, hair messed and eyes half-closed after pulling the pillow out from under them.

"Where are you going? Maude's going to sleep on the floor. You can stay in your bed."

"Oh. Okay then." She tossed the pillow onto her dolls. *Sorry!* "I'll just go brush my teeth now."

"You do that."

When Laurel was gone, Athena said, "No one has ever slept over here before. In case you couldn't tell."

"Yeah, I figured. No biggie."

"No, but I mean, no one has ever come over before. I've never had a friend over, ever."

"Ever?"

"Not counting my cousins, no."

"How come?"

"Homeschooling. Other stuff."

"So in other words, I'm the super guest of honor tonight."

This was a mistake. I should never have invited her over. Maude will figure out I'm impossible to be friends with. She'll start boxing me out of the lunch table, and then eventually I'll hear that she told all about what it was like in my house, how weird everything was.

"Hello? Athena?"

"Sorry, I totally zoned there for a minute."

"Well, as I was saying, you didn't miss much on the sleepover front. I'm pretty sure I was only invited to Hannah Stevens's birthday sleepover every year in elementary school so that they could scare me in the middle of the night. It happened like three years straight, and then I finally figured out to avoid the thing entirely."

"That's terrible. I promise I won't scare you tonight. Although Clover might try to snuggle at some point, and Laurel's morning breath will make you jump out of your skin."

"Noted."

Laurel returned and set about putting her dolls to bed, refusing to so much as glance at Athena and Maude. She waited until Laurel was under the covers, and then Athena said, "Laurel, we have a proposition for you."

Chapter 25

THE THREE GIRLS, DRESSED IN BLACKS AND BROWNS and navies, stood in the unlit attic bedroom. Athena's borrowed camera hung around her neck, a fresh roll of film loaded and wound. The clock read 1:17 a.m. Clover leaned against Laurel's leg, not fully awake.

"We can't take her. She'll wake up everyone."

"If we leave her here she'll whine and scratch the door and wake them up anyway. Here, look." Laurel unbuckled Clover's collar and dropped the clattering tags. "Now she's as quiet as we are."

"Fine, but you're in charge of her."

"All right, keep your shirt on."

Maude cracked her knuckles nervously. "Let's go already. Let's go."

They didn't click on their flashlights until the barn door closed behind them. Athena made a beeline for her father's table and the sheaf of hooks above it. Maude lifted her light while Athena gingerly peeled back layers of paper on the table.

Laurel's eyes swept around the barn—the baskets, the tool belts, the wall of drawers. "I don't think it's over there, Athena." Clover watched as Laurel opened the first drawer in the bottom row of the wall. Receipts, most dated 1989. She pressed her hand into each corner—no key. "Dad moves it around all the time. He uses it for a customer and then puts it away in the first place he touches."

Athena continued methodically dismantling and assembling the tabletop. "You're sure he doesn't keep it on him?"

"I'm positive. It's an old key, pretty small."

"Your dad doesn't keep a backup?"

"He does, but it's in a safe-deposit box in Catskill."

"Maude, why don't you look through those baskets?" Laurel aimed her light at three baskets hanging from the beam over the middle stall.

"Keep your voice down!" Athena whisper-yelled.

"I wasn't yelling!"

"Is there a stool for me to reach?"

"There's a chair you can stand on in the last stall." Laurel made her way through every drawer, finding ChapStick and matchbooks and countless doorknobs, but no skeleton key.

A loud crash made them all jump, including Clover. They froze, straining to hear any movements outside. Crickets, a faraway coyote, quiet. Clover slowly sniffed her way over to the basket of nails spilled across the floor.

Maude stood a few feet away with both hands on her head. "I'm so, so sorry. I didn't even touch it, I swear."

"It's okay. Laurel, check the house."

"It's like it jumped."

Laurel pressed her eye to a crack at the doorframe. The sliver of night on the other side was black and undisturbed. No lights in the house. No sound of her dad's shotgun cracking open to be loaded. "All clear."

"Clover, shoo. You don't want to chew on these." Maude began refilling the basket with handfuls of nails.

Laurel found work gloves and threw a pair at Maude. "Put those on so you don't get lockjaw."

Athena looked up from the desk. She watched Laurel boost herself up on tiptoe to see into drawers at eye level. Laurel's arm wormed through each compartment, rummaging through tulip bulbs, a harmonica, part of a cotton handkerchief, and there—small and cold, wrapped in a hankie—was the skeleton key, tarnished green and surprisingly heavy for such a little key. Laurel held it up in her flashlight beam. "Gotcha."

Athena crossed the room. "You found it?" She put her hand out.

As she handed it over, Laurel said in a sinister voice, "You can look anywhere you want, but don't go into the room that this little key opens."

"What?" Maude asked. "That's the point."

"Ignore her." Athena looked at the key in her palm. "Her brain's turned mushy with fairy tales."

This was the plan: Athena would be the one to go into Roxanna's grave. She was the photographer, and the wronged, so she would be the one doing the wronging. Maude would be the bouncer, watching the door, ready to open it when Athena knocked. Laurel would be the lookout up in a tree closer to the house. At any sign of a stirring, she'd whistle three times. Clover would stay in the barn until the deed was done.

This was what happened: Laurel slid open the barn door and Clover bolted.

"I told you to keep track of her!"

"That wasn't my fault!"

"Now she's out hunting possum and God knows what else. Catch her before she gets skunked or starts barking."

"What about the lookout?"

"We can get started without you. Just hurry."

Laurel could hardly see her feet as she tore up the Champs, softly clicking her tongue and praying Clover would obey. She wouldn't know what to do if she met a coyote. "Clover!" she hissed. "Treat, Clover! Treat!" No response.

At the end of the Champs, Laurel veered left toward her last best guess. *If Clover's in the woods, she's on her own. I'm not going in after her in the middle of the night.* Under the cover of overgrowth in the old quad, Laurel felt safe turning on her flashlight. Each footstep sounded deafening, snapping branches and crackling ivy sending up noise flares. "Clover," she whispered. "Clover, come!" A scuffing sound came in reply, a few yards down the row. *Definitely an animal, just please be my animal.* She thought of Charlie, his fear of mountain lions. Finally her light found Tamsen's door, and Clover stamping and leaping around excitedly on top of it.

"Clover Honey, you are in so much trouble! Come here." Clover came sheepishly, her drooping tail still wagging. With one hand firmly at the scruff of Clover's neck, Laurel walked to the door and knocked softly. After a moment, she knocked again. *He's gone.*

He'd taken her threat seriously—good. Home was where he needed to be. Laurel might still be able to see him now and then. Would he still want to go fishing? Could they meet up at the library maybe, if she could sneak away?

Then the doorknob turned and the warped wood rose a few inches. "Laurel? Who's there?"

"Charlie, it's me. And Clover." Relief filled her voice. He wasn't gone!

Charlie's head emerged, his voice weak with sleep. "What happened?"

"Clover got out, and she thought it'd be funny to wake you up. I'm sorry. You can go back to sleep."

"S'okay. Want to come in?"

"I can't let her go; I'm afraid she'll run off again." Laurel needed to get back and be lookout, but suddenly it seemed like the least urgent thing in the world. "Want to sit out here for a minute?"

Laurel and Charlie sat with their feet hanging into the grave, not talking about the ultimatum, or the single day left in the agreement. They didn't talk about Charlie's dad, or his mom, or school, or fishing, or the Snickers he still owed her from their bet. They didn't talk at all. They sat there, scratching Clover's belly, while clouds blew across the sky and the half-moon threw borrowed sunlight over the orchard.

It was unbelievably easy to break into someone else's grave once you had the master key. The discovery both terrified and thrilled Athena. Before she could pause to think about the differences between her door and Roxanna's, or the stale smell of someone else's air that folded around her as she descended the ladder, she was standing on the soft floor in complete pitch-black.

"Okay, shut the door."

Maude's silhouette gave a little wave and closed her in.

Athena switched on her flashlight. A white shag carpet covered the floor. At the head, a leather beanbag chair sat with a permanent punch to its gut. She had expected photos, tons and tons of photos, but the walls were covered in whitewashed cork, a single handwritten quote pinned to each wall. "You wouldn't worry so much about what others think of you if you realized how seldom they do," said Eleanor Roosevelt. "Never doubt that you are valuable and powerful and deserving of every chance and opportunity in the world to pursue and achieve your own dreams," said Hillary Clinton.

Another piece of paper had the same two words written over and over and over, covering the entire sheet: "Forgive yourself."

A shelf at waist height was lined with Moleskine notebooks that had been scratched and scarred, bent from corner to corner. Each spine marked a year, stretching back seven years. Athena picked up 2013, and a whole chunk of bound pages fell out. She read from a page in the middle.

> Last night at Jordan's, they cut my hair in the middle of the night. While I was sleeping. I bet they were laughing and being really obvious, but I didn't wake up. I found it in the morning. I sat up and my hair stayed on the pillow and for a second I thought all my hair had fallen out in my sleep.

Athena remembered Roxanna's dramatic haircut in the spring of sixth grade. She went full-on Natalie Portman and buzzed her hair completely. By the fall, she'd grown it into a flapper bob, which she'd kept ever since. The next page of the journal had a lock of hair Scotch-taped to the middle of the page.

As Athena examined cartoons drawn on the back of a receipt, or the empty jar of a used-up Yankee Candle, she realized that she was standing in a lived-in grave. She had expected to find dust covering every surface, unused grave-opening gifts still in their packaging, but everything about Roxanna's space felt deliberate—even loved. The beanbag chair was worn soft, same with the carpet. Pushpin scars pocked the corkboard walls. Roxanna spent time in her grave. A lot of time. Athena sat on her heels, feet folded beneath her, and skimmed through the rest of 2013, then flipped through 2014 and 2016. Roxanna had been journaling almost every day since she was nine. She wrote about her mom taking her for an ice cream sundae after school for no special reason, and keeping a supply of pads in the secret zipper pocket of her backpack for when she got her period, even though it could be years before she finally got it. She wrote about accidentally dropping her phone in the ocean when her family went to Hilton Head, and how spending the rest of the vacation in relative silence made time stretch like a piece of saltwater taffy. She wrote about the books she read, and how little she cared about college, how scared and how desperate she was to move to New York City. Each time she got a new lipstick, she kissed the page to document its color.

A gentle *tap-tap-tap* knocked Athena out of this other person's brain. "Yeah?"

Maude opened the door a crack and whisper-yelled, "Everything okay? You've been down there almost an hour."

And she hadn't even taken a single picture. "Sorry, I'll hurry up." Maude closed the door, but Athena didn't move. Turning the 2016 Moleskine in her hands, the leather corners gently curling up, Athena wondered if Rox Talks could be written by someone else, a snarky yet mousy girl at Greene Falls

High with a licensing agreement to use Roxanna's name. The voice of the diaries and the voice of the blog came from two different people—it had to be. Roxanna the blogger was snide and sarcastic, unimpressed by virtually everything. She was first chair in violin, but she resented it; her talent was thrust upon her by Fate. The Roxanna in the journals, though, complained of the ache in her pinkie and ring finger, how she stole a small baggie of ice from the trainer after soccer practice, not for her ankle, which felt fine, but for her hand, so she could practice the concerto she was working on in private lessons. Journal Roxanna worried and hoped and cared.

Athena stood the flashlight on the floor, working her way around. The strategy: take pictures that only Roxanna could identify, that other people wouldn't be able to tell was a grave, necessarily. A close-up of a Beanie Baby. An elegant angle on a rubber-banded stack of envelopes that had been worn soft by reading and rereading. A turquoise lap desk perched on her own outstretched legs. She trained the camera on a braided basket handle adorned with a sprig of dead pine. And of course, the row of journals, fat with ink, snapped from above.

With the last frame filled, Athena wound the film back into its canister and capped her camera. She stood for a moment and looked up at the underside of Roxanna's grave door. For so long Athena had wanted desperately, feverishly, to know Roxanna Dover, to be welcomed into her fortress of friends, to understand just one thing about her that no one else did.

Three short knocks, and fresh air whooshed into her face.

Maude's frantic whispers: "Did you get the pictures? What did it look like? Are you okay? You look pooped."

Athena held the camera in both hands. "I got 'em."

When the girls got back to Athena's room, Laurel and Clover were sharing a raw Pop-Tart in bed in the dark. The silver wrapper glinted on the floor beside the night-light. "How'd it go?"

"Thanks for checking on us, lookout. You really saved our asses."

"You were fine. Give me a break."

"I got a full roll, so we'll see."

"Good." Laurel clapped crumbs off her hands. "You have the key?"

"Catch." Athena tossed the charm-size key onto Laurel's blankets.

"I'll put it back in the morning. Dad won't be up too early on a Sunday."

Maude wormed down into her sleeping bag. "C'mon, Athena, tell me already."

"You'll see the pictures in a couple days. I want it to be a surprise."

Laurel yawned. "'It matters not what is in another's grave.'"

Laurel followed Clover into the morning orchard. She could feel the sun's warmth through her clothes before she slipped into the cool barn air and quickly tucked the skeleton key, in its hankie, in its drawer.

Last night's meet-up with Charlie clung to her like the memory of a dream. *Today is his last day. Tomorrow I'm telling.* She fought herself: *How do you say good-bye without saying good-bye? Should I find him? Should I go back inside?* She chose a chisel from the wall, flipped it from one hand to the other. Her stomach moaned for breakfast. Her teeth felt slimy with sleep. *It's not like he'll ever come find me.* Grabbing the hammer from Simon's work stall, she took off for the woods.

At Name Rock, there was no sign of Charlie. Everything was exactly how they'd left it, playing cards and fishing poles tucked into the crawl space underneath, coals damp in the fire ring above. She found a blank space toward the middle, away from the other initials, and set the chisel against the stone. She tapped a thin but deep *L* into the rock. Her fingers ached, the wooden handles slipping in her sweaty palms. She took one break, long enough to stand and look down the trail, hoping for an interruption, hoping the noise would bring him. The *C* proved tougher, and it came out jagged and angled. She blew away the powder and brushed dirt off the stone face. Sat back on her heels. Admired the lighter gray of the letters, how fresh they looked: *L + C.*

He would find it before he left, she was sure of it. Laurel spread her hands on the cool rock and waited.

Athena and Maude had slept until the sun was well above the trees, each taking turns waking up and checking to see if the other was awake yet before drifting off again. They brought their oatmeal bowls into the TV room to catch the last of a *Big Bang Theory* rerun, but Maude found *The Golden Girls* on TV Land and changed the channel. Had Laurel changed the channel, regardless of what Athena had been watching, Athena would've lunged for the clicker and fought a good fight. When Maude changed the channel, however, Athena merely thought, *This oatmeal needs more maple syrup.*

Laurel was nowhere to be seen.

EVERLASTING REST REQUIRES PATIENCE AND PRACTICE

I should tell you this part because what happened was my fault.

For over two hours, Laurel sat at Name Rock, waiting for Charlie to find her. Her stomach growled, more for water than food, but she melted herself to the rock, staying still until she absolutely couldn't. It hurt Laurel that Charlie might have slipped away without saying good-bye. Emotions radiated off her, a tide of hurt kept at bay by a gust of relief—she would have her freedom back. Her secrets would return to the everyday fibs about homework and bathing. She wouldn't have to constantly wrench her thoughts back from an unsealed grave in the orchard, and worries about providing food for Charlie, on top of her family. She could be a kid again, sort of. As soon as that feeling rose, a cold wave of loneliness washed it back.

When she got tired of waiting and slid off the boulder, I followed Laurel, knowing where she was going, willing her to go faster. Her ledge was my ledge. So often over the years, as I watched her there, sitting on the face of the mountain with so much air between her and a hard landing, I wished she would die. Every tumble from a tree, every dive off the broken dam, I wished and wished for her to die. Anyone's death was a prospect for company, but I was especially fond of Laurel. I daydreamed about a kinship with her the way aging parents daydream about grandchildren: nostalgia and future-hope in equal measure. All those scrapes and close calls and she never even got a concussion.

She barely even cried!

Around about her ninth birthday, as she was getting gutsier and more coordinated, more confident in her woods, I first hatched the idea of taking matters into my own hands. But how? But how? But how? But how? The problem throbbed through me. I didn't know the reason for my own existence, so how could I possibly replicate it?

My death was my only lead. If she died in the exact spot—if no one found her, the way no one found me—would I finally have company? Was that ledge the doorway to life as a ghost?

Laurel ran, light-footed as ever, hopscotching roots and rocks, slowing to a shuffle where the needles layered slippery. If she were in her secret place, it wouldn't mean that Charlie hadn't said good-bye; it would mean he couldn't find her when he looked. And of course he would look. Of course.

I waited to make sure it was just how it happened to me: a summer day, morning. Laurel climbed down the laddered rock, feeling carefully with her toes before shifting her weight. When she reached the third toehold, I swept the crumbled stone out from under her sneaker. She scrabbled at the cliff as she fell, ripping her nails and scratching her arms from elbow to wrist. I rode down with her, holding her to the cliff face, making sure she didn't tumble over the ledge.

I should also tell you that I planted the rock that was waiting for her head. I made sure she knocked her skull the very same way I had. And then I stood back and waited, giddily, watching for the dark puddle under her hair.

At the time, it seemed like the last possible option. Truthfully, I would have thrown myself off that cliff if there were any chance of a different outcome for me. I needed death like everyone else. Without death, life's significance is hard to come by. Some days I just wanted to burn everything to the ground. And people do that in certain ways—leaving families behind, fleeing countries, changing your name, your face, your past. You can get pretty far before the matches run out, and when they do, there's always that final choice. But not for me. So tell me you wouldn't be angry. Tell me what you would do after 381 years of that, when your options are as good as ash. Tell me you wouldn't haunt. Tell me I'm a terrible person for tipping the plates from the shelf, for tearing shingles from the roof, for dipping into people's graves and moving things around. Tell me it's a sin to leave the freezer door open all night, to invite moths into the attic, to rip the covers off Laurel's bed while she's trying to fall asleep. Tell me you wouldn't try anything, wouldn't give anything, to participate in life again. To have more than yourself. To have, at the very least, a companion.

If I had a breath, I would've been holding it. I watched Laurel the same way I had watched my own body, when all this was new. I waited for Laurel to join me, to ask what was going on. She would have it easier: there was someone waiting for her, ready to explain.

Chapter 26

"DO YOU GIRLS NEED ANYTHING FROM TOWN? YOUR father's dropping me at Suze's and then going to the hardware store for a while." Claudia had her braid coiled on her head and clipped with a long silver barrette. The string of her eye patch disappeared into the braid. She held her quilted purse with both hands.

"No, we're fine."

"No thanks, Mrs. Windham."

"So polite," Claudia fake-whispered to Athena, thumbing in the direction of Maude.

"Bye, Mom. Tell Suze hi." Athena brought her bowl to the kitchen sink and Maude followed. They stood rinsing the slimy oats down the drain until the truck's engine faded. "Soooo . . ." Athena drew out the word. "What do you want to do now?"

"I dunno. What do you normally do on Sundays?"

"Think in my grave, usually."

"After last night, we could think in anyone's grave we wanted." Maude laughed, but Athena didn't crack a smile, so she quickly backtracked. "I'm just kidding, I didn't seriously mean that."

"Oh, I know." Athena dried her hands on the dishtowel and handed it to Maude. "But it's not a bad idea. Want a soda?"

"It's eleven in the morning."

"So then of course you do. Come on."

The girls, still in their dark-camouflage pajamas, walked barefoot into the orchard and over to Athena's canopy. When Maude saw Athena reach for the doorknob, she put up her hands. "Wait a second, wait. What are we doing?"

"We're going to drink soda in my grave."

"I—uhhh—" Maude put one hand up to her bun. "This seems like a bad idea. We're pressing our luck this weekend as is."

"You were right, though. We could go in any grave in the cemetery, just about. I don't understand why they need to be so guarded. They're just graves."

"Your parents would not be happy to hear that."

"Yeah, but they're gone for the next couple hours at least. Laurel is somewhere, but she would care even less than I do. You're my friend, and I'm inviting you into my grave." Athena pulled the door up and over, propping it on two legs of the canopy. She descended the ladder with her can of Price Chopper store-brand cola tucked under her chin.

A moment later Maude joined her. She sat hunched over her folded legs, looking up toward the canopy, as if she were waiting for a tornado to pass overhead. "I've never been in a grave before."

Athena's eyes jumped to Maude's face. "You don't have a grave?" she asked.

"No, my parents aren't grave keepers. I wasn't raised with it."

Athena took a drink of soda. "I didn't know that."

"They have all these theories about land use and it being bad for the environment." Maude waved the notion away, clearly trying to cover up for the fact that she agreed with her parents' theories.

"Huh, I never thought about it that way before. I guess I assumed you belonged to a different cemetery. My family—" She was going to say *family business*, but it sounded like a euphemism for what her family did. "My dad's job must seem really weird to you. Running a cemetery."

"No weirder than others. Jordan's family running the ski slope. Frank Vandeveer's mom running the funeral home."

"Yeah, Suze. My mom's best friend—that's where she is right now."

"Oh." Maude released an embarrassed laugh. "I guess it is a little weird then. But honestly, it's mostly only weird because we actually understand what those parents do. My parents work for a consulting firm and an environmental nonprofit. And that is the beginning, middle, and end of everything I know about their jobs."

"They might as well be Russian spies."

"Just about."

"I guess we know as little about our parents as they know about us."

"Probably." Maude pinched the tab of her soda can and levered it back and forth, reciting, "A, B, C, D, E—" before it snapped off. "I'm going to marry a man whose name begins with the letter *E*."

"That trick is rigged. The tabs never last past *F*." Athena pawed through the plastic bag of unread magazines still in the corner of her grave, a whole month's worth that ordinarily would've been sliced and diced and tacked to the grave walls by now. "Want a mag?"

Maude chose *Marie Claire* with Kate Hudson on the cover. "All my problems solved, you say? Tell me more, Marie."

Athena paged through *Elle*, breezing past the thumbnail product descriptions she used to pore over, pausing only to lift a life-sized headshot of Gigi Hadid in front of her face. "Want to know a secret? I still text Joe Jonas sometimes. LOL."

Maude closed her magazine and held the Kate Hudson cover in front of her face. "Oh, Gigi," she said. "I still text Nick!"

Cracking up, accidentally kicking over Maude's soda can, laughing harder—her grave had never felt more like a home.

PARENTS SHALL KEEP THEIR CHILDREN'S GRAVES UNTIL THE CHILDREN REACH THEIR THIRTEENTH YEAR

I waited, but darkness never spread under Laurel's head. Her chest rose and fell, ever so slightly, and her eyelids cooled to a lovely lavender. The sun pulled its warmth away and a delicate breeze picked at individual strands fanned out around Laurel's head. Her baggy shirt had bunched up in the fall. In all my anticipation, I had never accounted for something so simple: her belly button, right in the center of her soft tummy, seemed like a revelation.

I thought about all the work it takes to hold on to your body—all the food and sun and stretching required to make a body go—and all the bodies that have to stop in order for new ones to start. For Laurel, the price of her life was Lucy's. Athena was meant to be the baby; Laurel was Lucy's understudy, called onto the stage at the last minute. Her parents would be too old to replace her now.

Most people don't think about the lives they need to fuel their own. Laurel did. She thanked the worms as she threaded them onto her hook. She honored the crawfish and trout with her make-believe burials, blessing their shells and severed heads with everlasting rest. When Laurel and her father went hunting, I played scout, running ahead to find the dumbest turkey of the flock, the one I could lull into a stupor. On a couple of occasions I was able to calm a deer to stillness. A kindness for the Windhams, but also for the deer. A kindness for me, if I'm being truthful. I needed a family in that farmhouse. If they left, if the orchard fell to an itinerant groundskeeper, I didn't know what would happen to me. Would I keep haunting if there were no people to be haunted?

Laurel slept on. Goose bumps rose along her arms, and the little dark hairs stood at attention in the chilly late afternoon air. All those phrases you hear about people on the brink of death—she was fighting, clinging to life, refusing to give up—Laurel was doing those things. She was waging the battle of her life, and suddenly I was embarrassed at my desperation and impatience. So selfish to think I needed her body to stop so I could continue. You would think that after death has come and gone, there isn't much to be afraid of, but that isn't true. Not for me.

And that's when a thought hit me: what if she died, but she didn't find me waiting for her? I would lose her as completely as her family would—I could be losing her right then and there. It wasn't until that exact moment that I realized I had anything left to lose.

Please stay, I told her. *I'll fix this.*

Chapter 27

Charlie had spent the afternoon at Name Rock, waiting for Laurel and playing game after game of solitaire. He figured she'd find him at some point. It was the day before Laurel's deadline, and he knew better than to doubt her threat. He paused to pull on a sweatshirt. Night always came to the woods first. He freed his head and put one arm through a sleeve as a wind came up, seemingly from the rock itself. It picked up his cards and swirled them in a mini tornado before engulfing him. He clapped at the cards speeding around him, trying to catch one, but they moved so fast they sliced his hands. Gathering speed, the cards swept into a swarm hovering over his head, fluttering like an unending shuffle, but the wind was still all around him, freezing. He thought back to the night of the fortune-telling and the storm. "Tamsen?" he said quietly.

The wind pushed at his back, pasting his T-shirt to his skin and making his eyes water. He staggered to his feet, and the wind raged with such force that it kicked out each foot in front of him as he stepped. Stumbling through the trees, still with one arm hanging out of his sweatshirt, an entire pack of playing cards flickering in midair above his head, the wind buffeted him across the creek and east, until he saw the cliff. His heart was racing—*I'm going to be blown off the mountain!* He lunged for the closest tree, tearing leaves from a low branch before staggering out of reach. He straightened his knees, bracing against the pebbly ground, and just like that, the wind let him go. He fell on his butt, like a tug-of-war victor.

The card swarm floated just off the edge of the cliff and unwound into a funnel, leading out of view. He crawled forward, ready to flatten himself in case this was a trick and the wind returned for him. He peeked over the edge into branches still as green as summer. The cards suddenly fell, as if their plug had been yanked from the wall, scattering red and white over the ledge below. *Well, forget that. I'm getting new cards*, he thought. And then he saw her hair.

Charlie climbed in a controlled slide down the cliff face to Laurel, landing on one of her feet. "Laurel, oh crap, are you dead?" He kneeled gently, refusing to glance over the edge but acutely aware of it nonetheless. A pulse pushed back against his fingers under her jawbone. "Laurel! You're alive! You're still alive!"

And just like in every fairy tale ever, the impossible happened. She opened her eyes.

"Shit," he said. "Now what do we do?"

Laurel blinked at the bald blue sky, but she didn't see it. She was in bed at home, waking up slowly, toeing the line of consciousness; she wasn't in her own bed, but Lucy's. The room assembled itself around her, pale pink walls tattooed with Magic Marker drawings in one corner, a window beside her bed with a unicorn sun catcher hanging from a suction cup. She felt the heaviness of the lavender quilt that her mother had sewn for her first daughter lying across her legs. Nothing felt strange to her—she knew where she was, and she was comforted by the familiarity, the menthol smell of the humidifier, the warm mustiness of her pillow. When she was younger, she used to beg to sleep in Lucy's room. The injustice of having a perfectly usable room, lovingly decorated, empty and waiting for her seemed too much to bear. Athena ruled the attic—could Laurel just borrow the extra bedroom? Her parents wouldn't hear of it. But now she was in that room—her room—in that bed—her bed—and a drowsiness settled into her body, soaking through to her bones. She had never felt more tired, or more at peace. She could lie there for eternity if they'd let her. *Let me sleep!* she shouted. Someone was rocking her awake, speaking her name into her ear over and over.

Laurel!

Laurel!

Laurel!

Charlie ran. He tore through the woods, arcing north toward Roaring Kill Road and the closest adult who would look past the missing kid standing in front of them and help Laurel. Vines and roots caught his laces, but he kept running, trailing a strand of leaves behind him. He plunged into the creek and out the other side, sneakers squelching up the bank. A stitch knit itself under his ribs, but his arms kept pumping; he sucked a bug down his throat and kept running; the hill steepened and he used his hands to pull himself faster. Zigzagging between trees, he caught his foot on a root and fell so hard his mouth smashed into the ground and he came up with the taste of dirt and metal. He ran and ran. If there had been any food in his stomach, he would have puked it up.

When he got to the door, the house was dark and shut. He banged the aluminum screen door with his fist, again and again and again, until the lock clicked. Van opened the door and spat through the screen, "What now?"

Charlie gulped and gasped, feeling gut-punched with every breath. "Help me," he rasped. "Please."

"Is someone chasing you?" Van stepped onto the porch and looked into the twilight.

"No, it's Laurel." The screen door slammed. "My friend. She's hurt."

"What happened? Where is she?" Van lifted Charlie by the

shoulders. "Where is she?"

"The cliff." Fighting to slow his breath, Charlie remembered what it felt like to cry with his whole body, like when he threw a tantrum as a little kid. "She's down by Painter's Point," he heaved. "But farther north. On a ledge. I can't get her. To climb."

Van didn't wait for Charlie to finish. He banged into the house and returned with two long rope coils crossed over his chest and a Maglite flashlight the size of his forearm. "I don't have a car. Let's go." Charlie followed him down the path he'd just cut, back into the dusk.

With excruciating care, Charlie helped Laurel sit. "My head feels like a broken watermelon." He didn't know what she meant exactly, but he let her rest it on his shoulder. "I'd like to take a nap."

"No, Laurel. Time to get up."

He helped her to her knees. "Seeing stars," she said. "I get it now."

"Laurel?" Van called down from the cliff top. "We're gonna get you home, you hear me?"

"Yes," Laurel answered, looking for his face. "Whoa." Her arms flew out, grabbing for the rock.

Charlie had her by the waist, her shirt bunched in his fist. "I gotcha."

"That is high."

"Mm-hmm. No sudden movements, 'kay? Let's take it easy." Charlie stood with his hands on her shoulders until she found a horizon. He wound the rope between her legs and crisscrossed it over her shoulders, following Van's directions as he shouted them. He walked with her, three steps back and forth along the ledge, until she mastered control of her legs again. And then he stood behind her, placing her feet in each toehold, saying, "You got this, you got this," while thinking, *Please don't let us die, please don't let us die.*

And the whole time, Laurel thought of Lucy's bedroom, the lavender quilt, how badly she wanted to burrow under it and never open her eyes again. When Van pulled her over the side, she dropped herself into his arms, and he told her, "You will be okay. You have to be. You have to be."

The woods had never been so vast. Van and Charlie each had an arm around her back to keep her up, coaching her over every fallen branch, every patchy moss colony. They stopped only to rest against trees, only for a minute at a time. Van grunted and strained, veins throbbing at his temples, half-carrying Laurel the whole way. Charlie was scared that if they let her sit down, Van would go down, too, and he would be the Scarecrow, all alone in the field of poppies, yelling, "Can anyone hear me?"

Van broke his focus to ask, "Why'd you come to me?"

"I knew you would help."

"Why didn't you go"—he hacked and cleared his throat—"to the Windhams? Call the police?"

"It would have taken them longer."

"True."

"Laurel told me you were a forest ranger."

"I was."

"And I knew you would help."

When Van looked over Laurel's drooping head, Charlie's eyes were there to meet him.

"I knew."

Athena stood over the sink, rinsing and piling wet cutlery onto a kitchen towel while her parents argued politely behind her.

"Five more minutes and then I'm calling the police."

"She'll turn up. She always does."

"It isn't like her to miss supper. She knows the rules. And Clover's here, she's been here for hours. That's not right."

"Just be patient."

"Something isn't—" The window over the sink flew open in a wind so fierce, it brought the curtains down, rod and all. One by one, every window in the house banged open, admitting a wind that knocked frames off the wall and set the ceiling fan spinning faster than factory settings allowed.

Athena dropped to the floor with her hands over her ears. "Is it a hurricane?" she shouted, but the wind tore her voice away. Her father had her mother under one arm, bracing the both of them with his free hand on the table. Her mother's braid whipped behind her like a banner.

The door flew open and slammed into the wall, breaking a pane of glass. Athena took the message and ran for the back porch.

"Athena, no!" Her father grabbed for her. Letting go of the

table, he stumbled back until he could gain footing. On the other side of the doorway, Athena was still, her hair motionless. She beckoned to them effortlessly, without bending into the wind. Walt hunched over Claudia, forcing their way to the back door, and as soon as they stepped over the doormat, the wind shut off, as quickly as it had come.

Claudia, Walt, and Athena stood on their porch in the still night air, watching the wind tear through their house. Pages ripped off the calendar. Claudia's spider plant tipped from the top of the fridge and crashed in a heap of pottery and dirt. All three thought it, but no one spoke: Lucy had never acted out this badly before. This wasn't mischief; it was an attack. Athena wished Laurel were there to help figure out how to turn it off. Clover whined under the porch. The tablecloth snapped like a flag, pitching the beaded lamp to the floor. Athena watched it all as if it were a movie. She heard someone shouting far away.

It took them almost two hours, but they made it to the orchard, and then Charlie broke open. "Help us! Somebody help us!" he shouted into the dusk. "Mrs. Windham! Mr. Windham! Athena! Clover! Help us!" Van staggered forward, a limp Laurel in his arms.

Athena got there first, and froze ten feet in front of them. "What? Who are you?" A strange old man held her sister in both arms. Mr. Windham was close behind. "Dad," she said.

"Walt," Van began.

"Everybody shut the hell up." Her father swept Laurel up,

her head lolling heavily, and half-ran, half-limped back to the house.

Claudia stood on the back porch with the portable phone in her hand. When she saw her husband barreling down the Champs-Elysées with Laurel's head bobbing over his arm, she shrieked, "No!" and Walt barked, "Dial!"

They lay her on the dining room table, pushing papers and textbooks and chewed pencils to the floor. The wind inside the house had stopped. Claudia squeezed both her daughter's arms, all the way down to her hands. "Tell me where it hurts, honey bee." Laurel blinked at the ceiling. "She's freezing. Get blankets." Claudia gripped her collarbone, her ribs, rotated both her feet to test her ankles. Walt returned with quilts and bundled every part of Laurel that Claudia deemed intact. When she reached Laurel's head, her daughter winced so fiercely, tears leaked from the outside corners of her eyes and dribbled down into her hair. Claudia locked eyes on Athena—"Ice, now"—and plunged her fingers into Laurel's thick curls, feeling for stickiness.

Athena brought in a bag of frozen green beans and placed it below her sister's head like a pillow. The image was so strange and so familiar: Snow White or Sleeping Beauty, stretched out asleep, on display, waiting for true love's kiss. Laurel blinked, her eyes unfocused. This wasn't a curse to be broken.

Her mother held Laurel's head in both of her hands, her face inches from her daughter's. "Laurel, honey, can you hear me? Talk to me, honey. Can you hear me?"

Walt had collapsed into a dining room chair, heaving. A

coughing fit sent him to the kitchen, where he put his mouth under the tap. He sputtered and choked, forcing the water down his throat and air down his lungs. When he straightened up, dripping water onto his shirt, he noticed Charlie standing on the doormat. "Hello?" he asked, as if Charlie had just called him on the telephone.

Claudia hurried into the room, saying, "Crushed aspirin," then stopped short. "Who is—oh!" The school photo she'd seen came into focus beneath Charlie's matted hair and dirt-streaked face. "Jesus, Mary, and Joseph. You're found."

Chapter 28

LAUREL REMEMBERED HAZY SNIPPETS OF THE BRIGHT white box that brought her down the mountain to Kingston and the faces that floated above her saying, "Keep those pretty eyes open, darlin'." She remembered a little bit of the first of several nights in the pediatric wing of the hospital. Nurses wore bright scrubs with cartoon dogs and cats on them. Murals of gigantic, smiling flowers swam in her vision and made her head pound. She wasn't allowed to sleep.

They had her propped up in a huge bed, big enough for two people to sleep in, and another faced her on the opposite wall. Once Laurel had been stabilized, Claudia and Walt were called across the hall for an interview with the police. Laurel was oblivious to everything that required more effort than it took to hold her head up.

Athena and Simon sat with their sister. Nurses came in and out. Doctors came morning and afternoon to peer into Laurel's face with a tiny flashlight. Watching them, pieces of an old bedtime story flickered in Athena's memory. There was a boy who could see Death—they were friends or something. The boy grew up to become a famous doctor because he always knew whether a person would recover or whether they would die. He cheated, though: if Death were standing at the patient's head, the boy could save the patient with a magical plant. But if Death stood at the person's feet, nothing could be done. And then she remembered her dad telling her that aspirin was made from the bark of willow trees. Magical plant.

As soon as the doctor left, Athena lounged beside her sister in the bed, flicking through the channels on the ceiling-mounted television, massaging one temple with her free hand. Simon pulled her empty chair in front of him to use as an ottoman.

"God, they have five thousand channels. What are you in the mood for, Sissy?" Athena landed on *Seinfeld*, mid–laugh track.

"Argh, noise." Laurel covered her face. Surgical tape pulled at the tubes on the back of her hand.

"I'll find something else, no worries." Athena hurried through twelve more channels. "I can't believe you were hiding that kid this whole time."

"Athena." Simon gave her a warning look over his Styrofoam cup of coffee.

She found PBS playing ancient reruns of *Thomas the Tank Engine*. "Maybe this, for old time's sake?"

A whistle blew and Laurel said, "Nuh-uh." Athena whizzed through the channels so quickly it hurt Laurel's eyes. She looked at her feet under the covers at the end of the bed. It seemed wildly impossible that they were connected to the rest of her body. They were so very far away. "I wasn't hiding him."

Athena muted the TV. Simon leaned forward in his chair.

"He was hiding. That's all."

Athena kept the TV on mute as she resumed her search. She bit her cuticle to keep from blurting out that their parents were basically under arrest for harboring a runaway and undermining a police investigation, which was unbelievable, even laughable, if not for the fact that Laurel was actually the one responsible.

"We know, squirt." Simon patted Laurel's forearm. "We know."

Athena spent the next three days in bed with Laurel, feeding her nibbles of Jell-O. When one of her parents came in to check on them, always with a police escort, they looked exhausted. Too scared to ask if they were in trouble, Athena clucked on and on about Laurel's progress and what they'd been watching that day. She told them about the MRI, and how you could choose a radio station to listen to while you were in the tunnel. She got permission from the doctor to paint Laurel's jagged nails after they healed a bit, something Laurel would never have allowed in regular life. Athena counted each passing hour that her parents weren't arrested a victory, a bright flag planted in rich, dark earth.

On the fourth morning, when the police and doctors agreed Laurel could be released, her dad signed Athena in late at school. The vacant hallway yawned behind her as she emptied her backpack contents into her locker. It all seemed so hollow now. Make-believe life, that's what high school was.

Of course everyone knew what had happened—the missing boy, Laurel's accident. It was all over the school. Hell, it was all over the news. Mrs. Adelaide, in sympathy for Laurel's ordeal, had given Athena an extension on her photo project. She was so grateful for the extra time alone in the darkroom, she hugged her teacher around her middle. "All right, then." Mrs. Adelaide patted Athena's back. "All right now."

The next day, waiting in the lunch line, a sharp finger poked Athena in the spine. Jordan breezed past. "Welcome back," she said, monotone.

Lindsay was right behind her. "Hey, Athena," she sing-songed. "Your sisters sure don't last too long, huh?" Their cackling continued as they crossed the cafeteria.

The following Monday, Athena spent her morning photo class tagging each print in her series "True Friendship," numbered one to twelve.

Mrs. Adelaide looked over her shoulder. "I really admire your courage, Athena."

Athena checked her face for any hints of sarcasm before

saying, "Thank you."

"It takes guts to turn the camera on yourself in such a nakedly honest way." She lowered her voice. "Most students care first about the object they're photographing, is it cool and all that. But you look for what that object represents, and you frame it to fit the emotion, not the object. That's advanced work, my girl." She moved behind her desk and rattled a box of pushpins. "Make sure you put your name on all of them! I'll be putting them up at lunch."

Laurel walked the grave rows in sunglasses to protect her eyes. After a week of absurdity, she was beginning to feel familiar to herself again. She remembered falling—the memory woke her up, night after night, with the feeling of rock and dirt under her nails. Charlie had been there—and Van. She didn't know how they fit in, but the dream-state reality only made it more plausible. There one minute, gone the next.

The first three days involved detectives and lawyers, Walt pacing and muttering about fees and being innocent until proven guilty. On the third day, after she had been allowed to sleep, two police officers sat in plastic chairs next to her hospital bed and asked her questions in the tone of voice of someone trying to put a baby down for a nap.

"Laurel, I'm Detective Toomy," said a woman with a tight bun, "and this is my buddy, Detective Rubin."

"Like the sandwich." The other woman smiled with cigarette-stained teeth.

"We'd like to hear about Charlie St. James. Do you remember Charlie?"

Laurel sighed and nodded once. She hoped people wouldn't treat her like she had been dropped on her head for the rest of her life. "Is he okay?"

The smiley detective jumped in excitedly. "Oh yes, he's gotten a checkup and a hot meal and"—she put her hand beside her mouth as if she were telling the whole room a secret—"probably a good long bath, 'cause boy, did he need it. He's home now. He's fine."

"We're wondering if you can tell us about how you met Charlie, and what he was doing with you when you fell."

"Whatever you can remember, sweetie."

"I met him at the creek," she began. Both detectives scratched down what she said in little notebooks.

Mr. Sturbridge, the family lawyer, sat in the corner while she told the detectives about Tamsen's grave, about Name Rock. She told them how she'd stolen food and candles, lied to Charlie's mother. She told them about sitting with Charlie in the middle of the night. She told them about their fight and her ultimatum. He had one day left. He was going home anyway.

When she got to the part about staking out Van's, all three adults came to life.

"Van, the old man who lives on Roaring Kill Road?" said Detective Toomy.

"Edwin Vandeveer?" said Mr. Sturbridge.

"Yeah, Van." Laurel knew they knew who she meant.

"Did you go inside his house?"

"Did you ever go anywhere with him, in a car?"

Laurel tried to wrinkle her face, but it hurt, so she closed her eyes. "No, we were spying. He caught us once and we ran."

"Was he there when you fell?"

"No. But he pulled me up."

Mr. Sturbridge absentmindedly patted his comb-over. "Why in the world would Ed Vandeveer help two strange kids, let alone a Windham, and almost fall off a mountain himself?"

The detectives exchanged glances. Rubin raised her eyebrows. "People do strange things out of guilt."

Laurel pushed herself up on her elbows. "Why wouldn't he? What's it matter that I'm a Windham?"

"It's nothing bad about you, honey." Detective Toomy rubbed the blanket over Laurel's shins. "We just figured, since the car accident, and your sister, it would be a little inappropriate of Mr. Vandeveer to"—she paused—"engage with you in any way. It might even be a parole violation."

Laurel lay back against the pillows. "Oh," she said. It would be many weeks before the significance of who Van was and what he'd done settled in her head.

The questions went on for almost four hours. They kept asking how she fell, who was with her when it happened. "No one," she told them, though she really wasn't sure. She couldn't explain her rescue, so who was she to say? The detectives wouldn't tell her anything more about Charlie, except that he was at home and safe.

He was safe with me.

Laurel slowly and purposefully walked every row in the western hemisphere of the orchard that afternoon, winding her way to Tamsen's grave. Her dad or Simon had sealed the door already, to keep out curious kids who'd read about the runaway online. To make things right. She never got the chance to ask Charlie if he'd actually been planning to leave that day. He never got the chance to decide. Her family talked about him as if they'd been visited by a ghost.

"There all that time, right in our own backyard."

"Thank God he was there, I'll tell you that much."

Her mind worked a knotted thought: *What if he hadn't been there? What if he'd already left?*

THE SEAL OF A GRAVE IS AN EVERLASTING SEAL

Here is another thing that happens when you die: you live in the world as the world.

That day at the cliff, I was the wind and the playing cards. I was Laurel, and I was Charlie. I was Van and his redemption. I was his muscle memory awakening as if from a decades-long nap. His days hiking up to the fire tower returning to his legs. His bark-hardened hands gripping the coarse rope without complaint. The breeze that cooled their sweaty foreheads. I was the Hudson River, a thin glint in the valley below. Of course, I was the terrible thing that happened, but I was the rescue, too.

Chapter 29

ATHENA AND MAUDE POKED AT THEIR SALADS, WAITING for the minute hand to reach twenty-five after. Maude took a bite from her apple, set it down. Athena fiddled with the loose button on her cardigan until it came off in her fingers. Her twelve black-and-white prints had a display board all their own, Mrs. Adelaide said.

"Let's go." Maude slung her backpack over one shoulder. "I can't stand this waiting."

They took up their post outside the girls' bathroom, where Roxanna stopped off every day after lunch. She would have to cross the lobby to get there, pass right by the new art display. If Roxanna didn't notice, Athena was afraid she might sit down

in the hallway and cry.

The bell rang. Kids tsunamied down the hall. Maude stood on tiptoe, balancing against the wall, searching for Roxanna's dark bob. Athena watched the crowd file past her photos. Most people only glanced, but for every ten people who strode past, one or two slowed down, squinted at the name tag. Athena's legs felt made of straw.

Maude deflated to her normal height. "Here she comes!"

Roxanna and Lindsay broke from the crowd, heading for the bathroom. Roxanna glanced up, did a double-take, froze. Her eyes roved over the display, digesting images as if trying furiously to calculate whether they were really there.

"Rox, c'mon." Lindsay beckoned. "We can't be late to Latin again."

Roxanna smoothed herself, squaring her shoulders, chewing her gum leisurely. When she met Athena's eyes, her face was casual, but she held eye contact until she swept into the bathroom without a word.

Maude herded Athena down the hall toward social studies. "She totally saw."

"She sure did."

"Now what?"

"Nothing. Now we pray she doesn't retaliate."

"What could she do? If she tells on you, you'll tell on her. She'll be in just as much trouble, and her sterling reputation as Susie Supercool will go poof!"

"Let's hope she sees it that way, too."

By the end of the day, Athena's hunger had regained its hold over her nerves. She scrounged through the pockets of her backpack for change and went to the vending machine. Passing her display in the lobby, she stopped short. All twelve photos of Roxanna's grave treasures were gone, the pushpins strewn like confetti across the floor.

Laurel sat at the foot of Tamsen's seeded grave, ripping grass up from the roots. She had decided to write Charlie a letter. She would tell him about how she'd been practicing shuffling cards, invite him to meet her at the creek before it got too cold. Her head was starting to hurt again. She nudged her sunglasses up her nose.

"Hey, it's the Phantom of the Opera." Athena plopped down beside her sister.

"Hey, it's Holden Caulfield."

"Why the hell do people keep calling me that?"

"I don't know, Simon just told me to say that. What are you doing here?"

"I figured you'd be here. Mom told me to give you these." She held out two pills and a juice box.

Laurel punched the straw through the foil, drank until the box crinkled up. "How did it go today?"

"Well, the photos were gone by the end of the day, so."

"Gone?"

"Someone ripped them all down."

"Not the principal."

"No, Sissy, probably Roxanna."

"Oh. Right."

"I checked—she already took down her blog post."

"That was fast." Laurel plucked a gray dandelion.

"I know, right? Maude and I are going to celebrate this Friday—a takeout feast at the library. Want to come?"

Laurel took a deep breath, blew dandelion seeds into the orchard with a wish. For a second, the world looked watery, then turned solid again. "I doubt Mom will let me leave the house for a while."

"I already asked. She said okay. I think she's feeling a little bad about keeping you here, friendless, alone."

"Gee, thanks."

"I'm kidding, but I do think Mom feels bad. It's been hard for her—this past week has reminded her of a lot. The hospital, the police, the reporters."

"I didn't mean to bring that all back."

Athena flicked her little sister's ponytail. "She knows that."

"Can I look at a book while I'm there?"

"Sure, Maude can sign you up for a library card."

Laurel crawled forward onto the hay and lay down on her back. *My own library card.*

"That door is ancient. Are you sure you should lie on it like that?"

"It's fine." Laurel spoke into the sky. "It'll hold."

ACKNOWLEDGMENTS

I would like to thank Seth Fishman and Jessica MacLeish for your insight and guidance; Bethany Reis, Maya Myers, Heather Daugherty, Allison Brown, the marketing and publicity teams, and everyone at HarperTeen for your hard work and care; my teachers, especially Jedediah Berry, Joanna Goodman, Noy Holland, Kelly Link, Nicholas Montemarano, and Patricia O'Hara; and special thanks to Sabina Murray for the summer I spent at your house (much of this story was written there).

Thank you to all my classmates and friends who read and helped me grow the story, especially Bryan Comer, Kristen Evans, Lauren Goodman, Khaled Khlifi, Annie Kleeman, Lech Harris, Ashley Nadeau, Leanna Oen, Greg Purcell, and Sean Rosenberg. And thank you in particular to Sarah Boyer and Ginger.

I am grateful to Maria Tatar for her edition of *The Annotated Brothers Grimm*, which was an inspiration and reference for me.

Thank you to Christine Fink, Lauren Fischetti, Kate McCooey, Tracy Taylor, and Deedi Yang, for all our (continuing) adventures. And thank you to the Kohuts, for being my second family.

Thank you to my sister, Amy, my first best friend: there is no one else I'd rather get in trouble with. Thank you to my parents, for being my first teachers, and for your encouragement, generosity, and belief; without you, this book wouldn't exist.

And thank you to Mike. Sharing this with you has been the true joy.